A FRANK DALTON THRILLER

DANGEROUS CURRENTS

JONATHAN SHIPPERLEY

CONTENTS

For Dad

I think you would have loved this.

For tho' from our our bourne of Time and Place
The flood may bear me far,
I hope to see my Pilot face to face
When I have crost the bar

— Tennyson

PROLOGUE

Under the dim glow of flickering fluorescents, Seaman Apprentice Jones manned the radios in the communications center at Coast Guard Station Port Aransas, just up the Gulf Coast from Corpus Christi, Texas. The relentless hum of machines and the occasional crackle of static were her sole companions during the monotonous twenty to twenty-four-hour watch. She shivered in the chilled room, a necessity to keep the computers from overheating but a constant battle for her to stay alert and warm.

She didn't like to be alone. Her nerves were always on edge during the night shift. Perhaps it was the way the shadows danced just out of reach of the station's lights, or the eerie scraping of palm fronds on the building when the wind blew a certain way. Whatever it was, Jones felt pleased as Petty Officer Hackman entered the room, breaking the monotony of the late shift and her introspective thoughts.

"Anything to report?" Hackman asked, surveying the room.

"Quiet night, Boats," Jones said, using the informal title for a boatswain's mate. She gestured to the radios with a flick of her wrist. "The usual idiots arguing on the radio."

Hackman smiled. "Yeah, they'll do that. Remind them about proper radio etiquette, if you want."

"I'll keep that in my back pocket," Jones said. "Especially if it becomes an issue."

"So, apart from idiots, nothing I should know about, then?"

Jones shook her head and stretched, glancing at the clock on the wall and holding back a yawn.

"Good. Let's keep it that way," Hackman said. He rapped his knuckles on a wooden desk out of superstition and picked up the weather report. "Did you check this out?"

Jones nodded. "Yes, Boats. It's calm near shore, but the further out you go, the worse it gets. There's a pretty big storm brewing. Looks like it'll be ten-to-twelve-foot seas. Pretty nasty until tomorrow."

Hackman scanned the report, confirming what Jones had said, and placed it back on the desk. "Right, I'm going to hit the rack. Gonna be a busy day tomorrow. Need anything before I leave?"

"No, I'm good, Boats, thanks. Have a good night," Jones said.

Hackman had his hand on the door handle, about to yank it open when the radio crackled to life.

"Mayday. Mayday. Mayday. Come in, Coast Guard..."

"Well, shit," Hackman muttered to himself. "I was so close. Should have tapped the desk harder." He let go of the door, walked back into the room and leaned on the communications console in front of Jones. "All right, let's get to work, Jones."

Jones stared blankly at Hackman and jumped as the radio squawked again.

"The radio, Jones. Answer the radio," Hackman said.

Jones blinked, then nodded, snapping out of it. This was her first ever mayday call, but she'd been trained well and keyed the radio's microphone, saying, "Vessel in distress, vessel in distress, this is Coast Guard Station Port Aransas, Coast Guard Station Port Aransas, channel one six. What is your position and nature of distress, over?"

Hackman nodded, giving her encouragement, and the two Coast Guardsmen waited for an answer. Jones stared at the radio's speaker, willing whoever was on the other end to say something. This was the awkward part of being on watch.

You couldn't help anyone if you didn't know what the problem was or where they were.

As the silence grew, Hackman paced in the cramped room, tapping his fingers on his pants. As the Officer of the Day, he was hoping this was another crank call, or maybe they'd picked up a transmission from outside their area of responsibility.

Seventy miles away, on board a fishing vessel far out in the Gulf of Mexico, wave after wave slammed against the hull as the boat steamed through the turbulent water, seawater roaring over the bow, splattering against the bridge. A nearby lightning strike lit up a lone fisherman standing on the bridge, his reflection a ghostly image painted in the windows, mirroring his terrified white face. He gripped the overhead tighter as the fishing boat pitched and rolled.

A soft incantation came from the fisherman's lips, muttering over and over, "I hope we make it. I hope we make it." The red bridge lights cast an eerie glow as he fumbled with the radio again. Raindrops fell from his slickers onto the bridge floor.

"Coast Guard! Oh, thank God!" he said. "This is the commercial fishing vessel *Reel Lady,* channel sixteen." The fisherman braced himself in a corner of the bridge, repositioning his grip on the overhead with one hand as he used the radio with the other. Squinting at the GPS in the dull illumination, he said, "We are an eighty-seven-foot trawler about seventy miles off the coast of Aransas. Coast Guard, our captain—"

Lightning struck again, and thunder rolled, drowning out the fisherman. He glanced out the stern windows and gulped, his fingers turning white as he held on tighter. Powerful floodlights on the vessel's superstructure shone bright beacons through the sea spray. The back deck was awash, and the surrounding ocean was awake, churning in time with his stomach. He could see the rest of the crew hanging on.

He keyed the microphone again, almost whispering, "Coast Guard, our captain is missing...I repeat, our captain is missing, he's gone. He's—"

Back at the station, Jones waited a moment for the transmission to begin again. When it didn't, she keyed the mike and said, "*Reel Lady, Reel Lady,* Coast Guard

Station Port Aransas, say again your last, your transmission was broken, over." Hackman had stopped pacing, the fright in the fisherman's voice making the hairs on the back of his neck rise.

When there was still no reply, Hackman said to Jones, "Try again."

Jones keyed the mic. "*Reel Lady, Reel Lady,* this is Coast Guard Station Port Aransas. Coast Guard Station Port Aransas, say again your last, over."

After a few moments, long enough for someone to answer, Hackman asked, "Did you hear the same thing I did? Their captain is missing? Did you hear that?"

Jones nodded. "Yeah, Boats. I heard the same thing. Weird how he'd say missing and not like it was a man overboard or something. What do you think?"

"I don't know. It's a new one on me. If he's missing, that would mean he's not on the boat. Until we get clarification, we'll go with a man overboard. I'd rather go with a worst-case scenario. We can always ramp down if they find he was asleep in his cabin or something." Hackman stood up straight and rubbed his face, coming to a decision. "Jones, wake up the boat crew and put them on standby. Then alert the air station. We'll wait to launch our boat. Seventy miles out is too far for our assets, but I want the crew awake in case the vessel is closer than reported. If it is, we may need to assist with search patterns, as we don't know how far out the *Reel Lady* was when the captain went over the side. We only know how far they say they are currently. We're also going to need air support. I think the air station should be able to fly in this weather without problems, but find out."

Jones nodded and flipped a switch on the control panel. A loud warbling alarm reverberated around the station. It lasted for about fifteen seconds before trailing off. Jones mashed the button on the intercom and said into the mic, "Now, ready boat crew lay to the command center. Man overboard, approximately seventy miles offshore." Speakers piped her words into all the berthing rooms and common spaces around the station.

"Jones, who's the RDO?" Hackman said.

"Mr. Frampton's the response duty officer on tonight."

"Thanks. Keep trying to get through to that vessel on the radio. We need to know where they are, more than just a vague seventy miles. That doesn't help much. Give it a few more tries. If you get nothing, issue a PAN-PAN and ask any vessels in the area to be on the lookout for her."

Hackman picked up the phone on the nearby desk and dialed Frampton's number. A moment later he said, "Hackman here, sir, Officer of the Day from Station Port A. We've received a distress call from a fishing vessel with a possible man overboard situation reportedly seventy miles offshore. We've put the ready boat crew on standby, but recommend we launch an air asset, as the distressed vessel is too far offshore for our small boats...Yes, sir, they didn't specifically say man overboard they said, missing...Yes, sir, it is weird...Yes, of course. I also suggest we divert the cutter *Glorious* from patrol. She's the nearest asset...Yes, sir. I've plotted their arrival time, and the *Glorious* can be on scene in a little under two hours. Once the air station has a helicopter up, they should be in the area in less than thirty minutes...Yes, sir. Roger, that." Hackman hung up the phone. "Jones, anything?"

"Nothing over channel sixteen verbally, but I did pick up a digital distress signal with a lat and long on channel seventy. It came in as the *Reel Lady,* so we know where they are."

"Good, that's good. They must have pressed the emergency button on their radio. The signal can bounce further than voice comms. All right, call the *Glorious* and divert them from patrol, tell them what's going on, and give them that position. Also tell them they have tactical control of the air station asset when it gets there, and to coordinate the search. You got that?"

Jones nodded and changed the frequency on the radio to contact the *Glorious* on a secure channel.

Hackman gazed out the window of the communications room while he listened to Jones on the radio. It was dark outside. He couldn't see the trawler from here, couldn't see much of anything except the parking lot and a few palm trees, but he could imagine what they were going through. Ten-to-twelve-foot seas, if the weather report was right, were no picnic. And that fisherman on the radio, he'd sounded downright scared. I hope they find their captain, and he just fell asleep in a locker or something stupid. All smiles in the morning. You called the Coast Guard? Man, now I feel stupid.

Hackman grimaced. It would be a nice turn of events on a night like this, but unlikely. If the captain did go over the side, no telling if they'd ever find him in this weather.

May God have mercy on his soul.

ONE

The palm trees swayed lazily on the night's light breeze, fronds moving in time with waves gently lapping along the shoreline. The moon played hide and seek, hidden behind a string of clouds, its absence leaving an inky blackness that smothered the world like molasses.

I was lounging on the starboard bench seat in the stern of my boat, the *Ghost*, moored up at the T-heads in downtown Corpus Christi, Texas. I had my feet propped up on the wheel and could just make out the faint strain of a country and western song floating toward me from one of the nearby restaurants. I nursed a beer, too lazy or too tired to grab another, I wasn't sure which.

I couldn't sleep. The gentle waves that usually lulled me, slapping against the hull, weren't working their magic tonight. I was still on leave from the Coast Guard, taking a well-earned break for a few days, a reprieve from the bustle of active-duty military life, and as much as I enjoyed the illusion of being free, restlessness was setting in.

The hatch to the main cabin was open a crack, the cool draft from the air conditioning raising goose bumps on my arms. I rarely left the air on and the hatch open, but I had a guest down below tonight. Peering through the crack, I could make out the shape of her curvy form nestled in a cocoon of sheets in the forward berth. Her chest rose and fell with each breath, almost in time with the swells from the waves. Such a shame.

Earlier that night at my local, run by my old friend Pete, she had sat down at the bar one stool over, and was obviously alone. I hadn't been looking for anyone or anything in particular, but after a little while we talked, and hit it off. She had an air of uniqueness about her I couldn't quite define, which was refreshing and intriguing. We went back to my place because it was closer, literally steps from the bar, and both of us had perhaps a little too much to drink.

Now, a mere couple of hours later, it felt like we were on the tail end of the relationship, although we'd just met. The air of mystery and uniqueness I thought she had had evaporated with each breath. Thinking about it now, perhaps I'd wanted to impress her with my boat, don't know why that was important, it wasn't like me to be so materialistic. But you do odd things when you've had a few too many. Fool reason though.

I took a swig of beer and sighed. I seemed to do a lot of that these days. Sighing, that is, although the drinking was vying as a close second place. It was starting to feel like I'd been in the Coast Guard for a zillion years, and I was thinking about retiring from active duty, even though I was still a few years out. Maybe move the *Ghost* some place else, maybe an island. Do some fishing, drink some beer, write a book. Who knows? I didn't have any fixed plans. I was still young, having enlisted when I was seventeen, but I hadn't quite hit the twenty year mark yet which was needed for a pension. Trouble was, the last few cases I'd finished had been soul-sucking, and I needed this time to get my head straight, which was why I was probably having thoughts of retiring.

My cell phone chose that moment to ring, shaking me from my melancholy. I'd left it inside the cabin on the little desk next to my laptop, its shrill noise abrasive in the calm night. I got up and pushed open the hatch some more, climbing down the few steps into the cabin. I walked past the dining table, more of a dinette really, the silhouette of too many empty beer bottles casting shadows, and silenced the phone as quickly as I could. I think most of the empties were hers, as I felt fine.

"Dalton," I said quietly into the phone. "Hold on." I glanced into the forward berth. The ringing phone hadn't stirred my guest, but I didn't want to push it. I walked back to the hatch, climbed up a couple of steps, and stuck my head out. "Go ahead."

"Sorry to bother you, Agent Dalton. This is Petty Officer Rogers from the Sector Command Center. I have a marine casualty to brief you on that may have a Coast Guard Investigative Service nexus." My gut —"immediately sank.

"What's going on?" I said.

"Sorry, sir. I know you're not on duty—"

"Actually, I'm on leave."

"Understood, sir, sorry again. But the SAC specifically asked for you."

Shit. Mr. Lewis, the Special Agent in Charge, was one up the chain of command from my boss. This was unusual, the big boss calling. I wonder what I'd done to deserve this attention. "The SAC? Okay, let me grab something to write on." I reached down and rummaged blindly through a cubby until I felt a pen and what turned out to be an envelope. Whatever works. I leaned on the hatch so I could write and sandwiched the phone between my shoulder and ear. "Go ahead."

"Roger that, sir. We've received a report from Station Port Aransas about a commercial fishing vessel, the *Reel Lady*. The vessel called over the radio to say their captain went missing while they were fishing in the Gulf of Mexico. The master is presumed to have gone over the side somehow. The *Glorious* diverted and arrived on-scene, along with a rescue helicopter from the air station. We're going to have a conference call with you, sir, the chief of response, and the SAC, at minute twenty, to go over our options. Mr. Lewis wanted you on the call, sir, because at this point the missing mariner is presumed deceased, and the vessel has some history that may need a criminal investigator." I glanced at my watch. I had about forty-five minutes. Thoughts of retirement and boredom melted away. I was a better person when I was busy.

"Fine. I'll take the call at the office. I'm not far," I said, and hung up. I needed to get dressed. The deck of the lounge was messy, as if a clothing explosion had detonated in the cabin. I gave myself a moment to focus and spotted my pants draped over a chair and shoved a leg in each hole. I picked up a bra I nearly tripped on, threw it on the couch with the rest of her clothes, and rooted around for my shoes.

Soon, I was dressed and ready to go, but there was one more thing to do. I walked through to the forward berth and sat on the edge of the bed. I contemplated the best way to do this. I didn't want to be an asshole. There was no need for that. She had done nothing wrong. On the flip side, I had little time to waste on niceties as I had to get a move on. And besides, it wasn't like I planned on seeing her again. I chose the middle road for now and rubbed her back, giving her a gentle shake to wake her thoroughly.

"Hey honey, you have to get up. I need to go to work," I said, not quite remembering her name.

"Hey," she said. She rolled toward me, her hand blindly crawling up my leg, not leaving the bed. "Ready again?"

I moved her hand and got up, hitting the switch for the dim overhead light, and pulled off the rest of the sheets, taking in her nakedness and making her squeak. Okay, asshole it is, then.

"I wish I had time. I truly do." I sort of meant it. "But I have to get to work."

I couldn't leave her on my boat. I didn't know her well enough, and I wasn't sure when I was going to get back. Besides, although attractive, I knew I'd never see her again, and figured ripping the band-aid off now would be less of a lead on. The more we'd spoken last night, the more apparent it had become we had nothing in common. I'm not opposed to a one-night stand, but I like to think there's always a chance to develop something more. There wasn't any redemption in this case.

I sighed. "Listen. I've got to go, but you can stay here." I made a show of looking at my watch. "For another couple of hours. After that, my wife is due back from her trip, and she won't be too pleased to see you sleeping in her bed."

Her eyes went wide as she inhaled sharply and scrambled out of bed, wrapping the sheet around her. Her hair was all messed up from sleeping, but on her, it looked pretty good.

"Where are my clothes?" she said.

I pointed to the lounge. "On the couch."

She walked through, grabbed her clothes in a bundle, and made for the bathroom, slamming the door.

I can't say I blamed her for being upset, but I couldn't talk about work. When she went to sleep, everything was fine. Anyway, she had to go now because if she stayed, she'd find out I wasn't married. I don't know why I'd said I was. Maybe I was trying to make her feel better about herself, give her a reason to leave, and a reason to blame me. Whatever.

There was some banging and muttered cursing, taps running, and what sounded like an attempt to flush the toilet. Heads on boats can be finicky things if you don't know what all the levers do.

She stormed out of the bathroom, making me wince as she battered open the door. Over her shoulder, she said, "You're a fucking asshole," as she sat down and zipped up her boots. Well, at least we agreed on one thing.

"Look," I said, softening the abrupt ejection. "The least I can do is offer you a ride home."

She made a little grumbling noise in her throat that may have been cute at another time, gave me the finger as she pushed past me and stamped through the cabin and up the stairs to the back deck, giving me a nice view of her perfectly formed rear. What was wrong with me? Get it together, Frank.

The boat rocked on its moorings as she stepped off, and I heard her calling for a cab on her phone.

I scanned the cabin to ensure everything was secure, gear adrift and all that. I retrieved my badge and P229 Sig Sauer pistol from the safe I kept under the bed, strapped the pistol to my side and slipped on a lightweight jacket, more to hide the gun than for the weather.

I heard a car drive up, so I poked my head out of the hatch, catching the neon of a rooftop taxi sign flicker off as she clambered in. Satisfied she was in competent hands, I locked up and headed to my car. I jumped in and took off. I drove fast, but not recklessly. It was still early enough in the morning that the roads were clear, but not late enough the drunks were spewing out from the bars. I wanted to get to work quickly. I didn't want to be another statistic.

I pulled into the sector underground parking garage and waited patiently for the guard to come out. After a minute that felt like ten, I beeped my horn. A muffled curse came first, followed by a chair scraping on the floor. A rumpled security guard shuffled out from the guard shack, yawning. He cast his bleary eyes over the badge I was holding out the window before he nodded and raised the barrier, waving me through. I parked and ran up the stairs to the fifth floor. It was quiet this early in the morning, and I easily threaded my way through the sea of cubicles to my desk. I sat down, pulled my chair up to the computer and rattled the keyboard to wake it up. The screen came to life, and I logged on, shoving my military ID card into the reader, so it could scan the embedded chip. Once I was in the system, I navigated over to email and found the one the command center had sent with the access codes for the telephone conference. I punched the numbers into the phone and grabbed a cup of coffee from the galley while it was connecting. I sat back down as roll call was starting.

"Mr. Lewis, are you ready for the brief?" Petty Officer Peter Rogers said through the line.

"Go ahead, Pete," Lewis said.

"Thank you, sir." Rogers cleared his throat. "Okay, at 21:30 yesterday, about five hours ago, the eighty-seven-foot commercial fishing vessel *Reel Lady* reported via the Rescue 21 system their master was missing. They were close to seventy miles offshore and the weather on-scene was...standby." I heard some rustling coming from the other end. "The weather, according to the National Weather Service, was seas of ten to twelve feet, winds from the north steady at twenty knots and gusting to forty-five, patchy fog and intermittent thunderstorms. According to the vessel's crew, they initiated man overboard procedures at once. We launched the MH-65 Dolphin helicopter, designation Rescue CG 6043, from Air Station Corpus Christi, and diverted the cutter *Glorious* from its routine patrol to assist."

"Understood. Go on, Pete."

"Based on the *Reel Lady's* automated track line, we were able to help them correct their course and successfully backtrack based on the set and drift of the tidal conditions. At 00:20, the master was sighted face down in the water by the crew of the fishing vessel. They pulled him aboard, but unfortunately, he was unresponsive. The *Glorious* was nearby by that time, conducting a reciprocal search on the same course, and sent their small boat over to the *Reel Lady* after they radioed they'd found him."

"What about the helicopter?" Frampton said. I'd forgotten the RDO was on the line.

"Rescue 6043 had to return to base to refuel. The plan was to refuel and head back out, but the helo was stood down when the missing fisherman was found deceased. Because of the amount of time the captain was reported to have been in the water, and that he was found face down and unresponsive, the flight surgeon didn't recommend CPR."

That didn't sound good. "Petty Officer Rogers, this is Agent Dalton," I said. "Let me see if I have this straight. What you're saying is the fishing vessel that reported the master missing was also the one to recover him?"

"That's right, sir," Rogers said. "The crew didn't know the exact time the master fell in the water, so we're estimating about four to five hours based on when they last saw him. Survivability for the water temperature wasn't an issue, but he wasn't wearing a life jacket or a Gumby suit. It's lucky they found him at all."

"How come they didn't know when he fell into the water?" I asked.

"That's not entirely clear, sir. According to my notes, the crew said they noticed he was missing from the bridge when one of them went below to cook dinner. The *Glorious* relayed that information."

Strange, they didn't know he was missing. "Okay, where's the deceased now?" I said, taking a swig of coffee.

"He was on the *Reel Lady*, but they transferred him over to the *Glorious*. The *Glorious* is going to escort the *Reel Lady* back to port, and then transfer the master to the medical examiner when they get back to base. They have an ETA of around noon," Rogers said.

"Very well, thanks, Pete," Lewis said.

"If I could, sir, there is one other item of note. When we ran the vessel registration through the Marine Information database, we got a hit for an expired lookout."

"What was the lookout for?" I asked.

"Hold one, sir." Rogers typed something in the background. "It says the lookout was posted because the *Reel Lady* had been involved in a prior drug smuggling case. During a boarding about five years ago, a law enforcement detachment from the *Magnificent* found two bales of marijuana in a false hold, but...scanning the report here...it looks like they've been clean since then. That's why the lookout expired."

That wasn't unusual. Fishing vessels didn't just always fish. Money was tight, like everything these days. Quotas were hard to come by and sometimes all it took was a little extra cash and the promise to look away. It wasn't always an intentional spin into criminal behavior, but there were more than a few boats out there that transport drugs and weapons and perhaps worst of all—people. The *Reel Lady* had probably changed ownership since, as it was probably seized by NOAA or customs and sold at auction.

Some deep rumbling conversation came through the speakers from the other end of the line. I couldn't quite make out what was being said, but figured since they'd asked me to be on the conference call, I was about to find out.

"Agent Dalton?" Lewis said.

"Yes, sir." Here it comes.

"I want you to take the lead on the investigations side of things. Get out there and figure out if this is an accident or if there's anything more going on. Nose around a little, see what you can come up with."

Called it. "Yes, sir," I said, reaching for the off button on the phone, a second too late.

"Oh, and one other thing," Lewis paused, probably knowing I wouldn't like what he was going to say. "I need you to take Agent Carter with you."

To my credit, I didn't say a word, but I could feel Lewis holding up his hand on the other end of the line as if to stop me.

"Now don't give me excuses," he said. "I know she's headstrong and thinks she knows everything, but not without reason. She graduated from FLETC, the FBI's training academy down in Georgia, with flying colors, after all…She has a good heart, she just needs a little guidance. I'm making it your job to guide her. It'll be good for you to have someone else to think about besides yourself. It's not healthy to spend all that time alone. See she stays out of trouble and learns a thing or two, will you?"

I didn't reply right away. I wanted to give at least one, 'but, sir,' although I knew it wouldn't do any good. Lewis had already decided. Carter's reputation preceded her like a foul wind. She may have had a 'good heart,' but she needed more than a 'little guidance.' From the scuttlebutt I'd heard around the sector, she needed mountains of guidance, and I didn't feel like taking a rookie, especially one as headstrong, arrogant, and argumentative as she was, under my wing.

"Still there, Dalton? Did you hear me?" Lewis said.

"Yes, sir. I heard you. Take Carter with me. Understood."

Ugh. Welcome back to work, I thought, and hung up the phone.

Two

I'd arranged to pick up Carter at a small park and ride near Portland, Texas. It was unnecessary to have her come all the way into the office; she lived on the way to Aransas and the *Reel Lady*. And anyway, that gave me less time in the car with her.

The only car left in the motor pool when I checked out was a nondescript economy-size Ford. I'm not sure what Ford was going for when they built this bad boy, but I nearly got flattened by an eighteen-wheeler when I tried to merge onto the highway, as it was so slow to accelerate. I jammed my foot flat to the floor, and the engine protested, sounding like a scurry of squirrels had taken up residence beneath the hood. I dunno, maybe they had.

I got out of that jam, my ears still ringing from the horn of the big rig, and settled down as I crossed over the Harbor Bridge, enjoying the view of the channel below, the Texas State Aquarium and the USS Lexington. If you ever visit my part of town, both are worth a look. The bridge connects to North Beach and through to the Nueces Bay Causeway, which is a beautiful drive. I pulled into the park-n-ride a little further up the road in Portland. Carter was standing on the curb, waiting for me. She was easy to spot. I got out of the car to greet her.

"Carter? I'm Dalton. Frank Dalton. We spoke on the phone last night."

I held my hand out to her, and we shook.

"Get in, and I'll brief you on the way." I opened the passenger door of the eco-friendly government sedan for her, and she muttered a brusque thanks.

Even dressed in civilian clothes, Carter had stood out among the handful of commuters. Her body language screamed, "I'm a federal agent and trying hard not to look like one." New agents were always easy to spot, and Carter was no exception. An oversized jacket covered a polo shirt and came halfway down the backside of her khaki slacks. Most rookies thought a baggy shirt or large jacket will hide their weapon. Instead, it drew attention, especially in the mugginess of South Texas. Her jet-black hair was pulled back in a bun so tight it looked like it might hurt and dark sunglasses rounded out the federal agent ensemble. She gave me a tight look, lips pursed together as she slid into the seat.

I pulled out of the park and ride and back onto Route 181 toward Gregory and the eventual turn to Aransas Pass. The squirrels manning the engine protested when I floored the accelerator. They eventually gave in, and I came up to cruising speed without killing us. I took small but perverse pleasure in trying to break the little engine that couldn't.

"So, Jessica, I wanted to go over a few things before we get there."

"Such as?" Carter had a sensual voice. It was deeper than I expected, husky and sexy, like I'd imagine a singer from a 1920s jazz club.

"Well, for starters, like how we're going to run this investigation."

"I'm going to take the lead," she said.

I paused for a moment, considering how best to reply, and decided on a diplomatic response. "That's certainly one option."

"What's the other option? Let you take the lead?" she said, almost snorting. "I outrank you."

Oh boy, it's going to be like that, is it? I clenched my teeth, gripping the steering wheel tighter. Although Carter was technically correct in her assertion, she was a mile away from how the world worked. Maybe this was what the SAC wanted me to sort out?

If we get down to the nuts and bolts of it, Carter was an ensign, the most junior of officers, fresh to the service. I was a chief warrant officer, a rank you can only obtain by growing up through the enlisted ranks, and had a lot more years of service under my belt. That usually gets you a modicum of respect as you've been around the block once or twice. A 'good' junior officer, although technically superior to a warrant officer, will come to them for guidance and advice. Now and again, however, the factory at the Coast Guard Academy churns out an individual who likes to play the superiority card and throw their rank weight around. Which is absurd when you realize these people have been in the service for about ten minutes and are super green. Fortunately, until now, I hadn't come across a, 'I'm better than you,' person since Diana Robinson—man, that's a story by itself—but it still grated. Games like these were what made me hate the Coast Guard sometimes. There was no need for them. What Carter was forgetting, since she was so new, was that as federal agents at our level, we superseded the rank thing and were equals in all but pay. I counted to ten before I replied.

"Sure, sure you do," I said. I didn't want to get into that conversation with her right now. "Thing is, this is a pretty sensitive case." I glanced at Carter, who didn't object, and carried on quickly. "I get where you're coming from, all your training, academy time and so on. The SAC tells me you did well down at FLETC."

"But?"

"But you need some field experience to go with all the training you have to round you out. You might have excellent technical abilities and book smarts, but you don't yet have the proficiency to go along with it. Listen, I was on leave when I got the call about this. The last place I want to be right now is here." The 'with you' didn't need to be implied. "But the SAC asked me to help, to give you some guidance." I bit my tongue. Damn. I knew as soon as I said guidance, I'd said the wrong thing. Out of the corner of my eye, I saw her staring blankly at me, her face impassive. I let her stew and concentrated on driving.

Queen palm trees flew past, clouds dark and pregnant overhead. I turned off the highway at the exit for Aransas Pass. There wasn't another car in sight for miles. I sped up, dust billowing behind me. I couldn't remember the last time it had rained. Everything had dried up and turned to dust. When it did rain, it was going to be all gooey sludge until it dried again.

When she finally spoke, her words were monotone. It didn't take a mind reader to sense she was seething underneath. "I can handle a sensitive case, Dalton."

I glanced at her. Whatever look I had on my face must have shown through.

"No, I can," Carter said. "I've done a ton of interviews and interrogations. Mr. Lewis asked *me* to help *you* in this case, not the other way around. He said we needed to work together and my high scores for fieldwork would be invaluable. I think perhaps you mistook what he said."

"Did I? I know you have high scores, Carter. Like I said, I get it, but this case is a little different. This isn't a classroom where, if you fuck up, no one gets hurt. This is the real world. We—"

"We were at the point where you were telling me why I can't do the job I've been trained to do," she said.

"Yes. No. It's not like that. The reason the command wants me to take this is because they're treating the death as suspicious."

"And?"

"And when they ran the captain's associations, it came back with a hit on a fellow called Timmy 'Batman' Black."

"Batman? Really?"

"Really. Not like the superhero, though, more like an antihero. Timmy was called Batman because he liked to close his business deals with a baseball bat if they weren't going his way."

She looked away. "Jesus."

"No, he was never involved. Just Batman." I risked a furtive look her way, but didn't get a reaction. Figures. I continued. "That's the reason the command called me in. I've dealt with these types of people before. They don't mess around, and they don't like us much either, or any feds, for that matter. I do need your help, though."

"Glad I can do something," Carter said, the sarcasm hard to miss.

I ignored her. "While I'm talking to these guys, I want you to keep your eyes open. I don't believe there's any actual danger. Not many people are stupid enough to go after two armed federal agents, but we don't know the whole story here. I want you to read their body language, see if we can isolate who's lying, if anyone, or who's more likely to tell us the truth."

"I didn't think there was anything suspicious about the death. I thought the master of the boat fell overboard. Slipped or something," she said.

"It's the 'or something' we're looking into. You're probably right, this could be routine, and we'll go home tonight, have a beer and think nothing more of it. However, we're mandated to investigate every maritime death, and based on the Batman connection, we need to look a tiny bit closer than usual."

She seemed to accept that. "You have any history on the crew?"

"No. Nothing popped up. All I know is they reported the captain missing, and it took a few hours to find him. This could all be a tragic accident. We just don't know yet." I needed to wrap this up, since we were getting closer to Port Aransas. "So, can we work together? Will you follow my lead?"

I glanced at Carter. Her face didn't give away too much. I hoped she saw it my way.

"Yeah. Sure. I'll be your little bitch."

Guess not. "Fuck, Carter. What's your problem? You're just out of school. You don't have any field experience. You've been in the Coast Guard, what, five minutes? I've been in nineteen years. I've been doing this job for the last ten. I'm experienced. I know what I'm doing. Why the attitude? What's eating you?" I didn't give her a chance to respond. "You know what? Don't fucking answer. I don't want to hear it."

I was seething. Fuck. I knew she was going to be trouble. A rookie agent with a big fuck-off chip on her shoulder about God knows what. This was all I needed.

A gray sedan barreled out of a side road, appearing from nowhere, not stopping, heading straight for us. I yanked the steering wheel and swerved, the tires protesting as I stomped on the brake and we skidded to a stop inches before impaling a palm tree. The sedan accelerated away.

"Shit. Did you see that fucking guy? Did you see?" I looked at Carter. "Shit. Are you okay?"

Carter was gasping and rubbing her right shoulder. "I'm fine. Shoulder hurts, is all."

"Shit. Sorry."

"Not your fault. I'll be okay. The seat belt did its job."

"Do you need to go to medical?"

"I said I'll be fine. Let's go."

I looked around. "Fucking guy's taken off already. Sorry. He came out of nowhere. Did you get a look at him?"

"No. I didn't see him."

"Guy came out of nowhere," I said.

"You said that already."

"Okay." I took a deep breath to steady my nerves. I sat there for a second, collecting myself.

"Are we going to sit here all day?" Carter said.

What was her issue? There had to be something I was missing. I ignored her and gently coaxed the squirrels back to life as the car had stalled. I put the car into reverse and maneuvered away from the tree, back onto the road, engaged drive and sped up carefully, scanning everywhere for any other ne'er-do-wells behind the wheel.

After a minute or two of silence, my eyes moving from mirror to windshield to mirror, the shot of adrenaline wearing off, I said, "All right...Where were we?"

She didn't answer.

The rest of the journey was in silence.

THREE

After driving down a few nondescript side roads for a few miles, the salt air struggling through the vehicle's air conditioning vents, we approached the port town of Aransas. Hulks of derelict fishing vessels dotted the landscape, rusting and sad, remnants from past hurricanes and storms. The occasional liquor and check-cashing store dotted both sides of the street, their garish neon lights enticing the downtrodden, all competing to take your hard-earned wages.

I rolled the windows down, and the incoming slug of humidity immediately battled with the outgoing air. The cooled air vanished instantly, and the rotting stench of fish rode in on a horse of heat and assaulted my senses. I quickly rolled the window back up.

I pulled into a parking lot and slowly drove past a shabby sign, 'Reel Fish Reel Quick,' swinging in a light sea breeze. Cute. This was the home port of the *Reel Lady*. They had a fleet of fishing vessels with catchy titles like *A Hook In Time* and *Catchin' Up*.

The *Reel Lady* had been heading into port ever since they recovered their captain, about a nine-hour transit. They were expected to arrive around noon, and even though I wasted no time in getting here, she had already beaten us to the dock and was moored up. Shit. I'd wanted to be here first. If that car hadn't delayed us, we might have made it.

I got out of the squirrel mobile and stretched. The stench of rotten fish wasn't getting any better, and it clung to the air like moss to stone. My feet crunched on the bleached, broken shellfish shells that paved their lot. The passenger door opened and slammed, and Carter appeared as I pulled out my go bag from the trunk. She looked frumpy in her oversized coat.

I think I hated her a little. It annoyed me I'd been saddled with such a cantankerous know-it-all, or anyone for that matter, preferring to work by myself. I put her out of my mind and looked around. There were several nice cars in the parking lot. Unusual for a small fishing company. Mixed in with the usual beat-up cars, trucks, and circa 1990s Toyotas, there was a Range Rover, a Maserati convertible, a sparkling Audi and a shiny new BMW, one of the large ones, complete with temporary tags.

"Hey Carter, fishing must be good, must be *reel* good," I said.

She stared at me with a vacant look.

"Get it? *Reel* good?"

No response from Carter. She stared at me like I had two heads. "Never mind," I said under my breath. I looked at my eco-friendly government sedan and sighed. It was a long way from a Maserati. I hoped the squirrels were resting up for the return trip.

Carter jerked me out of my reverie with her dulcet tones. "What are we waiting for, Dalton?"

I looked at her and shrugged. Maybe it was time to be the big man on the campus. "Just taking it all in, Carter. Just taking it all in. Look, I don't want to get off on the wrong foot here. Forget what I said in the car. I was pissed. It's been a long day already."

I started to walk toward the dock when Carter spoke up. "I've been thinking. About what you said."

I stopped and turned back. "Go on," I said.

"I was thinking I'm going to take the lead in this investigation."

My turn to stare blankly. "No. You're not," I said.

Her nostrils flared, and her cheeks flushed. She swallowed and took a deep breath, forcing it down. She looked at me.

"I thought we sorted this out," I said.

"For you, maybe. Hear me out, Dalton," she spat out the words. "Like I said, I had time to think." She paused and took a deep breath. "You might think I've only been in the Coast Guard for five minutes, but I spent four long, grueling years at the academy." I held back a snort. "Think on that. Four long, shitty years of swabbing decks that were already spotless. Four years of running and marching and classes and marching and push-ups and on and on. Knowing the whole time your friends from high school were living it up, getting drunk and high at other schools, but that was okay because I chose this. What did you do? Eight short weeks of boot camp about a bazillion years ago? I have more than enough time in service to know when I don't know something. I felt excited when Mr. Lewis asked me to help. Really excited. I felt like he was giving me a chance to prove myself. To show what I've learned, what I could do.

"You have no idea what it's like to be a woman in the service. We have to try twice as damn hard and be twice as damn good, just to feel like we're on the same level as a man. You cannot have any idea how grueling and goddamn demeaning it is to see men you know, you damn well know, that are not as good as you are getting the plumb assignments or promotions over you."

"Now hold on, Carter."

"No, you hold on, Dalton. I'm trying to explain. I'm trying to make this work. I'm not a bitch, even though it might seem that way right now. I realize I have a long way to go, but I thought...I was led to believe..." She spread her arms wide. "This was all mine. This was what I thought was the culmination of long years of hard work. The beginning of something. And what do I find? Some guy the SAC asked to guide me, who's almost old enough to be my dad, and admitted he'd rather be anywhere else, shot my feet out from under me before we even started. Fuck you and fuck him."

She's been punctuating each point she said with a jab of her right index finger. She was almost out of breath with the emotional toil of bearing her guts. I was smart enough to not say anything right away. This wasn't the time to argue. This was the time to let her vent. Maybe I was seeing the real Carter. I wondered how many others had ever seen this side of her. Honestly, apart from the part about being old enough to be her dad, I didn't disagree with her.

Carter ran her hands through her hair, realizing at the last moment it was in a bun. "And this fucking jacket? I look like a fucking blimp."

"I honestly hadn't noticed."

"Then you're a lousy investigator."

Carter ripped off the jacket and flung it on the ground, stamping on it and grinding it into the seashells.

That was going to be a tough dry-cleaning bill.

With the jacket gone, she already looked like a different person. She pulled her hair out of the brutal bun and shook it loose. Her hair wasn't black like I thought, but a dark shade of auburn, about shoulder length. Gone was the dowdy and tense rookie, and in its place was...a no-nonsense female federal agent. Looking every bit the part.

"Dalton," she said, hesitating. "I need this."

Now it was my turn to think. Despite what she said, Carter had a reputation for being a bitch. But the trouble with scuttlebutt is you never know where the information is coming from. I should know better than to let gossip cloud my judgment. She had to act like a tough cookie to get ahead. I could certainly appreciate that.

"Perhaps we've both come about this from the wrong direction," I said. "I have the field experience, but honestly, I have no idea what you've been taught. It's been years since I went to school. I'm probably a little rusty on new policy and guidance as well. How about I teach you how to apply what you learned in school to the real world, and you can educate me on new ways of doing things? Maybe we can learn from each other."

Carter didn't look like she agreed. Then again, she didn't disagree, either. Her internal shield was up again, masking her thoughts.

"How about we play it by ear for now and decide who leads later? Okay?" I said.

She shrugged. "Sure, we can try that."

She walked toward the building, and I followed her, catching up on the stairs and reaching the door first. The steps up to the building were old and gnarly, and like the sign, could have used a fresh coat of paint. The door was plain, wooden, blue paint peeling from years of neglect. I was about to knock but stayed my hand, as I could hear snippets of a loud conversation coming from inside.

"I'm sorry, Jimmy," said one voice from inside.

"I told you this wasn't the right trip," said another curt voice.

This was good intel and I might have learned something valuable, but Carter pushed past me, banged on the door with her fist and swung it open before I could stop her.

"Goddammit," I said.

I walked through the door after her, almost catching the rebound of the door in my face. We were inside an enormous warehouse with massive bay doors in the far back, flooding light into the building. Through those doors, I could see several fishing vessels unloading crates, a forklift moving busily back and forth. After my eyes adjusted from the brightness outside, I could see to the right of the door was a soda machine, and this is where two men were standing, staring at us.

"You there," Carter said, pointing at the men. "Who's in charge?"

The two men looked at each other and ignored her.

"I'm sorry. Did I stutter? I asked you who was in charge," she said.

One of the two men peeled off without looking and walked away.

"Hey, the lady asked a question. Where's the boss?" I said to the remaining man.

He shrugged and pointed to a large chair perched on the edge of the loading dock facing the water.

"Thanks," I said.

We walked over to where he had pointed, our shoes thumping on the stained concrete and echoing off the tin walls of the warehouse. As we got closer, I could see the chair was an executive chair, brown leather, massive. I doubt it could have fit behind a regular-sized desk. A thick plume of smoke was wafting upward, emanating from the fattest cigar I think I've ever seen, being held by the fattest fingers I've ever seen, from the fattest man I've ever seen. He looked, seriously, as if he'd been poured into this chair, he filled every possible crack and cranny.

I glanced at Carter as we approached the man. She looked a little contrite from her initial encounter by the door, so I pulled out my badge and introduced myself. "Sir, my name is Frank Dalton. I'm a Special Agent for the US Coast Guard. This is Special Agent Carter. Do you have a minute?" I smiled my most disarming smile to take the edge off the whole federal agent thing.

The man continued to puff on his cigar, looking us up and down. His beady eyes flickered over me but lingered on Carter a moment longer than was comfortable. I couldn't tell if he thought she was a threat, was dismissing her, or was checking her out.

Finally, he spoke. "Forgive me for not getting up. I'm not as young as I used to be." He was losing his hair, true, and what was left was gelled straight back. I placed him, not a day past sixty. Not so old. He was wearing a yellow jogging suit, like something that would have been comfortable and fashionable years ago. Hello? The 1970s called and want their jogging suit back. The front of the yellow ensemble was covered in ash, and his wrist jingled with gold bracelets when he reached forward to shake my hand. He had a firm shake, and his gold rings dug into my hand, squeezing. He held the grip for perhaps a moment too long, showing me who was the boss here.

"Tim. Tim Black. Pleased to meet you, agents." He nodded at Carter but didn't shake her hand. So, this was Batman, huh? The theme tune echoed inside my head. *Na na na na na na na na na na na na—Batman!*

I tuned myself out. "I'm sorry for the loss of your captain, Mr. Black," I said. "I understand the crew did everything they could for him."

"It is what it is." He shrugged, more ash falling on his voluminous stomach from his cigar. He didn't seem to notice. "Fishing's a dangerous business. People get hurt." He had a staccato way of speaking, as if the effort to get the air out of his lungs was too much for him.

"Were you on board when it happened, sir?" I said.

Black stared at me for a moment as if I was crazy and barked out a laugh, sounding like a seal.

"Me?" Black waved at his stomach. It jiggled in front of him like a large tub of lemon Jell-O. "No. No, I wasn't on board. I don't fish anymore. I suppose you'll want to talk to the crew?"

I nodded.

He flapped his hands at one of the moored vessels at the dock. "You'll want to talk to them over there. Tell them I said it was okay. They'll speak with you. You can use my office if you want. For privacy. Talk to Ricky. He's the first mate."

"Of course. Thank you for your help, sir," I said.

Black continued to puff on his cigar, never moving from his spot as we walked outside to the *Reel Lady*. Carter didn't say anything. I couldn't tell if she was upset about her interaction with the two guys when we came in or Black's obvious sexist dismissal.

On the dock, gulls floated lazily in the afternoon sea breeze, waiting to swoop in and pounce on some scraps. The waterfront was chock full of fishing boats, some moored up three deep, waiting to offload their catch. Aransas wasn't known for the cleanest fishing fleet in the world. Boats were dented and dinged, paint faded and peeling. It wasn't like the marina where I live, all glossy and picture-perfect. This was a working port, where real people sailed in weather most of us wouldn't go outside in. These were working boats, ran hard and looking like it. Fishermen were a proud bunch, and rightly so, it was a hard life and a hard job, but not something they'd readily give up for anything else.

I looked at the *Reel Lady* and suppressed a shiver. It would be super easy to slip over the side of one of these boats, far out to sea. A quiet splash. Coughing and spluttering, trying to catch a breath amid the waves. Head bobbing, barely above water, yelling at the crew, but no one to hear you over the racket of the engines and fishing gear. You can see them, but they're not looking for you. Not knowing you're in the water. Watching your only chance at survival steam away from you. Knowing you only have a small window. A slight chance someone might notice you're gone and raise the alarm. You tread water but know it's only a matter of time. No life jacket. Out of shape. You slip under. So tired. So tired.

It would be super easy to slip over the side, late at night, far out to sea. It would be super easy to be pushed too. Late at night, far out to sea.

Four

We stood on the dock and stared at the *Reel Lady*. "What do you think, Carter?" I was interested in her initial reaction and wanted to pull her back in from her introspection.

She glanced at me, shrugged, and continued to stare at the boat. "I don't know. Black didn't seem to be as brutal as you described him. I can't imagine how he even gets out of that chair, let alone wields a bat."

"Perhaps he has his first mate wheel him around," I said, and then imitating Blacks' voice, "Ricky, push me over there so I can break his legs. Hurry, man, before he gets away."

"And what? The victim doesn't run away? From a fat guy in a chair?" I could see Carter wasn't warming up to my idea. "Anyway," she said, "Black didn't seem to mind us talking to the crew, so there's that." She shrugged again. "I don't think we know anything else. We haven't spoken to anyone that knows anything."

I nodded. "I still like my chair idea, but on the whole, I'd have to agree with you on Black. Looks like his batting average is a lot lower than it used to be. Who knows? Let's go find this Ricky."

The *Reel Lady* was a hulk of a vessel. She was only eighty-seven feet long, but up close, looked much larger. Her superstructure was a delicate shade of rust, marred only by the original white paint peeking through, and her hull was a cool blue, although long faded by salt and sun. Dents and scrapes were apparent everywhere. She was no showboat.

Four men huddled together on the stern, talking quietly and smoking. We made our way over to them, mindful of large crates of shrimp whizzing above our heads, suspended on teensy tiny hooks, secured in place by a rusty green crane. The men scattered when we got close, except for a tall, skinny man who was leaning on the deck railing. He took a drag of his cigarette and threw it over the side as he looked at us, challenging.

"Hey, sir. Looking for Ricky. Is that you?" I asked. I had to raise my voice to be heard from the dock, over the whirring and clanking of the crane.

He nodded once. "That's me."

"Ricky, my name is Frank Dalton. This is Jessica Carter. We're investigators with the Coast Guard. Can we come aboard, so we don't have to shout at each other? We need to ask you a few questions about what happened last night."

Ricky nodded at me, and we clambered aboard using a makeshift gangway made of a couple of two-by-fours and a long stepladder. Not the safest gangway I'd ever used, but it did the job. I looked back when I got on deck to see if Carter needed any help, but she was managing fine.

"Pleased to meet you," I said to Ricky, after Carter joined me. We shook hands. He had a hard grip, hands rough and calloused from work. "Mr. Black said we should talk to you. First, though, let me say we're dreadfully sorry about the loss of your captain. I know it must be tough."

Ricky's eyes flitted between us and the warehouse, maybe getting confirmation from Black. I could tell he'd seen something as his eyes went blank as if they were shutters, banging closed on a stormy day.

"Had you known the skipper long?" I said.

Ricky's face remained impassive. "You'll want to talk to Jimmy. He's the one noticed Willis was missing."

"Sure. Sounds good. Who's Jimmy?" I said.

"Deckhand."

"Mr. Black said we could use his office for the interviews. Do you have any problem with that?"

"That's fine. It's back over there," Ricky waved his hands at the warehouse. "I'll send Jimmy over."

"Thanks. Appreciate it," I said.

Ricky nodded, walked to a hatch in the superstructure, and bellowed inside for Jimmy. For such a skinny man, his voice was pure baritone when he yelled, like the deep rumbling bass of a tuba.

Once Ricky was out of earshot, Carter said to me, "What the fuck is that smell?"

I sucked in a deep breath and smiled. "That, my dear, is the smell of money. Or rotting fish. Sweat. Saltwater. Low tide. Take your pick. It is pretty awful, isn't it? You never get used to it, though you learn to tolerate it."

"I can't wait."

Jimmy sluggishly shuffled into view through the hatch, mopping his brow with an old dirty rag, sweat dripping down the front of his coveralls, chest heaving. He was a big man, standing a good foot taller than Ricky.

Ricky jerked his head in our direction and Jimmy looked from Ricky over to us and back to Ricky. Jimmy mumbled something to Ricky I couldn't catch, and Ricky shrugged. Jimmy stared for a second and then lumbered over to us.

"Jimmy?" I said.

Jimmy nodded. "S'right."

"I'm Frank, this is Jessica. Mr. Black said we could use his office to talk. Shouldn't take more'n a few minutes." I smiled a quick, tight smile at Jimmy. "Perhaps you could show us the way?"

Jimmy clambered over the side of the *Reel Lady* and motioned for us to follow. He walked straight through the random puddles of fish run-off pooling on the concrete pier, seemingly oblivious to the slop, while Carter and I dodged around them for the second time.

He led us past Black, where I nodded to him. He ignored me, or rather, he stared straight through me without blinking. It was creepy. Jimmy also glanced at him, but I couldn't tell if there were any subliminal messages.

We came to a cramped office, invisible unless you knew it was there, tucked into the dingy back of the warehouse. A tiny air conditioner perched in a grubby window. It strained and lumbered, sounding like its last good day was a decade ago, and a small ceiling fan whirred listlessly overhead. Neither did anything to remove the smell of stale cigarette smoke and rotten fish, nor did they cool the room. Jimmy squeezed his bulk behind a small desk that took up over half the space in the room. When he sat down, he unzipped his coveralls part way to reveal a sweat and food-stained, once-white T-shirt. His large stomach eased itself onto the desk, and he sighed in relief and motioned me to sit, ignoring Carter's stare. I took out my pad to take some notes, while Jimmy took a long drag from a cigarette he had lit. Carter glared at him, still standing, and coughed, but he didn't even raise an eyebrow.

"Okay Jimmy," I said, "why don't you lead us through the events of yesterday?"

Jimmy said nothing. He looked like he was gathering his thoughts one by one. I didn't know how long that would take, so I prompted him again. "So...what happened?"

"Right," he said. "Well, I went up to the bridge to see if the captain wanted a mug of tea. He liked tea in the afternoons. He wasn't there."

Jimmy fell silent, appearing anxious. This would not be fun. I waited a few moments, then said, "And then what?"

"I looked out the bridge windows over the transom, but I couldn't see him. I thought he might have gone for a piss."

"Weren't you worried no one was driving the boat?" asked Carter.

Jimmy stared at her for a second before answering, as if he'd just noticed she was in the room. "No, Miss. I wasn't. Not at the time. The boat was on autopilot. It wasn't unusual for the captain to take a breather for a minute or two."

"And what time was this?" I asked, getting the conversation back on track. Routine questions always helped establish a baseline. No one was going to lie about what they had for dinner, for instance. I could gauge Jimmy's body language and compare it later to questions in which he might not be so truthful. It's not a difficult thing to do if you've had training.

Jimmy took a full five seconds to think while the ash lengthened on his cigarette. "About four in the afternoon. After that, I went back down below to prepare the evening meal."

"And what was for dinner?"

"Dinner was—"

"Never mind dinner," Carter said. "Why didn't you call the Coast Guard for help," she shuffled through some notes, "for another two hours?"

Jimmy stared at Carter like she had two heads. So did I.

Jimmy's eyes flickered to me, then back to Carter. Reluctantly he said, "I don't know, Miss."

I broke the tension and tried a different tack. "Jimmy," I said, to get his attention away from Carter and back on me, "what happened after you prepared dinner?"

Jimmy turned back to look at me, taking the last drag on his cigarette and stubbing it out in the overflowing ashtray on the desk. He blew the smoke in Carter's direction.

"I went up to the bridge to see if the cap wanted any grub."

"And did he?"

"He wasn't there, like I said. I looked around. We was still on course, and the autopilot was still on, but it was strange he wasn't up there by now."

"Okay. What happened next?"

"I went back down to the galley and asked the guys if they'd seen him. They were the ones working on deck while I was cooking."

"And what are their names?" I asked.

"Ricky, George, and Paul."

"What time was this?"

Jimmy appeared more at ease, less anxious. He didn't take as long to think. "About five-thirty. We always had dinner at five-thirty."

"Okay. Had the guys seen the captain?"

"No. They said they thought he was on the bridge. When I told them he wasn't and hadn't been earlier, Ricky, he's the first mate, he tells me and the rest of the crew to search the boat. Ricky goes up to the bridge, and I can feel the engines slow down."

Jimmy twitched. He was nervous again, but I couldn't tell if he was lying, tired, scared, or all three. "Tell me, Jimmy," I said, "what's your usual routine on board? You know, before any of this happened. Take me through a typical day."

Jimmy lit another cigarette, the action calming him. After a moment, he said, "Normally, I help out on deck. We all do. The cap—"

"I can't see the relevance of this," Carter said, looking at me. She turned to face Jimmy. "Tell me what happened when you found the master of the vessel."

"Excuse us, Jimmy, me and Carter need to confer for a minute." I stood up and took hold of Carter's elbow and ushered her out of the small office and down a narrow passageway to gain some privacy.

"Get off me, Dalton," she said, shaking my hand off her elbow.

"What do you think you're doing?" I whispered.

"Dalton, you're not asking the right questions," she whispered back, holding up her hand. "We need to know what happened to the captain. Who gives a rat's ass what his usual day is like? This is not how you interrogate someone." She huffed some more, and I gave her a moment to come down from the ledge.

"Finished?" I said.

She nodded.

"First, we are not interrogating the man. We're interviewing him. Second, he's not guilty of anything. Yet. We're trying to find out what the hell happened, and every time you jump down his throat, it takes us two steps back. These men have been through a tough ordeal. Maybe they topped the captain, but we'll never find out unless we build a rapport. We need to use a kid-glove approach. Understand?" Carter didn't say anything and walked back to the office. I wasn't sure if she'd heard anything I'd said.

"Sorry about that Jimmy—" I said, entering the room behind Carter, but stopped when I saw a woman standing next to Jimmy behind the desk. I couldn't tell you if I'd stopped talking because I was more impressed with her looks, that she'd found space next to Jimmy, or had snuck in without me or Carter noticing. The woman had intense blue eyes, piercing, even through the haze of smoke, topped by a shock of golden hair. A cute button nose perched above an upturned mouth as if she was always one step away from having heard the world's best joke.

"Hello, miss. I'm Dalton, this is Carter," I said, reaching over the desk and offering my hand. "What's your name?"

"Mr. Dalton, Miss Carter," she said, shaking my hand, "my name is Jamie Lancaster from Lancaster, Lancaster, and Mitchell. I'm representing the crew, and I'd appreciate it if you wouldn't ask them any more questions without me, or representation from my firm, present." She handed both of us a card and shook Carter's hand. "And I would like a word with all the crew first before we continue."

"Of course," Carter said.

"No," I said. All three of them looked at me. "I don't mean to be a pain, Miss," I glanced at the card, "Lancaster. I don't mind you being present when we interview the crew, but I can't let you talk to them alone. Not until we're done."

"May I remind you, Mr. Dalton, I represent the crew, and as their legal—"

"Sorry," I said, glancing at Jimmy. "Can I talk to you outside for a moment, Miss Lancaster?" I didn't stick around to see how she squeezed back around the desk. I didn't need the distraction. I marched back up to the cozy spot where I'd talked to Carter. Carter trailed behind.

As soon as she reached me, I said quietly, "Miss Lancaster, let me be clear. The Coast Guard is here to find out what happened. As such, we control the investigation, who we talk to and when. You're more than welcome to be involved in the interviews with the crew, but you can't represent them all, as that's a conflict of interest." I couldn't resist adding, "They must have covered that in lawyering 101."

"Mr. Dalton, this is highly irregular." She looked at Carter for confirmation I was off my rocker. Carter had her blank look on. I couldn't tell if it was by design or accident. Hopefully, she was taking some of this in.

"No, it's not," I said. "This is standard practice for an administrative investigation. This isn't a criminal investigation; no one has been arrested or charged with anything, so they don't need counsel. If you want to go ask someone, be my guest, but I'm not hanging around while you call. These people have been through enough, without this lasting all day." I looked Lancaster in the eyes.

"Then why did the Coast Guard send two criminal investigators, if this is just administrative fact-finding?" Lancaster said.

"In case it isn't," I said, "and at that point, I will advise whomever I'm talking to of their Miranda rights, and at that point, you are more than welcome to represent them. But you can't represent the company *and* each individual mariner."

She huffed and walked toward the office. "I'll be calling and confirming with my office," she said over her shoulder.

I was right on her heels until Carter pinched me by the elbow, holding me back.

"Can I have a word?" she said.

I was going to ignore her, but something stopped me, maybe it was the look on her face.

Carter inhaled and held her breath for a moment before starting. "I know you're not my friend."

I snorted. She ignored that.

"But I want to try to make this," she waved her hand between us. "I want to make this work, this partnership. I want you to explain to me why the lawyer can't be in the room." She looked at me plaintively.

"Okay." I resisted the impulse to check the time on my watch. "The issue is not simply her presence in the room, but her inability to adequately represent all parties involved. Given that this is a civil investigation, if she obstructs our progress, I have the power to have her expelled. I also don't want her talking to the crew alone and coaching them. Listen, as far as we know, the crew has done nothing wrong. But we do have a dead body. Our job is to figure out how it happened, and our best way of doing that is to put the crew at ease and ask simple questions. It's not like you see on TV, all stainless steel rooms with two-way mirrors, shouting and blustering." I ran my hands through my hair. "Did you catch how Jimmy hadn't seen the captain since the afternoon? And it wasn't until the evening they called the Coast Guard? He may have just gotten his times mixed up, or the master went below, and they missed each other in passing, but it doesn't smell quite right. Look, we have to get back in. If you follow my lead and don't interrupt, I'll coach you through it later."

"All right. I'll try," she said. "I really want this to work. And I really do want to learn so I can lead too."

I looked her in the eye and thought she was sincere. "Okay. Let's go in."

"Jimmy," I said, as we entered. Lancaster stood by his side again, glaring at me. I needed to change things up a bit. All these distractions had derailed the interview. I needed a fresh approach. "I'd like to get back on board the *Reel Lady*, get a feel for the layout, take some photos."

Jimmy looked at Lancaster. She shrugged.

"Sure," he said.

FIVE

We were back on the *Reel Lady*, standing on the stern, looking up at the bridge. It was hard to imagine that yesterday waves were spraying the windows, and all hell was breaking loose. The crew holding on to avoid slipping, searching the waves, massive spotlights beaming through the night. I shook my head and came back to the present.

The crew were smoking again and huddled together, whispering and watching me. I walked over to them with my entourage in tow.

"Jimmy. Can you walk us through where everyone was when you noticed the skipper missing?"

"I can do that," Ricky said, his deep baritone cutting through the quiet gossip of the crew.

"Before you say anything," Lancaster spoke up, "my name is Jamie Lancaster. I'm a lawyer and I've been hired to represent you. If you don't want to say anything, you don't have to."

While technically true, what she'd said was annoying. In a civil investigation, I couldn't compel anyone to talk, but I also didn't have to stop asking questions.

"What she said is true," I said. "And while Miss Lancaster has graciously offered her services, she cannot represent all of you at the same time. Now, if you don't want to answer my questions, that's fine. I'll come back with a warrant tomorrow and bring you in for questioning. But that's going to take time, probably a few days, maybe a week. A week where you're not earning money. Or you could just answer a few simple questions. All we're trying to establish is a timeline for when the captain fell overboard. And then we'll be out of your hair, and we can all go home this afternoon." I saw mixed results on their faces. "And your boss, Mr. Black, said to talk to me." I think that sealed it.

"Now, Ricky. Why don't we start with where everyone was last night?"

"Yeah. Sure. I don't see why it's important, though. Cap' Willis probably slipped over the side while he was cleaning some fish."

"Come again?"

"The overboard flaps get stuck up there on the side of the bridge. See it?" Ricky pointed to a piece of plastic or rubber secured to the side of the bridge, about ten feet up. I lifted my phone to take a picture. "We were shrimping, but if we caught a few fish he liked to clean them up there and throw 'em in a cooler. Sometimes we'd cook 'em up for dinner. The guts would fall in the sink and over the side out that plastic flap. Sometimes it gets gummed up. He was probably reaching round to clear it when he slipped." Ricky pointed at a section of open deck near the bridge secured with a single line right next to the sink. "Sometimes the crew take a piss right there, if they're on watch. Easier than going down below. One time I slipped, and nearly went right in. There's nothing to stop you. I reckon I was lucky that night. I guess it coulda happened like that." The rest of the crew mumbled in agreement and nodded. One of them crossed himself.

"So that's what you think happened?" Carter asked.

"Yeah," he shrugged. "I guess. As likely as anything else."

"What was the weather like, Ricky?" I said.

"Wasn't too bad," he said. I made a mental note to check the NOAA weather report when we got back.

One of the crew snorted. We all looked at him at the same time. "That's Paul," said Ricky. "Pay him no mind. He's new. Only been on the two trips." Ricky raised his voice. "Ain't that right, Paul?"

Paul looked down and mumbled. "Yeah. I s'pose. Seemed rough to me, though. I was hanging on for life when I called the Coast Guard."

"That was you, Paul? Called the Coast Guard?" I said.

He looked up, saw everyone staring at him, nodded, and looked down again. "Yeah. That was me."

So the new guy had been the one to reach out. I filed that away and turned back to Ricky.

"So, Ricky. Humor me. I have a ton of paperwork to do, you know? I have to have exact times for whatever went on. Keeps the old man off my back. So why don't we start with where you were and what you were doing before any of this happened?"

"Yeah, sure. Not much to see. We were trawling." Ricky pointed to the outriggers, now secured upright. I snapped another picture. "The outriggers were down, nets were out. Looking for shrimp."

"Who was with you?" I said.

"It was me, George, and Jimmy. Then Jimmy went inside to make supper. Paul was sleeping."

"What time was this?"

Ricky scratched at his stubble. "Maybe around five. We usually have supper sometime 'fore six."

"And the captain was on the bridge?" I asked.

Lancaster, silent up to this point, sprung to action. I wasn't sure why this particular question had triggered her. "You don't have to answer that, Ricky. You couldn't possibly know where the captain was," she said.

"Sure," he said, ignoring her. "The cap' was on the bridge. While we work the nets, he drives the boat. Same way we've always done it. No reason to think he was anywhere else."

Lancaster walked away, pulling out a phone, no doubt to call her higher-ups. I jumped on the chance to get away from her. "Ricky," I said, "which way is the galley?"

"Forward, through the hatch. You want to see it?"

"Yes, please."

Ricky walked thirty feet or so to the galley door. The door was really a watertight hatch, so it was dogged down to keep it shut tight. Ricky knocked the dogs loose with his right hand so we could go through. I stepped over the lip of the door and followed Ricky into a short passageway that ran into the galley, my shoes sticking to the floor as we neared. The galley spoke of rough days at sea. There was a brown, crusty stain running down the side of the stove. The fridge had countless dirty fingerprints around the handle, and a dent low down that made me think it was usually kicked closed. The sink was stainless once upon a time, but that time had long since passed, and a few dirty dishes lay piled up inside. The air was thick with the smell of rancid grease, and every time I swallowed, it felt like lumps went down my throat. I'm sure that wasn't on the recommended Keto diet list. A small table secured to the floor in the opposite corner with bench seats finished the kitchen.

Jimmy had followed behind Carter down the hallway. I looked back at Jimmy, his bulk pressed into the narrow passageway. There was no way he was getting past Carter, so I turned and spoke to him over her head, "Jimmy, you said you were cooking dinner?"

"'S'right."

"And then you went to see if the captain wanted tea?"

"Yeah."

"Which way did you get to the bridge?"

"I went—"

"He went up the ladder here, through the other side of the galley," Ricky said, cutting off Jimmy.

I turned to Jimmy. "Is that right?"

Jimmy glanced at Ricky before he answered. "Yeah. Yeah, it is." Damn. Now that he wasn't alone, he'd be harder to question. I should have realized. Idiot. All this back and forth was throwing me off my game.

The ladder to the bridge looked narrow. I wasn't sure if Jimmy could make it in that tight a space. "All right, let's go up."

Ricky went up first, followed by me, Carter, and then Jimmy. It wasn't pretty, but I guess he could make it, after all.

I had the feeling though, Jimmy hadn't climbed the ladder yesterday. Ricky was coaching his answers. I wasn't sure why how he got to the bridge was important enough to lie about. Or maybe…Maybe, it was because he hadn't come up to the bridge. Another thought to file away and think on later.

Soon we were all standing on the bridge, looking out over the boat and port. The others had stayed out on deck. If they'd ever had a meal in the galley, they probably didn't want to spend any more time in there than they had to, as gross as it was.

With all of us up here, it was crowded. I eased myself over to the wheel so I could look at the instruments. "Ricky, can you turn on the GPS for me and power up the rest of your electronics?"

"Sure. It'll take a moment to come up," Ricky said, flipping breakers and pushing buttons.

I looked out the bridge windows. The dry salt spray made the windows hazy, but I could still see all around. It would have been easy for the captain to see the crew working on the stern deck. Come to think of it, it would have been easy for the crew to see the captain, too. I took a couple of steps to the rear hatch.

"Ricky, is this the cleaning station you were talking about?" I gestured to a dirty sink, partially covered by an old block of wood, streaked in fish guts, with a short, blunt-looking knife attached to the sink by a string. A series of rubber flaps hung in an opening behind it.

"Yeah. That's right. The flaps behind the sink get stuck sometimes," Ricky said, moving to the sink and pushing on the rubber flaps. "When you're cleaning fish, or shucking scallops, the guts an' shells an' what have you are s'posed to go over the side, like this, but sometimes they get caught. The only way to fix it is to reach around and yank the flaps."

"Show me."

Ricky reached around the open side of the bulkhead with his right hand hanging on with his left, caught hold of the flaps and gave them a quick tug. As if to prove his point, a couple of loose scallop shells fell into the water below.

"That's quite a way to reach around, Ricky. You guys do that underway?"

"Yeah. It's the only way to loosen the flaps, like I said. Captain coulda been reaching round and slipped."

"You're a shrimper, right? A trawler?"

"S'right."

"So how do you get scallops up in the nets? Aren't they stuck down in the mud?"

Ricky shrugged. "Get all sorts of things in them nets. Shrimp, fish, scallops. We sort it out, throw back what we don't want. Sometimes the cap' would keep some bits and pieces for dinner."

The GPS beeped, and I looked back to see the electronics powered up. They looked impressive, as good as some of the gear the Coast Guard had. I thought of the cars I'd seen in the parking lot.

"You've got some sweet navigation gear here, Ricky. A lot more'n most fishing boats I've been on."

"We go a lotta different places. Need to know where we are. Where we're going. Got to get home, too."

Cool as a cucumber, this Ricky. "No doubt," I said. "All right, can you pull up your track line on the electronic chart for me?"

"Yeah. But Paul's more of the electronics guy. Hold on, and I'll get him." Ricky walked back out to the cleaning station and shouted in his booming base again. "Paul, can you help out the Coast Guard? I've got to use the head."

I looked back to where Paul was. I could see him look up at the bridge when Ricky yelled, and he shuffled over, climbing the outside ladder. Lancaster hadn't followed us to the bridge, and now I could see why. She'd been talking to Paul, gesturing urgently.

Interesting.

"Hey, Paul," I said when he made it to the bridge.

"Agent." Paul nodded at me but didn't offer to shake hands.

"Paul, Ricky tells me you're the electronics guy. Can you bring up your track line for me, please?"

Paul shrugged, leaned over the console, and pressed a few buttons. A few moments later, I was looking at a line on an electronic chart that showed me where the boat had been. I pointed to an area that looked like a toddler had scribbled in crayon. "Is that where you started the search?"

Paul shrugged again. "Guess so," he said. I took a couple of close-up shots of the screen with my phone. It would be useful to compare it to the track line the intel guys would get for me.

"Do you have an AIS system on board?" I asked.

Paul gave me a blank look.

"You know," I said, "it records where you've been, and sends out beeps so other vessels can tell who you are on their radars. Like on an airplane?"

"I don't know about that, sir. This is only my second trip, and I'm just getting used to what everything is."

"That's all right." I slipped my bag off my shoulder and pulled out a small thumb drive. "I'm just going to slot this into the laptop here, and download your—"

"You can't do that."

I turned and looked at Lancaster. She'd climbed the outside ladder. She was glaring at me.

"I can, Miss Lancaster. Like I said before, this is merely a fact-finding mission. I can take any evidence off this boat that's pertinent." I turned back around and slid the thumb drive into the back of the laptop.

"My boss, Mr. Lancaster Senior, told me you cannot take any evidence off this vessel."

There was a momentary silence, only punctuated by the sound of the keys I was tapping. I didn't turn around and spoke to her over my shoulder while I continued to type. "Well then," I said. "He's wrong as well. Listen. I don't mean to be a pain in the ass, but you guys need to brush up on your Admiralty Law. I'm not the lawyer here, but I seem to know more than you do. If you keep getting in my way and impeding my investigation, I will have Agent Carter here escort you off the vessel."

Carter did a double take, but was quick enough to hide it from Lancaster and the crew.

Lancaster's phone rang, saving me from carrying out my threat. She tried to retreat gracefully down the ladder, but it was hard in heels and on the phone at the same time. She almost made it, but messed up the last step and did a little dancing, bobbing movement, trying to regain her balance.

The data finished downloading, and I popped the thumb drive out and slipped it back into my bag. I took a few more photos of the bridge layout and the view from the bridge windows. You never know what might be relevant later.

"All right, Paul. So, you called the Coast Guard last night, right?"

Paul nodded.

"Did you call from in here?"

"Yeah. I was scared. I thought we were going to sink. It was so rough, the waves were pounding, and we'd just lost the captain."

"So, you were sleeping when he disappeared?"

"Yeah. I'd worked the last shift and was getting some shuteye. Or trying to. It was so rough I wasn't resting well."

"Did you hear anything? Anything strange go on before you hit the rack?"

"No. Not really."

I looked at him. "Not really, or no?"

Paul looked down at his feet, clearly uncomfortable. "No. Nothing happened."

"Okay." I rubbed at my face. Time for plan C. "Carter, do you have anything?"

She looked at me for a second, gauging if I was testing her. "Yes. I do. Paul, what was the captain like? Did you get along with him?"

"He was all right, I guess. Didn't talk to him too much, you know. This was my second trip, and everyone told me to stay out of his way." Paul said.

"Why'd they want you to stay out of the way?" I asked.

"I dunno," Paul said. "I think they just wanted me to keep clear, as I was the new guy."

"Well, apart from that, how was the captain? Did the other crew get on okay?"

"I—"

"You shouldn't be talkin' 'bout stuff you don't know, Paul," Ricky said, walking back up the ladder from the galley. Ricky looked at me. "You done with him?"

"Yeah, I think so, thanks. He was a great help." What was Ricky trying to hide?

"Is that it then?" Ricky said, "I've got things to do, so does the crew."

"Almost. Give me a minute here with Carter, and I'll catch up with you out on deck."

"Make it quick. We've got work to do." He turned to leave.

"Oh, Ricky?" he stopped. "I almost forgot. Where's your other crew member? George, was it?" I hadn't forgotten.

He shrugged. "Dunno. I wasn't on George watch, maybe he slipped ashore. George can be like that sometimes."

I smiled tightly to his back as he and his pals shuffled out, not believing a word of it. I scanned the bridge once more. I wasn't sure what I was looking for. Nothing looked out of place. I just had a feeling something wasn't quite right. Like when you're walking down a dark alley and the hairs on the back of your head rise and scream at you that a crazy person is running up behind you with a big-ass knife. But when you turn around, it's just a cat. That feeling. There was something not quite right. Something fishy, *Reel Fishy*.

"Carter. What do you think?"

"I don't know. Ricky doesn't want the crew to talk for themselves."

"Yeah, I saw that. I'm not sure if he's keeping secrets or if he's naturally controlling. I don't think there's a lot more we can get here now, especially with Ricky breathing down their necks. We can always come back later. Why don't we do our due diligence, have a quick look in the engine room, and the other spaces, snap a few more photos and call it good? With nothing more to go on, I don't see any way of making this a criminal investigation. Perhaps he did slip and fall over the side. We'll check in with the medical examiner on the way back though, tie a bow on this case. If she doesn't have anything…" I shrugged.

"Yeah, okay."

We descended from the bridge, went through the galley, and found the captain's cabin. There wasn't anything that immediately stuck out, but we gave it a quick once over, anyway.

"Oh, look at this," I said. I pulled out a new-looking iPhone from underneath the dirty mattress. When I glanced up, I saw Ricky hovering in the doorway, watching us. Lancaster was behind him.

I waved the phone at him. "Seen this phone before, Ricky?"

"No."

"Well, since it was stuffed under the mattress, it must have been the captains. Carter, can you sort out an evidence receipt for me?"

"Sure," she said.

"I strongly object to you taking any evidence from this vessel," Lancaster said.

"Oh hello, Miss Lancaster. I thought you'd left already." I smiled at her.

She didn't smile back. The cute, almost joking curve of her mouth I'd noticed when we first met was turned into a face I bet her mama wouldn't have approved of.

"No. I'm still here," she said. "Listen, it's one thing taking some computer track lines or whatever, but taking a phone, essentially a minicomputer that could have company proprietary information on it, is another. I cannot allow you to leave the vessel with that phone." She stood as if to block me. Even Ricky got out of the way.

"Miss Lancaster. Once again, we are investigating the circumstances of the death of Mr. Willis, the captain. We have the authority to use anything that may help us discover those circumstances—"

"But he simply fell overboard. How much information—"

"As I was saying. The Coast Guard investigates every death on board all US flagged commercial vessels. There is no evidence as of right now anything other than the obvious happened, but that does not prevent us from pursuing our investigation. I'd be happy to talk this over with you at the office and show you the applicable regulations and so on. Perhaps tomorrow?" I smiled at her. I think she could tell I wasn't sincere. Either way, it didn't matter. I knew I was in the right.

Carter had finished filling out the evidence receipt and handed it to Lancaster. I bagged the phone and sealed it. I wrote the details of where and at what time I'd found the phone on the bag.

"After the investigation is finished, you can have this item returned, along with any other evidence we may seize," I said. "Now if you'll excuse us."

I poked my head out into the corridor. I saw Ricky slip around a bulkhead. That feeling I had earlier, that something was wrong, came roaring back. I quickly followed him. Carter was right on my heels. I thought he'd headed down the ladder into the engine room, but when I looked down the steps, it was dark. I fished my flashlight out of a pocket, flicked it on and climbed down, shining the light around the engine room.

"Ricky? You in here?" I didn't hear anything, but when I shone the light into the far corner, I saw something move and heard Carter's sharp intake of breath.

I moved the flashlight back to where I thought I saw movement. "Hey. Who's in here? US Coast Guard, come out into the light," I said.

A wraith appeared in the circle of my light and stood motionless. I almost backed up a step but stopped myself as I realized it wasn't a wraith, but a man. A man so pale he could have passed for dead, his eyes deeply sunken and black, a long beak-like nose.

Six

I'd spotted a wraith-like man in the engine room. "Who are you?" I said.

"George," he said, in a rasping whisper. He was wearing overalls like Jimmy's, but stained and far more ragged.

"George. Why don't you come out where I can see you? Keep your hands in view buddy, don't reach for anything and no sudden movements."

"Okay," George said, and he made his way silently over to where we were. He looked even worse up close.

"What were you doing back there in the dark, George?" I said.

"Maintenance. On the engine. Lights went out. Was looking for the switch when you came down."

"All right, George. Find the switch and let's talk."

I followed him with the beam of my flashlight and in a moment, the overhead lights flickered to life. The engine room was large, but like the rest of the vessel, needed some serious TLC. Soot stained the walls presumably from an exhaust leak. The engines were streaked with oil and the bilges looked like they had at least a couple of feet of oily water in them. They'd probably pump that straight over the side when they got offshore.

"George, what do you do here on the boat?" I said when he came back to where we stood. There was barely enough room to stand up straight.

"I'm the mechanic and deckhand. Mostly deckhand," George said. I couldn't tell if George was thinking or not, as his expression never changed. He didn't seem to blink either. Maybe he was a wraith, after all? And why hadn't Ricky, or the others bothered to mention there was a George?

"What were you doing when the captain went missing?"

"I was working the nets on the back. With Jimmy and Ricky."

"When was the last time you saw the captain?"

"I don't recall. I don't keep track of what the captain's movements are...were...above my pay grade."

"Right," I said. I looked at Carter, hoping she'd pick up the lead.

"How well did you get on with him?" Carter said.

Nice, I thought.

George shrugged. An almost infinitesimal movement of his shoulders. At least I think it was a shrug.

"Never had any complaints."

"What do you think happened to the captain?" I asked.

Another small shoulder movement. "Don't know. Not my place to guess. Maybe he slipped."

"And maybe he didn't?" I asked.

George didn't say anything. He didn't move. He didn't blink.

"You done?" Ricky said, coming down the ladder to the engine room. "I thought you'd be gone by now."

Ricky had broken the moment, and I wasn't going to get anything useful out of George. I wondered if he had been waiting, out of sight, listening. I looked at Carter, and she nodded.

"Yeah. I think so," I said. "Look who we found, Ricky. Guess he didn't slip away after all." And I bet you knew where he was all along. "Where'd you run off to Ricky? We were looking for you."

"Wasn't nowhere."

"Sure," I said, ignoring the lie. "Guys, is there anything else you believe we might need to know, that we may not have asked you yet?"

George did his almost shrug. Ricky shook his head.

"Well, thanks for your time, gents. Once again, I'm sorry for the loss of your captain. We'll be in touch if we need anything else." I shook hands with both of them. "Oh. One last thing. When do you guys plan on going fishing again?"

"Don't know," Ricky said. "You'll have to check with Mr. Black. He runs the shop."

"All right, I will. Thanks again."

We left the *Reel Lady*. Mr. Black grunted at us as we passed his warehouse seat that they'd be fishing again in two days. I filed that away with all the other nuggets I'd saved. We slung our bags in the trunk, and I slid behind the wheel, starting the car to cool it down but not driving anywhere yet. I left the door open as it was hotter in the car than outside. I was trying to figure out what to say to Carter. In the end, I decided just to get on with it.

"Let's talk," I said. "I know we got off to a rough start this morning, but I appreciate your help. Once you got your rhythm, you were asking some good questions." I let her digest that for a moment, then continued. "I couldn't explain a lot earlier, but I've got all the time in the world now, so do you have any questions for me about what we did, or what went on?"

Carter turned in her seat to look at me and was silent while she thought. I gave her time.

"There was one thing I didn't understand," she said finally. "Why were you so interested in what they had to eat and what their routine was? It sounded stupid. I thought we were investigating a death, not their eating habits?"

"We are, and we were," I chose to ignore the antagonism. "That's a good question, though. I explained a little of this before. Broadly speaking, when we interview someone, we're trying to build a rapport, trying to make them feel comfortable. They're much more likely to open up if they think we're on the level with them or have something in common. It's also useful to gauge their body language on easy questions, then—or if—they're not telling the truth we have something to compare. It's not foolproof, but it's a useful skill to develop." I took a swig of lukewarm coffee I'd left in the car. Gross. "There are some classes you can take, if you'd like, to help with interviewing, that you wouldn't have gotten at the academy or FLETC. Reid interview and interrogation is a good one. They talk a lot about micro-expressions. Too much to go into now, but I can set you up with the details later if you want?" I closed the car door as the AC had caught up.

"Thanks." Carter looked at her feet, deciding. "Listen, Dalton. I know I wasn't helpful in the beginning, I just...I just like to know what's going on. I thought I was going to be in charge, and then you tell me you're here to babysit...I saw red. I'm not like this. I worked so hard at the academy, had amazing scores at FLETC, and when Mr. Lewis called me, I was so excited. I know I've said this already. I guess I let it get to my head a little. When you said you were running the show, I flipped. I'm sorry. You've been nothing but helpful."

I studied Carter for a second. It takes a lot of guts to admit when you're wrong. I admired the hell out of that.

"Apology accepted. I believe you. And thank you for clearing the air. I think we can make this partnership work. I wasn't joking when I said you could teach me some new things, and if you work with me, I promise to always keep you up to speed when and where I can. Deal?"

We shook hands, awkward in the confines of the small car. "Deal."

I looked out the window. "I don't see a reason to hang out here any longer. Let's head over to the ME's office and see what Doc Hutchins has come up with." I backed out of the space and took a last wistful look around the parking lot at the cars. Maybe one day, I thought.

I turned onto the road and headed back in the general direction of Corpus Christi. I flicked the knob on the radio and the lonely wail of an '80s techno band whose name I couldn't recall warbled from the tinny G-ride speakers. I started to hum. After a minute, Carter leaned over and turned it off.

"You're showing your age," she said and buried her nose in her phone. I wasn't sure about that, but said nothing. I didn't feel old. Did Carter have a sense of humor?

Surfacing from whatever had caught her interest on her cell, she said, "Can we talk about the case?"

"What's on your mind?"

"I don't know what exactly, but they're trying hard to hide something."

"Could be they pushed the ol' boy off the boat," I said.

"Yeah, maybe. Maybe that is it, but I have a feeling they're hiding something more, something else."

"Like?"

"I don't know yet."

"If it helps, I got the same feeling. Maybe the ME will have something for us."

The Medical Examiner's Office of Corpus Christi was nothing like you'd imagine from watching movies. It wasn't dank and dark and depressing, nor was it all glass, gleaming polished stainless steel, and swish sound effects like a CSI episode. Instead, it was an unassuming brick building, pleasantly painted and landscaped, set back from the local police station. From the fifth floor, you could see Corpus Christi Bay on one side and downtown on the other. The Shining City by the Sea. We, however, stayed on the main floor. I guess it was easier to wheel the dead bodies in if you kept it all on the ground level.

Doctor Kelly Hutchins was an odd bird for a medical examiner. She was a whirling dervish of bustling activity, wrapped up in a diminutive package, and despite the frenzy, her compassion belied her size. I'd seen her move from defending the cause of death on the witness stand as an expert witness in front of high-powered attorneys, to hugging relatives that had come in to identify their lost ones. In a word, she was the consummate professional—well, in two words. I'd known her for years, and she'd been the ME well before I'd ever come along. When we walked in, she was going over some notes on a clipboard.

"Hey, Doc, how are ya?" I said.

"Frank! Goodness, I haven't seen you in ages. I'm doing great. How've you been, love?" She put down the clipboard, hugged me, and I was simultaneously wrapped in her arms and enveloped in the lingering smell of disinfectant coming from her lab coat.

"Can't complain," I said. I stepped out of the hug and smiled. "Doc, this is Jessica Carter, my new partner. Carter, this here's the best ME in all of Corpus."

Hutchins snorted. "Pleased to meet you, Jessica. Pay no mind to Frank here. I'm the only ME in Corpus, and Frank's getting old."

"I told him that in the car," Carter said.

"Did you now?" Hutchins said, raising an eyebrow. "And what did Frank say?"

"He didn't say anything. I think he's probably going deaf, too."

"Oh," Hutchins said, clapping her hands together, "I believe we'll get along splendidly, Jessica."

I rolled my eyes. Was Carter coming out of her shell? "Ladies. Can we get down to business?"

"Party pooper," Hutchins said, "But okay. So, I'm assuming you want to talk about the dead fisherman?"

"You assume correctly. What can you tell us?"

"Follow me."

We walked over to the shiny steel refrigerated racks, and Hutchins, consulting her clipboard, found the right numbered drawer and pulled it open, a body-shaped sheet sliding out. The faint odor of decay came with it. It wasn't as bad as people make out, but it wasn't something I'd want to breathe in all day. Mind, I hadn't been there for the actual autopsy. That could get pretty stinky.

Hutchins read off her clipboard. "Captain Frederick Lucius Willis, age 49, found in the Gulf of Mexico by the crew of the *Reel Lady*," Hutchins said.

"Yeah. That's right. The crew said he must have slipped over the side."

"Did they? I suppose he must have gotten in the water somehow, but I don't think he slipped. That's your job to figure out, though. Here, let me show you."

Hutchins pulled back the sheet, exposing Willis and the familiar Y incision, the hallmark of every medical examiner's investigation. I'd seen some dead bodies before, but this one looked rough. His skin was pale and bruised all over.

"His organs appeared normal, except for his liver, which was enlarged, indicative of someone who likes his booze a little too much," said Hutchins. "Add to that, his skin was yellowing, which makes me believe he was in the first stage of liver failure." She raised his right arm and pointed to the left. "He was also an intravenous drug user. The track lines are prominent on both arms."

"What did the tox report say?" I asked, pointing.

"Patience, young man. I'm getting to it," Hutchins said. She rapped my knuckles with her clipboard as I tried to read it upside down. "His blood pathology report suggested he'd recently injected opiates into his system."

"So, he was high and fell overboard," Carter said.

"Well. I don't think so," Hutchins said.

"What do you mean?" I asked.

"The amount of opiates in his system would leave me to believe he was still functioning, albeit at a diminished capacity, and although his lungs showed some water intrusion, I can tell you he wasn't breathing when he fell into the water."

"So, if he was high as a kite, he'd still be breathing and would have drowned had he fallen in the water, which would have shown up in his lungs?" I said.

"Exactly. You know, the offer to be my assistant still stands."

"Another day, Doc."

"What are you saying? That he was dead when he entered the water?" Carter said.

"Yes."

"So, what was the cause of death, then?" I asked.

"Asphyxiation."

"He was strangled?" I said.

"Not exactly. Look here, at his neck. There are no ligature marks or post-mortem bruising, so he wasn't strangled." Hutchins pulled out a small penlight from her top pocket and pried apart one of Willis's eyelids. "But if you look at his eyes, see the marks?"

I leaned in closer and pulled on my reading glasses.

"Old." Hutchins and Carter said together.

I ignored them, trying to see what the doc was pointing out.

"Deaf." They both said in unison.

I huffed and ignored them again. Willis's neck was covered with tiny red spots, like he'd been bitten by insects. "What am I looking at?"

"Those little red marks are petechiae, basically broken blood vessels that show up during suffocation," Hutchins said.

I leaned back and took off my glasses. "Let me get this right. He was high but didn't OD. He was in the water but didn't drown, but he was asphyxiated or suffocated somehow. Thanks for the puzzle. Could he have had a heart attack when he fell, that's why there's no sea water in his lungs? It's not unusual for an overdose to cause a heart attack."

"I looked for that," she said, not minding the question. "There were no signs of a myocardial infarction. So no, on the heart attack."

I cracked my neck, letting out some of the tension. "Anything else?" I said.

"Yes," Hutchins said. "And perhaps this is the most interesting. It's hard to tell, but I don't think he died on board the vessel."

"Why not?"

"Time of death."

"I thought it wasn't that accurate, especially since he's been in the water?" Carter said.

"Well, it's a bit more exact than stuffing a thermometer into him like you're cooking a ham, but there are more scientific ways. I extracted part of his tissue and ran an analysis through the mass spectrometer and gas chromatograph. The results lead me to believe he was frozen for several days."

The silence stretched out for a moment while I absorbed this little nugget. "Shit. He was killed on land and dumped at sea," I said.

"It certainly looks that way," Hutchins said.

I blew out a breath and rubbed my face. "Okay, Doc. Any other little tidbits?"

"No, I think that's about it." Hutchins snapped her nitrile gloves off and shook hands with Carter. "It was a pleasure to meet you, dear. I hope you'll drop by again?"

"I'd like that," Carter said, nodding her head. "Just under better circumstances."

"Oh. Of course. Sometimes I forget as I'm in here all the time. Frank, Nice to see you again too, dear. Don't be a stranger."

"I won't, Doc, I won't," I said.

"And be kind to Jessica. Teach her the right way. Not the way you had to learn."

I looked at her, then Carter, hoping she hadn't heard that last sentence. "Sure, Doc, sure."

We made our way out into the sunshine, and I took a moment to lean into a conveniently placed palm tree and breathe the fresh sea air. It made me feel less annoyed at what Hutchins had said at the end.

Although it was humid, it also made a pleasant change from sucking in the artificial air inside the morgue. I had the utmost respect for Kelly Hutchins. I didn't know how she did it, day after day, looking at death and destruction.

"What did she mean in there, when she said to teach me the right way?" Carter said.

Damn. The back of my neck itched. Sometimes, every so often, I wish I still smoked. This was one of those sometimes. "Well, you don't want to be taught the wrong way, do you? Come on, Carter. Looks like we have a bad guy to catch."

I started to walk back to the car. Carter followed, but she didn't press me for an answer, and for that I was thankful. We jumped in the car and drove back to the office, parking the squirrels in the underground parking lot.

I was grabbing a cup of coffee from the galley that looked suspiciously like the coffee I had made last night when my boss walked in, Assistant Special Agent in Charge Tobias Smith. That was a super mouthful, so I either referred to him as the ASAC or by his name. Whoever came up with these titles didn't say the acronyms out loud.

Smith leaned in the doorway, not quite committing to entering the room. "Frank. Long day. Talk to you guys when you get a chance?" he said.

"Sure, Tobias. I'll grab Carter and catch up with you in the conference room in a minute, if that's okay?"

"No rush." He left. I took my mug to find Carter.

I wound through the cubicles and found her making googly eyes at a puppy someone had brought in.

"Cute dog," I said, after a moment. I watched Carter with the puppy. She appeared relaxed for the first time since I met her. "Hey, the ASAC wants to see us. Can you grab the case folder off my desk and I'll meet you in the conference room?"

She nodded. "Sure. Where's your desk?"

I slapped my head. "I'm sorry. I'm such an idiot. I didn't even show you around. I'll give you the nickel tour and then I'll grab the case folder and we'll go to the conference room together."

I did just that, showing Carter her desk, the galley, where the heads were, and we still beat Smith to the meeting. Carter had to use the head, so instead of looking like a lurch outside the bathrooms, I told her where the conference room was and went on ahead. I sat down in an ergonomically challenged chair someone had probably ordered for hundreds of dollars more than it was worth, and a moment later Carter came in pulling up the next most uncomfortable chair and sat next to me.

Smith walked in through the door, closing it behind him. "You must be Carter," he said, offering his hand as she stood. "Sit, sit, please. I hope Frank has been looking after you? He can be a little set in his ways sometimes."

"Hey," I said.

Smith flapped his arms at me, smiling. "I'm kidding, I'm kidding."

"So, what have you got for me?" Smith asked, sitting across from us.

"Well, at first splash, it looked like the captain of the *Reel Lady* fell overboard. The crew recovered him a few hours later, deceased. We interviewed the crew and Mr. Black—"

"What did Batman have to do with it?" Smith said.

"Oh, you know him too?" Carter asked.

"I think the whole Coast Guard in South Texas knows about Mr. Black," Smith said. "He's famous, or at least infamous, should I say? Frank, did you bring Carter up to speed on why we call him Batman?"

"I did. He was well-behaved today, though. But here's the thing. We interviewed the crew, your usual selection of half-deadbeat fisherman, but nothing super unusual. That was until we went to see the ME."

Smith smiled. "How is the good doc? Been a while since I saw her."

"She's good. Feisty as ever. She says Willis didn't drown, though. She thinks he was frozen and died sometime well before he was found. So, we're looking at murder. The crew's looking good for dumping him at the least, but we've got to figure out where he was iced, so to speak, before we can arrest them."

Carter and Smith both groaned. "Really?" Carter asked.

Smith smiled at her. "Glad you're on my page, Carter. Thankfully, he's a better investigator than a comedian. Don't give up your day job, Frank." Smith stood and leaned on his desk. "Okay. Nice work, you two. Keep me up to date. I'll brief the SAC and let him know what's going on. He may need some more details so he can brief the director, but we can handle that later. If you need anything, you know where you can find me. This is your top priority."

"I like him," Carter said as we left the office.

"I'm sure," I said.

SEVEN

We drove back to the *Reel Lady* to see if we could dig up more clues, now we knew it wasn't a straightforward drowning. It was early evening by then, the light starting to wane. The port had a desolate feeling to it, the earlier hustle and bustle knocked off for the day. Batman's chair was where we had last seen it, but no Batman. I guess after they had finished off-loading the vessel, he didn't need to sit there and watch anymore. The vessel looked deserted when we climbed aboard, although I wasn't announcing our presence. I had a feeling someone was watching, though.

"Where is everyone?" Carter said.

"Trust me, they're here. They'll be out as soon as I do this," I said. I reached for the hatch to the fish hold, the most likely place I thought they could have stowed a frozen Captain Willis.

"Need help?" Ricky's baritone rumbled from his skinny body as he appeared from the door to the galley. If I looked closely, I thought perhaps I could see his ribs vibrate as the words came out.

I winked at Carter.

"Yeah. Ricky, I need you to open the hatch to the fish hold for me."

"What for? I thought you'd looked at everything earlier?"

"Just a couple of follow-up items. Shouldn't take long. Say, where is everybody? Place looks deserted."

Ricky stared at me. I could see him deliberating about helping and how much trouble he might be in if he did or didn't. Finally, he bellowed for Paul to come out. "Bring the T-bar with you when you come out," he added. There was a muffled acknowledgment from inside the galley, and a moment later Paul came out with said T-bar.

"If I open this for you, is that it? We need some time to grieve, and you keep interrupting."

"Maybe. Can't tell until you pop this bad boy open. So...the quicker we do this, the quicker we'll be outta your hair."

"Whatever. We don't use the fish hold much," Ricky said. "What are you hoping to find?"

"I'm not hoping to find anything," I said, "but we didn't look in here when we came aboard this morning, and when we got back to the office, I remembered I can't complete the paperwork until we have a quick look in all the spaces. You know? Just to say we did. Shouldn't take long." I gave him what I hoped was my most disarming smile.

"You'll be wanting to look in the laz and forepeak then too," Paul said.

I noticed Ricky glaring at Paul. "Yeah. Sounds good. Thanks for offering," I said.

Ricky grumbled something under his breath, but I let it go. "Open it," he said to Paul.

Paul popped the hatch open. I let it air out for a minute and made Ricky go down first. If the air was foul, I didn't want to be the first one down there.

"All good, Ricky?" I said from the deck. I heard a rumble of thunder from below that I took to be his affirmative and climbed down into the hold. I had my four-gas meter attached to my foot, so if there was anything toxic down there, my foot would beep and vibrate, giving me enough time to evacuate. My foot stayed silent as I descended the ladder, so I figured I was okay. That and Ricky was still standing and breathing.

The fish hold was a space about twelve feet long by twenty wide and about ten feet deep, following the contours of the hull. There was an anchor, silently rusting in a corner, and a few coils of line hanging from wooden hooks. Various boxes full of machine parts were strewn around. When a fishing vessel goes offshore, they work until they can't anymore. Often that means fixing whatever is broken so they can carry on. If they had to come back to port every time they broke down, they'd never make any money.

"You don't keep fish down here when you're underway?" I asked Ricky. I could see Carter's flashlight bouncing around as she came down the ladder, blocking the light from the overhead hatch.

"No. Use it as a storeroom, mostly." Ricky waved his hands around. "Engine parts, damage control stuff."

The floor was damp, and it smelled of mold and mildew. When the hatch was closed, it didn't look like there would be any ventilation. Carter cleared the ladder, but slipped as she made her way over to me.

"Easy," I said, as I caught her from slamming her ass on the steel floor. "Okay?"

She gave me a brief smile. "Yeah, thanks. Slippery."

I shined my light around looking for any evidence Willis had been stashed in here, but there was nothing to see. It looked just like a dank storeroom. I could have called our CSI guys to check the place out, but they had to come down from Houston, and there was so much crap in here it would take months and months to sift through this. I knew we couldn't hold the *Reel Lady* that long unless we came up with something a bit more conclusive. Since we knew they'd dumped Willis, we could have held them on illegal dumping of a body, but that was weak, and Lancaster would bust that up quick.

Burial at sea was legal, for sure, but you were supposed to get a permit, and the body should have been weighed down. But I didn't want to hold them on that. I wanted to find who'd murdered Willis. And I didn't want to jump the gun. Right now, they didn't know we knew anything, and I'd like to keep it that way.

There was a hatch leading from the stern bulkhead of the fish hold into the lazarette, and I got Ricky to undog it for me. I poked my head inside and shined my light around. Apart from the steering ram and rudderpost, there wasn't enough space in there to hide anything.

We made our way back up the ladder of the fish hold to the deck and then forward to the forepeak, but there was nothing there but some old anchor line and more spare parts.

"Ricky, can you do me a favor? I need to talk to all the crew. Can we meet up in the galley? Shouldn't take more than a few minutes," I said.

"Again? You said you'd be done when you looked around."

"I will be after this."

"Can't it wait? We're all pretty tired," Ricky said, "and anyway, Jimmy's not here, he's on a parts run."

"I thought you just said you were all tired," Carter said, "now one of your crew is out getting parts?"

Ricky scowled. "Jimmy never needed much sleep."

"Well, let's talk to who's here. It won't take long," I said. I felt reiterating it wouldn't take long, might sway him. I was lying of course. I had no idea how long it would take.

Ricky scowled some more to let me know he thought he was the boss, and then we convened in the grease-stricken galley. I looked at Paul, Ricky, and the wraith-like George. Paul was the only one staring at me. The rest looked around uncomfortably, looking wherever Carter and I weren't standing.

"So," I said, "why don't you guys sit at the table, and I'll lay it out for you." They sat. Carter and I remained standing. "I won't sugar-coat this. There are a few inconsistencies in your captain's death, and I wanted to see if any of you had any ideas why?"

I wanted to see if we could shake something loose. Ricky continued scowling, Paul looked surprised, and George's expression didn't change.

On the ride over, I'd discussed my plan with Carter and at my nod, she slid out some documents from a folder she was holding. They didn't have anything important written on them. I just wanted to see if we could shake something loose.

"It says here you reported the captain missing at 21:30 and then you found him," she said, shuffling the papers in her hand, "at approximately 00:20. Does that sound about right?"

Curt nods from around the table. "If you say so. I wasn't watching the clock. Too busy, you know?" Ricky said. Wraith George didn't move. Perhaps he was asleep with his eyes open. Couldn't tell. Paul fidgeted, wringing his hands.

Carter continued. "When you recovered him from the water, you reported he was already deceased. You told the crew from the *Glorious* he must have slipped, perhaps when he was cleaning fish, although no one saw him. Still right?"

More nods. I didn't want to tip my hand we knew he was previously frozen, but something had to shake loose. Paul hadn't looked up since Carter started talking. I took over the questioning.

"Paul," I said. "When was the last time you remember seeing the captain?"

"Well, I—"

"Paul didn't see much of the captain. Paul was busy out on deck most of the time or sleeping." Ricky said.

"Thanks, Ricky," I said. "Paul managed to answer my question without moving his lips. Impressive trick. Let him answer the question, please." Ricky frowned but didn't reply. I turned back to Paul. "Is that right, Paul? Surely you saw the captain driving the boat, for meals, cups of tea?" Shooting up?

"I—" Paul said.

"Already told you that—" Ricky said.

Goddammit. "Carter. Could you escort Ricky and George here outside for a moment, please?"

"All right, you two, let's go get some fresh air," Carter said.

Ricky glared at Paul on the way out, and Paul looked down. Something was going on here.

I sat down across from Paul. "Hey, Paul. Look at me, buddy. I know this is nerve-racking for you, talking to a federal agent, your captain dying. I'm sure it's pretty weird, and the guys are acting strange, right? Look at me, Paul." He finally looked up from studying his hands. He had a hangdog look to him. I couldn't tell for sure if he was ashamed or guilty. "I need you to answer my questions, okay? Need you to be the big guy here." He nodded. "So, really, when did you last see the captain?"

Paul rubbed his face. "Well. It's like Ricky says, I was working a lot on this trip. And sleeping."

"Come on, man. You're telling me you didn't see him even for meals?"

Paul thought about my question. When the answer came to him, I could see it was a surprise. "Actually, no. George said he wasn't feeling well, and Jimmy took all his meals to the bridge or his cabin."

"Well, what about when you were working on the back deck? Surely you could see him on the bridge, through the windows? Or when he was cleaning fish?"

He looked more confident. "Sure. Sure, I did."

Knowing that was impossible, I pressed Paul. "Are you sure you saw his face, actually saw him? Or could it have been someone else?"

"Why...why would it have been someone else?"

I slapped my hands on the table. "Did you see his face?" I said.

Paul looked shocked at my outburst, but it made him think. "Well. Now you mention it, I don't think I ever did. His back was always turned when he was on the bridge." He thought some more. "And I never saw him for meals, neither."

Finally getting somewhere. I hoped Carter could keep those other idiots out of here for a few more minutes. "Did you ever go up to the bridge?"

"Well sure, I stood watch and stuff, but I never relieved the captain. It was always Ricky who was on watch before me."

I thought maybe I could trust Paul. It was worth a shot. I looked him right in the eye. "Let me float this one by you. Is it possible the captain was already deceased when you went out fishing the other day?"

Paul's face went pale. "What? What do you mean already dead? Why would you say such a thing? That's stupid." He stood up.

"Sit down Paul and listen. Get off your high horse. Look, I'll be upfront with you, but you've gotta hear me out. I think I can trust you, but I don't think I can trust the rest of the crew, so here it is." I dropped the bombshell, hoping my instincts about Paul were right. "It's entirely possible Captain Willis was not alive when you set sail."

He processed that for a minute. "But I can't see how…"

"I get it sounds weird. I'm telling you this because I think you're being honest with me, and I want to tell you what's going on. We believe Captain Willis was murdered before your trip and dumped when you were out to sea."

"No," Paul said, his eyes growing wide. "No, that's…stupid. Right? It can't be. Wait…You…you don't think I could have anything to do with that, do you? Why would we rescue him if he was already dead? No," he started to shake his head. "No, it doesn't make any sense."

"I can't answer why it happened for certain just yet. Possibly to make it look like an accident." I shrugged. "We don't know. What I do know, though, is I think you're one of the good guys. I don't believe you're mixed up in all this."

Paul shook his head. "No. I'm definitely not mixed up in this. This was only my second trip. I was thinking of quitting anyway, I don't think this life is for me." Paul rubbed his face and took a deep breath, blowing it out. "Jesus. I can't believe this. The guys have been so kind to me. How can I tell them you think they tossed the captain over the side?"

"Well, that's the thing, Paul. You can't say anything—"

"What do you mean? Of course I have to say something to them. This is ridiculous." He stood up again.

"Sit down." He deliberated and finally acquiesced, "You can't tell them a thing. If they think you know, I can't guarantee your safety."

"They would never—I don't want to be here anymore. I think I'm going to be sick." Paul lurched, and I grabbed his arm.

"Sit down. I'm not gonna keep telling you. It's getting tiresome, Paul. You have to be here. I'm sorry, but I've put you in a tricky situation. If they think you told me something—"

"But I didn't," Paul said. "I didn't tell you nothing."

"But if they think you did, your life could be in danger. You could end up like your captain."

"I don't like this," Paul said. "Why would you even tell me something like that? What am I supposed to do now?"

"I told you because I don't think you're wrapped up in any of this—"

"—I'm not. I told you that."

"I know. You're the innocent one in all of this, like I said. Trouble is, if this case goes to trial, would the prosecutor believe you? These guys are going to go down one way or another. You'll go down as an accessory or maybe as an accomplice after the fact. That's still jail time, even if you didn't do anything to Willis. How believable is it that you were on the same boat and never saw anything? It's not like this boat is the size of an ocean liner."

Paul's color came back to his face now he was agitated. "You said you believed me."

"I do," I said, "but I'm not the prosecutor. I'm an investigator. If you maybe, saw something, or heard something, in the next day or two you think may be useful. Well," I spread my arms wide and smiled. I hoped it looked sincere. "That information would probably help the prosecutor decide you were innocent after all."

I wasn't a fan of railroading anyone. Paul just happened to be in the wrong place at the wrong time, or for me, the wrong place at the right time. The long and short of it was that I didn't have a lot of good leads right now, and I was willing to use whatever leverage I could to get to the truth. "Listen, here's how it's going to play out. You have to act normal, go about your daily routine. If it gets too much, or you hear anything suspicious," I handed Paul my business card, "call me. My number's on the card; you can reach me anytime. If anything comes up, at all. Call."

"I'm no grass," Paul said.

"I never said you were, Paul. But it's like this. Someone murdered your captain. I need to find out who. If you can help me and save yourself from being locked up at the same time," I shrugged, "it's a win-win for both of us. Do what you feel you need to do. Listen, my partner's been out there talking to those guys. No one will know what we discussed if you don't tell them. They'll ask though, so throw them a bone. Tell them I asked all the same questions I did earlier today. That'll match up with what Carter asked them. It'll seem believable."

"What if I tell them the truth?"

After all this? I gave him a condescending look. "Then don't be surprised if you end up the same way as Willis," I said.

I left Paul in the galley with his thoughts. I didn't like pressuring him, but sometimes that's the way investigations rolled. I went out to the back deck to check on Carter. She'd finished with both of them.

"Thank God," she muttered under her breath when I approached her. "I didn't have anything left to keep them," she said to me, and then louder, "glad you're here, Dalton, I was about to cut these two loose. You done inside?" She nodded in the direction of the galley.

"Yep, all good. Just like you thought," I said in a loud voice for the benefit of Ricky and George who were listening. "Paul doesn't know anything." Hopefully, that would help Paul some.

As we stood on the back deck, I saw Jimmy coming up the gangway carrying a cardboard box. When he looked up and saw me his steps faltered for a second, but he came aboard anyway, as he was committed by then.

"Jimmy," I said, looking pleased. "Where've you been?"

His eyes flickered to Ricky. "Parts run," he said. "Needed some spares for the engine."

"I thought George was the mechanic," Carter said, turning to George.

George, as usual, didn't move a muscle. He'd be great in a poker game. Ricky came to his rescue. "Jimmy's the only one with the company credit card. He gets all the supplies," he said.

"Sure he is," I said.

We let Ricky and George go but made sure to talk to Jimmy to keep up appearances, knowing we wouldn't get anything out of him. Just going through the motions. None of them apart from Paul had anything useful to say.

We got back in the car and drove toward the office. We'd pass the park and ride on the way, so I'd drop Carter off before returning to the office and retiring the squirrels for the night. They'd had a long day. I was looking forward to going home. It was only day one of the investigation and I could already tell this case was going to be a headache.

EIGHT

The office wasn't far away, so I expected a quiet car ride, but Carter soon piped up. "So...Frank," Carter said, "tell me something about yourself. Why did you join the Coast Guard?"

I groaned in a silent huff hidden by the whine of the engine. Why is it everybody asks that question? I wondered if I worked in a different profession like in a bank, would everyone still ask me why I'd joined the banking profession? I couldn't imagine getting the same questions.

"I don't know. I needed a good job at the time, I guess." I gave a half-shrug, my eyes on the road.

"Come on. I can tell that's your generic, leave me alone answer. The standard one you give at parties."

"Parties? I don't go to parties," I said.

"You know what I mean. That's your canned response. I'm interested. Really. Why did you join?"

"What can I say? I like blue."

Carter sighed and looked out the window. I could tell she was frustrated. I don't like to talk about myself, never have. I glanced over at her in the passenger seat, studiously studying the view out of the passenger window. I could see the back of her head and her reflection simultaneously. She wasn't smiling. I gave it some thought and decided I should at least put some effort into this partnership.

"My great-great-something granddaddy's name was John Franklin Dalton," I started, "but he went by Frank. I guess he was the first Frank Dalton, or at least the first one with any infamy."

Carter stopped pouting and turned in her seat to face me. "Go on," she said.

"Well, he was a Deputy US Marshal back in 1887, but he got shot and killed when he went to arrest a suspected horse thief and bootlegger called Dave Smith. His partner, Deputy J.R. Cole, escaped and later came back with a posse. From what I could gather, looking through some old reports, no one expected it was going to get rough."

"Where was this?"

"Oh. Out in the Wild West, some place in Kansas called Coffeyville. The story goes, as they rode up to arrest the guy, my namesake got shot in the chest, which knocked him off his horse and he didn't get back up. Cole returned fire and killed Smith, but someone back at Cole, and hit him, but not seriously. Wounded himself, Cole, thinking Dalton was dead, left to get help. Dalton wasn't dead, though, and recovered enough to engage in another brief gun battle with the rest of the gang before they shot him again, this time for good. Cole came back soon after with the posse, took control and rounded up whoever was left alive, although it didn't matter much as they hanged the survivors later."

"That's some story."

I looked at her. It surprised me to see she was genuinely engaged. "All true. Look it up. What I think is even more interesting is Frank was the oldest Dalton brother. After he'd died, there was nothing to keep his younger brothers in check, and they formed the Dalton gang, later nicknamed the Desperate Daltons. They terrorized railroads and robbed banks. They were quite famous in their time. Eventually, during a double bank robbery, they all got caught and killed in a gunfight by the local law."

"Wow. So, you're famous. That would make a really good book, you know. You should write it. Sort of like an ode to your namesake."

I snorted. "Me? Have you seen the way I write reports? I can barely string two coherent words together."

"That's all you need to write a book. You start with two words, then two more, and so on."

"Said the woman who's written…how many books?"

"Touché. But I'm not the author, you are."

I snorted again and cleared my throat to cover it up. "No, not me. Anyway, back to your original question. I joined the Guard because I felt like law enforcement is in my blood."

Carter turned to look out the windshield.

"It's more than that though," I said. "This will sound stupid." I hesitated for a moment and took a peek at Carter. She had turned back to me, looking expectant, so I plowed forward. "I can feel when I do something right or wrong. And sometimes I can feel it in other people too," I blurted out in a rush.

She punched my shoulder. "Now you're having the new girl on. You're teasing me."

I held up three fingers together in a Boy Scout salute. "No, scouts honor. I can sometimes feel…stuff. Stuff that isn't quite there."

"You were a scout?"

"Well, no. But that's not the point. I was trying to be honest. Listen, I'm rambling," I changed the subject. "How about you? Why'd you join?"

"I needed a good job at the time," Carter said.

"That's my line." I smiled when I looked at her.

She smiled back and shrugged. "I guess I felt obligated. After 9/11, everything changed. I felt like I wanted to do something to help. I didn't want to join the Marines or Army. I dunno. I've always liked the water and felt what with the Coast Guard being so small, I could have more of an impact, get more field time maybe."

"Well, that's true. You should be able to stay in the field if you stay an agent. A lot of people can't handle it, though. We have our fingers in a lot of different pots. It's still the military, and some people can't handle the responsibility and rules."

"Don't forget the high paycheck," Carter deadpanned.

"Right. That too. How could I forget?"

We made it back to the park and ride in what felt like a decade since I'd picked her up that morning. I told her I'd call her if anything came up and drove myself back to the office. I checked with our DOMEX digital forensics guys, where I'd dropped Willis's phone earlier, but they hadn't had any luck yet. Tomorrow, they said. Maybe.

I drove home with the windows open. It had been a day of awful smells, and I wanted to wash them away. I pulled into the marina parking lot at the T-heads where *Ghost* was docked and parked. I looked at my watch. It had been a long day, but it wasn't super late. The neon sign of Pete's bar beckoned me from across the lot and after the day I'd had, I figured a nightcap was probably in order. I locked up and walked over.

"Hey, Pete. How've you been?" I said as I walked through the door.

Pete squinted as he looked at me. "Frank? Long time no see. How did it work out with the lady last night?"

"I don't want to talk about it. Let's just say it wasn't meant to be."

"That good, huh? All right, what'll you have?"

"Oh, the usual."

"Always one with the words, this man," Pete said, deadpanning to the mostly empty bar. I rolled my eyes.

The bar overlooked the marina, half of it open to the outside, palm trees dotting the area. It was really more of a beach shack, placed in a marina. There was an old jukebox in the corner, a few white plastic tables and chairs dotted the available space, more solid-looking stools surrounded the bar. Pete served nothing fancy, beer, well drinks and shots. Strictly functional, he liked to say. He catered to the liveaboard boating community and the occasional transient tourist who wandered in. He knew they wanted something simple to combat the overpriced foo-foo drinks you could find in town, and that's exactly what they got.

I eased myself onto a barstool at about the same time a bottle of Pete's local brew slid its way down the bar to me, falling neatly into my outstretched hand. I grinned despite myself. Pete's Brew was the best beer on the menu.

"Pete. You're a lifesaver," I said, taking a long swig, and then holding the sweating beer up in a mock salute.

"Tough day?" Pete asked.

"No, not really. A long day is all. And I met my new partner."

"Oh yeah. What's his name?"

"He's a *her*."

Pete was silent for a moment, which was rare, then his eyes got wide. "Oh. Right, right. Don't ask and don't tell and all that. Gotcha."

I sighed. "Jesus, Pete, you show your age sometimes. They repealed 'Don't Ask, Don't Tell' years ago, and no, you've misunderstood me. She hasn't transitioned; she has always been and still is a woman. And I highly doubt you know her, old man. She's younger than the number of years you served. Her name's Carter. Jessica Carter."

He pretended to think about it for a minute as if to prove me wrong, then said, "Nope. Don't know her. What's she like?"

I thought about that. "I don't know, to tell you the truth. She's only been on the job for about ten seconds. I swear, in the academy, they must teach you to believe you're superior to everyone else. Anyway, I think we worked through that and ended the day with her listening and willing to learn, which is about all I could ask for at this point." I hesitated, knowing what I was setting myself up for, but added, "she has a cute voice too."

Predictably, Pete jumped on that snippet with both feet. "That all that's cute? Just her voice?" he said, coming round the bar and slapping me on the back. He sat on the stool next to me. I gave him a withering look.

"Relax. I'm kidding."

"What makes you think I'm not relaxed?" I said.

"I've seen that look in your eye before. Seriously, though, it's great she has you to learn from. I remember taking you under my wing all those years ago."

"Ha. Here we go." It was true, though. I'd had a rough time when I'd joined the Coast Guard. Back then, it was well and truly the Old Guard. You do it my way or the highway mentality. If it wasn't issued to you in boot camp as part of your seabag, and fill in the blank here—spouse, kids, debt, dog, whatever—it didn't belong in the service. Back then, no one cared about your life outside of the Guard. Your life was the Guard. If you had marital problems, or your kids were sick, it was just tough shit.

That's a hard nut to crack for any new enlistee and drove many people out. Hell, I was going to get out after my first tour because the leadership just plain sucked. Thankfully, most of that bullshit has changed, hence the Old Guard moniker.

After I'd transferred to my second unit, Pete was there. An old salt, but fair. He wasn't like a lot of the others. He was a chief petty officer, and my supervisor, but he didn't subscribe to the adage of, 'I was treated badly, so I'm going to treat everyone else the same way.' He showed me the ropes, and how it could be, how it should be. Pete retired shortly after, but we kept in touch in the intervening years, and his advice was instrumental to me applying for a position with the Coast Guard Investigative Service. I knew he had a bar here at the marina, and after I'd received orders to the CGIS office in Corpus, I moved *Ghost* here.

Pete got up and attended to the other two customers in the bar, swapping brief small talk, probably about the weather or the Astros, his favorite baseball team. After a time, he came back over. "So, what's this case about you're working on with your new sexy voice partner?"

"Knock it off," I said.

He put his hands up in mock surrender. "Okay, okay. I'm sorry."

I contemplated how much to tell him and settled with the basics he could pull from the news and could put together himself if he thought about it. It wasn't like I didn't trust my old mentor, but he'd been out of the service now for years, owned a bar, and was known to wax philosophical at times. "It's a murder case. A guy fell off a fishing boat, and it was reported as a missing person, a man overboard, but it turns out it looks like someone killed him earlier and then dumped him over the side. Made it look like a man overboard situation. It's got some complications."

"Sounds like it," Pete said. "Anything you can share?"

"I'll tell you this," I said, making sure no one was within earshot, and leaned in closer to Pete. "You remember Batman? He's involved somehow."

"Shit. He's got his fingers in everything." Pete knew him well. Batman was notorious among the boating community. Nothing substantial ever stuck to him, and so far he'd stayed out of jail. But word on the street was he was a player in the Boston mob at some point and moved down here, either to set up his own criminal enterprise or at the behest of his mob brothers.

"Finished?" Pete asked, pointing at my beer.

I drained the last dregs. "You know it. Last one, though, I've got to get an early night, busy day tomorrow."

He passed me another beer and nodded. "Okay, Frank. This one's on the house. Old times."

"Pete. You say that every time. You're never going to get rich."

"Don't want to get rich. Would have opened a bikini bar if I wanted to get rich. Let's just say I still appreciate your company."

"All right, thanks." I threw some money on the bar, anyway. "Take it easy Pete. I'm taking this one with me."

Pete waved from across the bar, already deep in conversation with another customer. I did a quick double-take as it looked like George the Wraith at first. It wasn't, but could have passed for his brother, the deep-sunken eyes, the paleness. It stood out in South Texas. I made a mental note to ask Pete about him the next time I was in. For now, I needed some rest, or else I'd start seeing George under my bed, too.

Two minutes later, I bounced down the dock and across to *Ghost*. I know it's not a mega yacht or anything, but it was home to me, and I always got a feeling of deep calm when I stepped aboard. Perhaps the previous owner was a Zen master or shaman or something. Whoever it was, I enjoyed the tranquility they'd bestowed upon my boat, and it felt special. Comforting.

I went below and made myself a ham sandwich, added some thinly sliced English cucumbers, a slather of mayonnaise and a dash of Colman's mustard to the bread and took it back to the stern to enjoy the sunset and the rest of my beer.

Tomorrow was going to be a long day, and I turned in early. I didn't see Wraith George's doppelgänger watching my boat from the shore, but I figured out later it had to have been him.

NINE

I swung by the DOMEX lab when I got to work the next morning. Mark Malone, the tech guy, had left me a post-it note on my desk asking me to come see him. He'd signed it, 'M n M,' after his initials, hoping people would call him Eminem, like the rapper. I didn't know anyone who did that, but it never stopped him from trying.

I looked around the bullpen where all the agents had their desks, including mine, but didn't see Carter yet. Her desk was in front of mine and looked empty of the usual detritus an agent brings into the office with them every day: car keys, coffee mug, water bottle and so on, so I walked over to the lab alone.

Malone was sitting at his desk, wearing a lab coat and wearing thick spectacles. "What have you got, Mark?" I asked.

He peered up with anticipation. "Did you see my post-it note on your desk?"

I knew what he wanted. "No," I said. "Just thought I'd drop by."

Mark looked a little deflated, but it didn't stop him from playing a little rendition of *The Real Slim Shady* on his phone. I ignored it.

"Well, anyway," he said, gathering himself. "That iPhone you gave me? We did a chip-off and retrieved some data."

"A chip what?" I said.

"A chip-off. Come on, I must have explained this to you before. How long have you been working here, anyway?"

"I swear I have no idea what you're talking about," I didn't. I'm not a Luddite, but Mark's tech explanations sometimes ran long, and my mind wandered. "Please elaborate."

Malone muttered to himself and shook his head, but continued, "Basically, we take the phone apart, isolate the memory chip by carefully heating the phone to melt the solder, and then we can extract the data. Ringing any bells?"

"No. Go on."

"It takes a while for this to happen. For the data to transpose, it's laborious." He went for the kill as I'd not called him Eminem. "Remarkably similar to watching you type out a report."

I let that pass. "And."

"Does everything go over your head, Agent Dalton?"

I let that pass too, smiling inwardly. "So, what's your point?" I said.

Malone threw up his hands. "Ugh. Has anyone told you how exasperating you can be?"

"Frequently."

"The point is, Agent Dalton—"

"Special Agent."

"There you go again. The point is, *Special* Agent Dalton, is that I don't have anything yet."

"Gotcha." I paused a beat. "I thought iPhones were unhackable?"

"We're not hacking it. We're fooling it. We use that and another program called Celebrite. It's from the Israelis."

"Figures. What did you have to do, bribe a Mossad Agent?"

Malone looked shocked. "No, of course not. I—"

"Just kidding, Mark. Lighten up."

"Right. Of course." Malone faked a laugh. "How silly of me. You and your Special Agent humor."

I sighed. "So, what did you get?"

"Right." Malone pushed his spectacles further up the bridge of his nose. It was a tell that he was concentrating. "Come over here, and I'll throw them up on the big screen."

For whatever else Malone might be, he was a tech genius. The department budget didn't stretch to a lot of new technology, too many crusty old Admirals stuck in the Dark Ages of wooden ships, typewriters and carbon copies in triplicate or something. Somehow, Malone had got the DHS to fund him a small grant, as long as he shared whatever results he obtained with other government agencies. Something he would have done, anyway.

Malone waved his hand. At least that's what it looked like to me, from the computer screen to a giant, almost transparent screen hanging from the ceiling. At the same time, the lights dimmed, and the giant screen came to life, with streams of hex data scrolling through.

Malone watched the data scroll for a moment and then, with another swoosh of hands, stopped the data on a sixteen-digit hash. I didn't understand what it all meant, but I didn't have to. That's what Malone was for, and I appreciated that. Even if I didn't appreciate his jokes.

"This hash represents one photo we took off the phone," he said.

I gave him a blank look. "Don't tell me you forgot this too," he said.

"No," I said, "of course not. Just pretend, though, for the moment, I have no idea what you're talking about."

Malone huffed in frustration but told me, anyway. I think he saw through my thinly veiled deflection. "Each hash or group of data represents a photo."

"Gotcha. Hash equals photo," I said. I didn't get it.

Malone looked at me like I was stupid. "No. But let's just go with that for now."

"Good. Okay. Let's see it."

A photo appeared of what looked like a group shot of several men standing around something blurry in the background. "Can you enlarge or enhance or whatever it is you do so I can see the background?" I asked.

"Can Eminem sing?"

"More of a rapper, I believe."

The image pixelated, enlarged, and cleared up. I was staring at the faces of a trimmer, younger Batman Black, the unfortunate, but vastly healthier-looking Captain Willis, and a still wraith-looking, sunken-eyed George. I didn't recognize the background. It looked like some sort of tropical setting, with a few palm trees in the background, lusher than Corpus Christi, somewhere in the Caribbean maybe. I didn't know.

"Shit," I muttered.

"You know them?"

"Maybe. Can you enlarge those boxes they're standing around?"

Malone manipulated the image once more, and the boxes came into focus. They looked like shipping crates, and there must have been half a dozen in the photo. One crate was open, and inside there were three empty slots. The other slots were full of ominously dark rifles, and Batman, Willis and George looked like they were holding the three from the crate.

That didn't give me a good feeling, but it sure gave me something to think about. "Yeah. I know them," I said. It looked like the three compadres were not only old buddies but gunrunners, too. I'd seen a crate or two of illegal guns in my time. I couldn't tell how long ago the photo was taken, but they were all younger-looking. Is this what Willis was killed over? They appeared to be friends in the photo. Maybe they'd had a falling out.

"Can you print me out a series of those shots, Mark, please?"

"Sure can."

"Any chance of dating the photo?" I asked.

"I can try, but it wasn't taken with this phone. It's a copy or something. I'll look at the metadata and see if I can get something for you, but no promises."

I nodded. "Thanks. Did you find anything else of interest?"

"No, not really. Just some family shots. I can print those up too if you want."

"Yeah. You never know. Did you get an idea of where the phone's been?"

"Working on it. I told you the chip-off was slow. Usually, we can identify where the phone's been by looking at the geocache data on the photos and if he accessed any GPS apps. He might have deleted all the data from the phone, but nothing is ever truly gone. I don't have it yet. But I will."

"Thanks. Remind me to use a burner phone when I go to the dark side."

"That doesn't work either," Malone said. "You still have to take out the sim and destroy it, then take out the battery. Otherwise, you can still be tracked even when the phone is off, and—"

I looked at him. "I'm kidding."

He looked surprised for a moment, then rolled his eyes. "Oh, of course. Special Agent humor. Again."

"Let me know when you get that data," I said and left the lab. I walked over to my desk and sat down. Carter still wasn't in, so I called her.

"Carter," she said, on the first ring.

"Hey," I said. "Where you at? We've got things to do."

"Yeah, I know. Sorry. I had a couple of errands to run." She sounded a little flustered.

"Are you okay?"

"What? Yes. Yes, I'm fine, thanks. Listen, I'll be there in two minutes." I would have replied, but she hung up on me and then the office line started to ring. I looked around, but no one else appeared in a rush to pick it up, so I did.

"It's all right guys," I said to the room, "I've got it." Muppets. "Special Agent Dalton, Investigations," I said into the phone after I picked it up.

"Frank? How's that for luck? Just the guy I wanted."

It took me a second to place the voice. "Pete? What's up?" Pete never called me, at least never on the office line.

"Can you swing by when you get off shift? There's something I want to talk to you about."

It was early to call, especially for someone who runs a bar. I don't think I ever remember him calling me at the office.

"You okay, buddy? We can talk now if you want," I said.

"It'll be better in person, Frank. Listen, I don't want to worry you. It can wait until your shift is over. I just wanted to give you a heads-up."

"All right, if you're sure it can wait. I'll catch up with you this afternoon. At the bar?"

"Yeah. That's great. Thanks, Frank. Later."

Another intriguing phone call. I was thinking about what Pete might want when Carter flew through the door and sat at her desk in a disheveled heap. I hadn't known her for long, but this seemed out of character.

"Hey," I said.

Carter jumped.

"Sorry. Didn't mean to scare you," I said.

"It's okay. It's nothing. Forget it." She spat out. Woah, sailor.

I got up, went around to her side and spun her wheely chair to face me, then sat down on the edge of her desk. "What's going on?"

"It's nothing."

Like anyone would believe that. "Look. You're late. You're short with me on the phone, and you're jumpy. We have a lot to do today, and I need your head in the game."

"I'll be fine," she said, staring at the floor.

I thought about it for a second, taking her entire demeanor in. Something wasn't right. "Keep your jacket on. Follow me."

"Where are we going? I've got things to do."

"Just follow me."

We walked downstairs, and across the street, to a hole-in-the-wall coffee joint I favored, aptly named Jitters. It wasn't gourmet six-dollar-a-cup coffee, nor was it a skinny macchiato, two pumps of caramel, cinnamon and whipped cream, or whatever the hell people ordered. All you got was a big, strong, steaming mug of house coffee. But it was good. I told Carter to get a table in the back while I went to the counter and ordered. It only took a moment before I had two oversized mugs of steaming hot coffee. I worked my way back to Carter and gave her the mug that was slightly less chipped sitting down across from her. There was creamer and sugar on the table, and I let her doctor hers for a minute, letting her settle. She took a sip.

"Now," I said, "What's going on? If we're to be partners, we speak the truth to each other, and we trust each other. If we can't talk to each other and trust each other, we won't work well in the field. I need to know you. You need to know me. I need to know you've got my back and vice versa."

"I have your back, Dalton."

"After yesterday? Call me Frank."

She smiled a little. "Jessica."

"Okay, Jessica. What's going on?"

She hesitated. "I don't want to be a burden."

"You'll never be a burden, as long as we're open and honest. Go ahead. I'm listening, not judging."

Carter sipped some more of her coffee. "This is good."

"I know. Stop stalling. What gives?" I didn't want to be so brusk, but we did have a murder to solve.

She looked down at the cup. I waited. Finally, she met my eyes. "It's my mom. She's not doing well."

"I'm sorry to hear that," I said. I was, truly. She said nothing more. I waited again. Gave her time to talk. To gather her thoughts. After several false starts, she told me the story.

"My mom and I were close when I was younger, but...when my brother died, we drifted apart. I didn't see it. I was angry. Angry at her, angry at the world, how unfair it was. I was only twelve, my brother was sixteen. He'd just gotten his driver's license." She took a deep breath, held it, and let it out. "It was a drunk driver. He came out of nowhere. T-boned him. From what I remember, he didn't suffer."

"I'm so sorry, Jessica." I reached across and briefly held her hand, squeezing it.

She sat back, pale. "My dad couldn't handle it, and he took off shortly after my brother died. When he walked out, it simply added to my teenage angst. I like to think I didn't get on with him anyway but grown up me doesn't know anymore. Looking back, it hit my mom hardest. Her son was ripped away from her, her husband walked out, and she was left alone with bitchy me. It took years for my mom and me to reconnect. I went through a teenage rebellion I'm sure was hell for my mother...I was a wreck...I hung out with the wrong crowd." Her eyes glistened. She paused for a minute to use a napkin and wipe her eyes. The world shrunk into the surrounding space until it was just us in the café. "It wasn't until I was seventeen, a year older than my brother was when he died, that I sorted out my life..."

She fell silent for a moment. When she didn't look like she was going to continue, I said, "I think you're being too hard on yourself, Jessica. You were just a kid. Rebelling is normal." I gave her a moment to compose herself. "What were you saying about getting your life together?"

A deep breath. "You're going to find this stupid..."

"Try me. I have a large capacity for what some people think is stupid," I said, thinking about my Zen boat.

Jessica took a deep breath. "All right. One night...I had a vision...of my brother. Billy. I don't know if it was truly my brother, or if it was my fucked up subconscious, or what, but it felt like my brother, you know? He told me to cut the shit, sort my life out. He told me how lucky I was that I was actually alive and had already lived longer than he had. He said he would totally swap places with me, just to see a sunset, to feel the breath of the wind on his face..." She paused and I handed her another napkin. She took it and dabbed at her eyes. "Whatever it was, a vision, my subconscious, I don't know, but it had the right effect. It was the right time, maybe it was fate, I don't know. But I turned my life around. I got back on my feet. I quit the lowlifes I'd been hanging with, and I tried to be a better person. It took a long time. It wasn't easy. I'd not just burned a few bridges, I'd demolished them and then buried them as well. But I did it. I also reconnected with my mom. She's such a good person she forgave me instantly. She's been my rock and my biggest fan ever since, although I know she never stopped loving me. After all, it's just the two of us now."

Carter blew her nose into the napkin, and I gave her a moment while I went to the counter to get refills.

"Thanks," she said, as I sat down again. I nodded.

"So, that brings us to today. What happened?" I said.

Carter sighed. "My mom has Alzheimer's. She's forgetting who I am, keeps asking where Billy is. Frank, it's been years since he died, but she doesn't remember. The hospital called me this morning as I was coming to work. She'd had a particularly bad night, and they asked me to go in. Although she doesn't always remember me, I seem to calm her down. When I got there, though, she didn't know me. She kept screaming, over and over, and they had to sedate her. It was a terrible morning all around."

"I'm so sorry, Jessica. You know, you can always talk to me if you need to."

"Thanks, I appreciate it, Frank, but to be honest, we've only just met. I'm surprised I've said this much, as I usually keep it together a lot better. It's not the sort of thing you dump on someone who you've just met—" she stopped talking, looked at me. "Shit. I did, though, didn't I?"

I smiled. "It's okay. If you need some time..."

"No. I can't. I'm sorry. I didn't want to come off as needy on my second day, especially after our rocky start. And besides, we have a murderer to catch," she said.

"Look. There's nothing needy about it at all. We're a team now. Partners. We look after each other. Have each other's backs, remember? Listen, why don't you take the day off, sort out what you need to and come back tomorrow? I can handle what's going on."

"Really?"

"Yeah, Go. I've got it."

Carter sighed again, straightened her shoulders some and lifted her head. "I'd love nothing more than to crawl back into bed, but I can't. I need to work. It'll keep my mind off what's happening with my mom. And besides, we have a murderer to catch, don't we?"

"I think you already said that," I smiled. "But I definitely could use the assist. If you need to take off later or whenever, let me know."

"Yes, boss."

I put our empty mugs on the counter, and we walked back across the street.

Ten

On the walk, I filled her in on what Eminem had shown me.

"Guns? How old was that photo, do you think?"

"Malone said it was hard to say. He could tell it was a photo of a photo, but there's no telling when it was initially taken. The copy was made a few months ago. Judging by the way Batman has aged, it had to be at least ten years ago."

"Do you think they're still running guns?"

"Again, hard to tell. We didn't see anything on the *Reel Lady*, but who knows? We could check out some of their other vessels, put a lookout on them, see if the *Glorious* or *Magnificent* pick something up."

"Makes sense," Carter said.

Back at the office, we grabbed another economy-sized box from the underground lot and sped out, powered by rubber bands, hopefully recharged squirrels, and a certain amount of willpower.

Captain Frederick Lucius Willis was divorced, but I wanted to go see his ex. They would have been married about the time the gun-running picture was taken if it was ten years or so ago, so I wanted to see if she knew anything. Perhaps she had a score to settle?

We drove in what I always felt was a northerly direction, but what the car's compass told me was east, along the beautiful and winding Ocean Drive. On my left, the bay sparkled in the sunlight, dotted with the occasional shimmering sail on the horizon. On a good day, you could see clear across the Bay to Aransas. Both sides of Ocean Drive were home to multimillion-dollar houses, condos, and the occasional small hotel. Palm trees lined the middle of the street, and it was a pleasant drive to Willis's ex-wife's house.

We arrived at Willis's ex's—who had remarried at some point and now went by the last name of Rivas—estate off of Ocean Drive and drove through an ornate entrance gate down a long winding driveway, the tires crackling and crunching on the shingles. In front of us were two stories of an exquisitely sprawling house, with massive double front doors opening onto a wraparound porch. The buzz of a weed whacker came from around the side of the house, and I could see a swarthy, suntanned guy with a backpack leaf blower moving leaves and grass clippings around. I parked, and we got out of the car, walking up to the front door. The doorbell chimed somewhere deep inside the house when I pressed the button.

"Nice house," Carter said.

I nodded. "Not too shabby. A little out of my price range, though."

Carter smiled. "Just a little?"

A moment later, an honest-to-God butler appeared at the door. He was dressed in a tuxedo with tails and was wearing white gloves. The inside of the house was a single step up from the porch, and the butler looked down imperiously.

"Can I help you, sir, madam?" he said.

I held out my badge. "I'm Special Agent Dalton, this is Special Agent Carter, we're here to see Mrs. Rivas."

The butler barely glanced at our badges. Instead, he said, "Is Mrs. Rivas expecting you?"

"No, we just dropped by. However, I'm sure she'll see us. Please tell her it's about her ex-husband."

"Mr. Dawson?"

I didn't miss a beat. "No. Captain Willis."

Butler-man raised an eyebrow, the only indication he was surprised. "If you'll follow me to the library, I'll inform Mrs. Rivas you're waiting."

"Say, how many exes does she have, anyway?" I said, following Jeeves into the house. I didn't know his real name, but Jeeves was the only famous butler I could think of. You know, Wooster and Jeeves?

"I wouldn't presume, sir." We walked into a large foyer with a gigantic spiral staircase. Jeeves led us through a door underneath the stairs into a massive library.

"She'll be along shortly," Jeeves said. He left and closed the double doors of the library behind him.

"Damn, Carter," I said, looking around. "A library. In a house."

"I know, right?" she said. "I don't think the public library I went to as a kid had this many books."

I walked around the library, admiring the furnishings and rubbing my finger across the spines of several books. It was a big room with dark paneled wood and red carpeting. At one end of the library was a leather couch and three leather armchairs, next to a fireplace. For the library's large size, it still felt cozy. I turned as I heard the doors open and in strolled a vision in white. She was dressed in a white chiffon dress, a cross between a pool cover-up and something you might see at a nightclub in Miami. There were just enough layers to cover her lady bits tastefully, and she walked like she was floating, even though I could see heels that went on forever.

She glided over to us and stretched out her right hand to shake. In her other hand was a martini glass half full of clear liquid, two large olives skewered on a stick, and an unlit cigarette in one of those holders they used to use in the '20s.

"Mr. Dalton?" she said, as she shook my hand. She had a firm grip. No limp fish there.

"Special Agent," I said. "This is Special Agent Carter." She shook hands with Carter.

"Forgive me, Special Agents," she said. "Roberts forgot to mention that part. He's getting somewhat on in years."

Now I had a real name for Jeeves. "That's quite all right Mrs. Rivas—"

"Oh please. Call me Julia. Shall we sit?" She gestured to the leather seats. Rivas sat on the couch, kicking off her heels, and folded herself into its comfort, flicking her feet up underneath her. Carter and I sat on leather chairs. I tried to perch on the end so I could write notes, but kept sliding back and sinking into the chair. Awkward. I could feel who was getting the upper hand already.

I glanced over at Carter. She seemed to be managing. "Have you always lived here?" Carter asked.

"Yes. It's the family house. Daddy was a whiz in the stock market, did rather well for himself and retired here when he was still in his forties."

"Mrs. Rivas," I began. She stared at me and raised her eyebrows. It took me a second to remember. "Sorry, Julia. Did Jee—Roberts," I caught myself, "say why we were here?"

"He said it had something to do with my nefarious ex-husband, Freddie. Did something happen to him?"

"What makes you say that?" Carter said.

"Well, I'm not a special agent, but I can't imagine they make house calls just to say hello."

"You're right, Julia." I paused. This was never easy to say nor to hear. "I'm sorry to inform you your ex-husband Frederick Lucius Willis fell overboard from a fishing boat late yesterday evening and was found unresponsive in the Gulf, quite a ways off-shore. I'm afraid he didn't make it."

Rivas didn't look fazed. "I'm not surprised. Mind if I smoke?"

"It's your house," I said, a little disturbed by her lack of reaction. "Why aren't you surprised?"

"Be a dear and get me that ashtray off the mantelpiece?"

I wouldn't normally cater to the whims of an interview subject, but in this case, being helpful would get me more information than being antagonistic. I got up, found a heavy glass ashtray above the fireplace, and handed it to her. She balanced it on the armrest and retrieved a lighter from the hidden depths of her bra, taking a long drag as she lit up. I sat back down, tried and failed to stop from sliding backward again. I gave up fighting. Carter was still perched on the edge of her chair.

"It's been so long now. I don't suppose there's any harm in telling you. Freddie was always living on the edge when we were married." She inhaled and blew out a long stream of smoke. The library didn't smell stale, so she either didn't smoke much or Roberts was a whiz with the Febreze. "I suppose that's what attracted me to him. He was a bit of a rebel, and I was a little rich girl looking to act out. It was a mutual attraction. He traveled so much back then that every time he came home, the sex was new all over again." She smiled tightly at me, perhaps wistfully. "I'm sorry to hear of his demise, but we hadn't been married for years, and I hadn't seen him for longer than that. Tell me, was that Mr. Black figure involved?"

"Why do you say that?"

"Oh, come on, don't be difficult, dear. He was always hanging out with that ne'er-do-well. I can't imagine he would have left his business partner."

That was interesting. "So, they were partners back then, Mr. Willis and Mr. Black?"

"Much to my disgust, yes. That was the one thing I didn't like about Freddie. His association with that man and that henchman of his, Geoffrey or Gerald or something like that."

"George?"

"Yes. That's him. Dreadful man. I always thought he looked like he was dead or dying, the way he could stare at you without blinking."

I nodded. "What was it about Mr. Willis's relationship with those two you didn't like?"

"Have you met them? What was to like? No, Freddie was always a bit fly by night, but I don't think he truly turned into a bad apple until he got involved with them. You do know Mr. Black's reputation, don't you?"

"We're familiar with it." I glanced at Carter. She was furiously scribbling notes. I'd have to try to remember to ask her how she didn't sink into the chair.

"Yes. Well, you see, that was the last straw. Freddie told me he had to run a few errands for Mr. Black. I was terribly upset because we were invited to a private art exhibition that night. A new up-and-coming artist, I hear he's doing rather well now. Anyway, I'd just bought a new dress, and I hated to disappoint... I know that sounds all sorts of frivolous, but it was important to me. I ended up going alone."

"Freddie ever tell you what errands?"

"No, and I never asked, not at the time. I was too furious. I was getting ready and heard tires crunching on the gravel outside. It was too early for my limo, so I looked out the window. I saw a car that was most certainly not my limo, and then I saw Black sitting in the back seat. Freddie ran out and got in, and the car sped off. I didn't see him for three days. When he came back, he smelled like he hadn't showered in three days too."

"What happened after Freddie got back?" I said.

"Well. The first thing I made him do was delouse in the shower. He stayed in there for what felt like a week. When he finally came out all pink and scrubbed, wearing a dressing gown, I marched him down here and demanded he tell me what was going on. He hemmed and hawed and hedged for a while until I threatened to cut him off from this lifestyle."

Carter looked up from her notes. "What did he say?" she said.

"He actually laughed at me," Julia said with a scoff. "Can you believe that? He laughed at me."

We both shook our heads. I'm not sure I could imagine anyone ever laughing at her.

She sighed. "He said he didn't need my damn money. Said he had a sweet deal going with Mr. Black. The trip he'd taken was the first of many, and he was going to be stinking rich. As if to prove it, he pulled out two huge rolls of cash from his dressing gown. Why he had the money in his dressing gown I can't begin to imagine and then he threw them at me. I was too shocked to move, and they bounced off my chest and rolled to the floor. I stared at the money and asked him if it was from drugs. He laughed again, said it was better than drugs. He was getting stuff people wanted, although he used a more vulgar word. This was so unlike Freddie. I told him to get out. He told me to watch myself. I picked the money up and threw it back at him, screamed at him to get out. He left.

"That was the last time I saw him. I kept tabs on him for a little while after. It was stupid of me, but I did still love him. That wore off about the same time I found out Mr. Black was beating people up with a baseball bat. I couldn't condone what either of them were doing after that. I knew Black must be connected, and now he had his hooks in Freddie. I just never realized how awful and evil Black was."

"You don't know where he got all that money?" I asked.

"No. I believed him when he said it wasn't drugs. But really, I have no idea what it could be. It was a lot of money he had with him, though."

"Could you make an educated guess?" Carter said.

"Darling, all my guesses are educated, but sadly, no, I can't, not in this case."

I sunk deeper into my chair, thinking over everything she'd said, looking for other leads. "Do you think your butler might know?"

"Roberts? I couldn't think why he would. They didn't speak to each other. Freddie thought it was pretentious I had a butler, and I don't think Roberts liked Freddie's brash behavior."

I hadn't cared much for the butler myself. After a few more questions that didn't go anywhere, I thanked her for her time. "Oh, anytime, darling," she said, and we left.

We sat in the car, but I didn't immediately drive anywhere, just started it to get the AC running.

"What do you think?" I said.

Carter flipped back through her notes. "She's not shy."

I smirked. "No, she's not."

"I don't think we got an awful lot. We did get confirmation Black and Willis were tight once upon a time and were definitely up to something besides fishing."

"Yeah," I said. "I wonder if all that cash came from those crates of guns I saw photos of?"

"I guess if we can get a date on those photos, we can match it to what Rivas told us," Carter said.

"Good thinking."

I pulled out of the driveway and drove back along Ocean Drive, deep in thought, heading for downtown. I didn't see the gray sedan pull out and follow us until I slowed down for a light. I looked in the mirror and the car peeled out from behind me, tires chirping on the smooth tarmac, and took a sharp left turn as the light turned red.

"Did you see that car?" I asked Carter. She shook her head and turned to look at where I was pointing. "I think it was the same one that drove us off the road yesterday," I said.

I thought about following it, but I wouldn't be able to catch up with it now. It was moving too fast, especially for this slow-ass car.

"Why would it be following us? We didn't even know what was going on yesterday," she said.

"*We* didn't know what was going on, but someone else did. Black had to know we'd investigate. But you're right, it is weird they'd have someone run us off the road on the way there." I shrugged. "I don't know. It feels like we've been two steps behind this thing from the start." I thumped the steering wheel in frustration and drove off when the light changed.

"I'm not sure I feel the same about being two steps behind. I'd prefer to remain optimistic."

"You do that," I said. We stopped at another red light, and a moment later it changed color. I accelerated, and the squirrels complained again. "Remind me to switch out this vehicle when we go out again. We need something with a bit more oomph."

"You should write these things down. You're giving me so many things to remind you about, I don't remember what they all are."

"What good are you if you can't remember stuff?" I said, teasing.

"What good are you? You're the one asking me."

"Touché. Really, though. We need a better car."

ELEVEN

When we got back to the office, there was another post-it note on my desk, this time from Smith telling us to go see him ASAP. I think we kept the post-it note company in business in this office. I showed Carter the note, and we went in to see him. He was sitting at his desk, holding a phone to his ear. He lowered it when we entered.

"Hey, Tobias," I said.

"Frank, Jessica." He nodded at us. "I have the SAC on the line, and he wanted to get an update on what's going on with your case. Hold on, let me put him on speaker." He pressed a button and put down the phone. "Are you still there, sir? I have Agents Dalton and Carter with me."

A harried voice came through, sounding at once bored and stressed, as if he had a million other better things to do, but this was important enough he couldn't leave it to someone else to mess it up. "Agents," he said. "I apologize for the abruptness, but I'd like to get a round turn on this before it gets out of hand. What have you got?"

Before what gets out of hand? I was puzzled by the turn of phrase but wasn't going to quiz the boss. I launched into my brief. "Not a problem, sir. At this point, we know Mr. Willis didn't drown, and we know Mr. Black is involved, but we're still in the preliminary stages of the investigation and are trying to run down all the leads we have. I have to say upfront that Agent Carter has been a huge help."

"Glad to hear it. Keep up the good work, Carter."

"Yes, sir," Carter said, smiling at me. It felt nice.

"Do you have anything specific you can tell me for the assistant director's brief tomorrow morning, Frank?"

"Nothing conclusive sir, although our DOMEX tech retrieved some old photos from the captain's phone that had been deleted and it confirmed a long-running relationship with Mr. Black and others in the crew. The picture we saw appeared to show that Mr. Black and Mr. Willis were gun runners, or at the very least, in possession of a large number of weapons."

"Now, that's interesting," Lewis said. "And these pictures came from the phone you took? Are you sure we had the authority to take the phone?"

"Yes, sir," I said.

"Very well. Have you alerted the ATF and our partner agencies?" Lewis asked.

I chose my words carefully. "Although we don't have a lot to go on right now, we're still the lead agency, and I'd like to keep it that way for as long as possible, sir. Right now, we wouldn't have a lot to share with ATF, just some photos and suspicions."

"Of course, Frank. I just want you to be aware if Willis and Black were running guns, after all, it could take this investigation out of our jurisdiction. We might have to hand the information over and take a step back."

"Yes, sir." Shit. I didn't want to give this one up. It was just starting to get interesting, something I could get my teeth into. And besides, Carter didn't seem to be as bad as all the rumors suggested.

"For now, though, I want you to continue," Lewis said. I felt a strange sense of relief that I got to keep my murder case. "Keep me updated on what you find out, and we'll play it by ear."

"Yes, sir," I said, pleased.

"Good work, Frank. Listen, I have a meeting I'm running late for, but keep me up to date, and if anything important happens, call me directly. Don't go through the chain."

"Roger that, sir."

Smith hung up the call and gave me an odd look I couldn't decipher.

Carter left the office and went to organize her notes from the interview.

I stayed put. "What's up, Tobias," I said.

Smith hesitated, but then said. "If anything important comes up, you'll call me and I'll call Lewis. Don't bypass me, okay?"

"Sure thing. That it?"

He nodded, and I got up and left, closing the door behind me. I walked over to my desk and thought about what the SAC had said. Something wasn't ringing true, but it was probably over my paygrade. A pissing match between Smith and Lewis, perhaps.

I put the thought away, checked my emails for a few minutes, letting the details of the case percolate around my head. I was pretty sure at this point Batman was good for this, but I didn't know if he'd murdered Willis or just orchestrated it. I also didn't know the where or why. Once I nailed down a motive, I felt like the other things would slide into place. At least Paul appeared to be shooting straight. Maybe he'd have something to tell me. I hadn't heard from him, so had to assume he was still okay. If I wanted to keep the case, and not hand it over, I had to solve it quickly, but right now I was looking at a lot of dead ends.

My phone vibrated in my pocket. It was a text from Pete.

Don't forget to drop by when you get a chance.

It reminded me of the way he was on the phone this morning and, as I didn't have any new information on the case, I figured it would be as good a time as any to go see him.

I went to the secure locker that held all the keys to our G-rides and punched in the code 1790 to open it. I rooted through for a second and selected something a little more fitting. Grabbing Carter, whose notes didn't tell us anything we didn't already know, we went down to the underground garage. I pressed the lock button on the key fob to make the car beep so I could find the behemoth I'd chosen, and soon we were off and running. We burst out into the sunlight, the engine roaring in a black Ram Crew Cab with a 5.7L V8 Hemi and tinted windows. I screamed around the corner and settled into the short drive to Pete's. This was more like it. Sorry, not sorry, squirrels.

It was a short drive, so I gave Carter the Cliffs Notes version of how I met Pete and what he does now. I wanted to let her know it wasn't usual to dash out in the afternoon to a bar. It wasn't unusual either, but in this case, I had a different reason than alcohol.

I pulled in front of Pete's and noticed one window was boarded up. That wasn't like that the night before. We went in and saw Pete drying a few glasses with a dishcloth and putting them up behind the bar.

"What's up with the window, Pete?" I asked.

Pete waved his rag. "Oh, nothing. Wind slammed it closed, and it cracked earlier. Is this Jessica?" I didn't believe him, but if he didn't want to tell me, that was his right.

Pete smiled at Carter and came out from behind the bar, throwing the rag over his shoulder. He took her offered hand in both of his. "Extremely pleased to meet you, Jessica. Frank was just telling me all about his new partner last night."

"He was?" she said, turning to me and smiling.

"Don't get too excited, Carter," I said. "I just told him I had a new partner, is all."

"Oh, that's not all," Pete said. "What he didn't say was how utterly gorgeous you were."

"Pete, you old flirt, stop. You're embarrassing yourself," I said.

"No, please go on," Carter said, warming to him.

"Oh, where to start, where to start," Pete said, looking Carter up and down.

"If you can turn your lecherous gaze away for a moment, how about you start with why you called me down here, Pete?" I said, rubbing my eyes. "It's not like we've got a murder or anything to solve."

Pete sobered immediately. "Yes. Right. Can I get you two a drink? Coffee, soda?"

"I'm good. Stop stalling. What gives?"

Pete looked around nervously, even though we were the only ones there. "Okay, okay," he said in a low voice. "You remember that guy that was in here when you left yesterday?"

The only person that looked out of place was the guy that looked like George. I'd forgotten about him until now. "The thin guy you were talking to when I left?" I said.

"Yeah, that's him," Pete said.

"What about him?"

"Well, he was asking about you."

"Asking what?" I said.

"Where you live, when you come in, what time you go to work."

That was creepy, but I recognized the behavior. "He was trying to squeeze you for information," I said.

"Yes, he was. But he wasn't doing it directly. He was subtle. Asking about boats in the marina, if anybody lives aboard, what the dock fees are, if I get many people in here, that sort of thing. I must be getting old. I didn't put two and two together for a little while. Not until he came back this morning."

"What did he want this time?"

"He had the audacity to try to shake me down. Came in with a bat, of all things. He told me he'd be coming around much more, and he thought we could come to a nice business arrangement. I told him where to go."

"Is that when he broke your window?" I said. Carter looked surprised.

He sighed. "I should have guessed you'd see through that. No. He didn't break it. Well, in a manner of speaking, he did. I shoved him when it was obvious he was trying to shake me down. I might be old, but no one's going to hold me upside down and collect my loose change. When I shoved him, he tripped and landed against the window."

"Seriously? Jesus. Are you okay?" Carter said.

"Me? I'm fine. I should have waited 'till he was outside. I liked that window."

I smiled. Classic Pete. "What did he do after that?"

"That's the strangest thing," Pete said, scratching behind his ear. "He didn't say a word. Just got up, shook himself off and walked out. I was expecting something a bit more, you know? One push from an old man, and he takes off. Weird."

"Where'd he go?"

"No idea."

"Did you call the cops?" I asked.

"I called you."

"Come on, Pete. You know I'm not a cop."

"You're all I need," he said. I knew that look from when we worked together. There would be no convincing him.

"Fine, do me a favor, though, and file a report. If he ever comes back, you'll have documentation."

"He won't come back, but sure, I'll call it in if it makes you happy."

"It does. Was there anything else?"

"No. No, I don't think so. I just wanted to let you know he was asking questions about you. Be careful, Frank. Someone's after you."

Unfortunately, I already knew that. "Thanks, buddy. I'll see you around." Carter and I turned to go.

"See you, Frank," he said. "Oh, and Frank?" I turned back. "Sorry about not telling you the truth about the window. Didn't want to worry you. And look after Jessica, will you?"

I nodded at Pete. "Of course," I said.

"Enchanted, Jessica," said Pete.

"Bye, Pete. Pleased to meet you." Carter waved.

We walked back to the truck, but instead of getting in, I put the keys back in my pocket. That bad feeling had returned, stronger than ever. I knew to trust it when it came.

"Come on," I said to Carter. "I want to show you something." I walked with her down to the marina.

"Where are we going? Shopping for a boat?" she said, looking around.

"Not quite. I want to show you *Ghost*."

Carter looked at me. "Is that a boat?"

"Yeah, a small one. She's a 47-foot Gulfstar Sailmaster. Two cabins, two heads, galley, living room. I live aboard."

"She doesn't sound small."

"No, I guess not. I suppose it depends what you compare her to."

We walked along the boardwalk to where *Ghost* was moored up, and I stepped on. As soon as I laid a foot on her, I knew something was wrong. I signaled Carter to stay quiet and unholstered my pistol. She followed my lead and drew her piece, giving me cover, and nodded she was ready. Moving carefully to not rock *Ghost* and further alert anyone on board, I carefully pushed open the hatch and eased down the steps to the main lounge. If I went forward, someone could come up behind me from the master cabin, so I had to check that first. I edged over to the port side and crouching down, shimmied closer to the cabin door. Entering low so I was less of a target, I poked my head through the door and hastily back again. No shots. No one was in there.

I entered the cabin and nudged the head door open with my foot. Shower, sink, toilet. Nothing else. I let out a deep breath I'd been holding and made my way back to the lounge. Confident now no one was going to sneak up on me from behind, I crept forward toward the other cabin. I passed through the galley. There were very limited places where anyone could hide. I peripherally took in the surrounding mess. I wasn't the cleanest, but it looked like this place had exploded. Someone had been here. I followed the same procedure in the forward cabin as I had in the stern. Nothing. I blew out another breath and made my way back to Carter.

As I poked my head out of the hatch, I saw Carter crouched on the boardwalk. "Hey, all clear," I said. I went out on deck.

Carter stood up and holstered her weapon. "What's going on?" she asked.

I felt my cheeks redden. "You'll think this is weird, but the moment I stepped foot on *Ghost* I knew the Zen had gone."

"The what?"

"Zen. *Ghost* had a lot of Zen. Well, I call it Zen. I'm not sure what it is. I'm probably using the wrong word. I just know whenever I come aboard, I always feel safe and secure, like a big fluffy blanket hugging me." I felt my cheeks get a little red saying that out loud, but I shrugged it off. "Stupid, I know. But when I stepped on her just now, I didn't feel it, and knew something was wrong."

"It's not stupid," she said quietly. "I saw my dead brother, remember."

Oh, I'm an idiot. I mentally slapped my forehead. Maybe she did understand. I nodded, feeling less embarrassed. "Yeah."

Carter coughed, seeming a bit uncomfortable herself. "So, was somebody here?"

"Yeah. They turned the place upside down. Here," I said, holding out my hand to her for balance. "Come aboard."

Carter stepped lightly onto *Ghost* and peered through the hatch. "Frank, I didn't know you were such a neat freak."

I grimaced. The boat was trashed, drawers were opened and dumped, paper strewn all over. The place had been completely ransacked.

"What do you think they were looking for?" Carter said.

"I don't know. I don't think it was a coincidence that guy was asking Pete all those questions, though. And we've been followed by whoever is in the gray sedan. I think they've just upped the game."

"I'm sorry, I'm bursting for a pee. Can I use the head?" Carter asked.

"Sure, it's through there," I said, pointing forward.

Carter went to use the head and after a moment called out to me. "Frank, I think you need to see this."

I followed Carter and opened the door to the head a little wider to see. Someone had left a message written in red lipstick on the mirror.

"Back off, Dalton," I read aloud. "That's certainly cryptic."

"You mean you don't always have that written on your mirror?"

"No. I usually go with don't burn the toast again, or something similar." I went to the fridge and found my beer stash was still intact. Then went and checked underneath my bed. My safe was intact. Priorities, you know? These clowns weren't good at searching, were interrupted or were looking for something else.

"I hate to ask," I said, "but I can't leave the place like this, now I've seen it. Would you mind giving me a hand cleaning up real quick?"

"And I hate to give you the same advice you just gave Pete, but don't you think we should call this in? The mirror is evidence, and if someone's threatening you…"

"Fuck." I ran my fingers through my hair while I thought. "You're right of course, but I don't want those CSI assholes rooting through all my shit. I'm sure whoever wrote that message wore gloves so there wouldn't be any prints. From what I'm seeing they were trying to scare me off." I gave it another run through the brain box to make sure I was tracking. No prints, nothing taken, just a message. "I'm good with some photos of the mess and a few of the mirror. There's not much more anyone else could do. We'll tidy up a bit and give the office a call."

"You're the boss," she said.

We did the best we could. Carter kept asking me where this thing or that thing went. She coughed at one point to get my attention and I could see she was holding up a skimpy black thong suspended on the end of her pen. "Ew, Frank, you wear some weird underwear for a guy."

I tried to hold down a blush. "Those aren't mine. And I don't know how they got there, and I plead the fifth." Dammit.

"Duh! I know they're not yours. And you don't have to pretend to be a saint. We all have lives outside of work," she said, flicking them at me.

I picked them up and threw them in the trash. "Well. She's not coming back." I'd seen to that by telling her I was married. Carter didn't say anything, and I couldn't tell how she was processing this information.

With us working together, the place soon looked as good as it ever did. But it bothered me more than I wanted to admit that the place had been ransacked. This has been the one place free from all the bullshit. I'd have to find that shaman now so I could get the Zen back on my boat.

TWELVE

We drove back to the office, feeling much less cheerful than before. I'd used a digital camera to take photos of the mirror and the mess aboard *Ghost*, instead of my phone because if the photos had to be used in evidence, it was easier to prove I hadn't manipulated them if they came from a camera. That, and if they did end up in evidence, I could just hand over the memory card, whereas if I'd used my phone, the whole thing would get stuck in some evidence locker for years. And I kinda didn't want to have to buy a new phone.

Carter offered to put the photos onto a CD while I filled in Smith, and we talked through what our next move should be.

"What about surveillance at the marina?" he said.

"CCTV? I thought about it. They have cameras, but as far as I know, they don't work. They're more of a deterrent for vandals and weekend boaters, so most of them are pointing at the transient docks than the liveaboards. I'll check with the marina manager when I go home, though, see if they have anything."

Smith didn't have any other thoughts, so I grabbed the finished CD from Carter and went in search of Malone. He was in the same spot as last time. I think he lived there.

"Hey, Mark. I've got some images on this CD I want you to look at when you get a chance," I said, handing him the CD.

"A CD. Wow. Thanks. That's so two decades ago. What are they of, anyway?" he said, rolling his eyes and throwing the CD on his desk.

"Someone broke into my boat and wrote some shit on my mirror. I took some photos and put them on that disc. I didn't want to use my phone for obvious reasons. What was I supposed to use instead of a CD?"

"Oh my God, I'm so sorry. Is anything missing? You could have used a thumb drive or emailed the photos. Should I be worried if it's related to this case?" Malone said, all in one long breath.

I took a moment to process that. "Thanks? No. Noted. It may or may not be related to this case. Listen, at this point, I don't know who left the message, so I have nothing to compare the writing on the mirror to, but maybe you can turn something up?" I changed the subject. "Did you manage to get any more photos off Willis's phone?"

Mark motioned for me to come back to his state-of-the-art screen.

"No, not yet. It takes a while for the chip-off to do its magic. If you could put a good word in about budget, and we got faster computers, it might help."

I waved him off. "You're preaching to the choir, buddy. Heard of sequestration? Continuing resolution? The whole military is broke."

"So, it would seem if you're the best we've got."

"Ha ha." I nodded at the screen. "What have you got?"

"Right. I've been going through the records of Mr. Willis, and he appeared to be the owner, CEO, CFO, partner and so on of a whole slew of companies. One's that don't exist."

"Shell companies. What was he doing? Laundering money?"

"It looks like it. You know what they say, follow the money. The money he takes in illegally has to get turned into good cash he can use, so it gets spent through the guise of a purchase through a legitimate company, and then the product that was bought is sold, and you get usable 'clean' money—"

"Thank you, Captain Obvious," I said, interrupting Malone's spiel, "is that how money laundering works? Do you have anything actually useful to add?"

Mark ignored my jibe. "Yes, these shell companies—would you like me to explain what shell means?" he asked, not so innocently. I rolled my eyes and motioned for him to get on with it. "These shell companies are linked to an offshore bank in the Caymans. The rest of them appear to be related to accounts that track the movement of shipping containers, or at least several large cargo and container vessels."

"Why would Willis be interested in that?" To say that seemed a little out of the depth of a commercial fishing captain was like saying your average household pet could drive your car and go grocery shopping for you.

"Again, hard to say exactly until I do some more digging, but his name does crop up quite a bit. Along with your Mr. Black, too."

"Figures. Anything I can pin on Black?"

Mark shook his head. "Right now, all I have is supposition. Nothing illegal to be the CEO of a lot of companies, just unusual. But if you know what we know, you can bet your bottom dollar it was probably illegal in some way."

I scratched my chin. "Those ships he's tracking. Can you get names or doc numbers for any of them? I don't suppose any of them run under the US flag, do they?"

"I haven't got the names or documentation numbers for all of them yet, but I got partial details on a 450-foot cargo ship that sailed out of Grand Cayman a week ago and is pulling into Ingleside soon. She should be with the pilots right about now. None of them are US flagged, though, but it does fit with having accounts in Cayman. Could be an easy way to transport cash."

Nothing's ever easy. It was never a mobster in a suit standing over a dead body with a smoking gun, 'Jimmy had it coming to him, ya hear.' it was all accounts and wire transfers, subterfuge and misdirection. "Isn't all that stuff done by wire transfer these days?" I asked, inwardly sighing.

"Sure. But if you're making off-the-book deals, it would be easier to keep with cash. Less traceable than wire transfers, and the beauty of the banks down there is they don't ask questions. It's illegal to move more than ten grand in cash in or out of the US, but if you have your own transport vessel..." Mark shrugged.

"What's she called?"

"The *Bold Endeavor*."

"Cute."

An hour later, Carter and I were on a Coast Guard 45-foot Response Boat-Medium out of Station Port Aransas en route to the *Bold Endeavor*. We had teamed up with some of the enforcement guys and were going to piggyback off their boarding. They had bigger guns than we did.

We'd made the vessel stop at the anchorage just outside the port before she came alongside the pier in Ingleside, as I wanted to ensure nobody, and no cash, conveniently hopped off before we got there. The ride out on the 45 RB-M with its twin Detroit Diesel 60s and Rolls Royce Jet drives was smooth and fast, and although it had a nice, air-conditioned cabin, I preferred to stand on the well deck aft of the cabin and take in the salt air. Lately, it felt like I was always riding a desk or riding in a car and the drone of the engines and beautiful blue-green water relaxed me. Carter stayed in the AC, chatting it up with the boat crew. They seemed to like her.

The afternoon was already rolling on by the time I sighted the *Bold Endeavor* at anchor, barely moving in the chop. It was a huge boat, about six times the size of the *Reel Lady,* the size feeling magnified by how low we were in the water compared to them.

Pulling up on the leeward side of the freighter, the giant steel hull of the ship minimized the wind and flattened the seas, making it easier to clamber on board. The ship's crew had lowered the gangway, so it was a relatively simple job to move from the smaller vessel Coast Guard vessel to the larger ship. Not quite like the old days when all they would do was throw over a Jacob's ladder, essentially nothing more than a rope ladder with wooden rungs. I hated climbing up those things. I'm not scared of heights, but scaling what feels like a thousand feet straight up the side of a steel boat on nothing more than a rickety rope ladder freaks me out.

Not by nature a team to stand idly about, the enforcement guys were already conducting an initial safety assessment by the time I'd hoofed it up the gangway. I left them to it, as they had this down to a science, searching accessible spaces on board to ensure no one was going to jump out and kill us with a machete or whatever. I wasn't expecting that scenario, but it never hurt to check. This was all routine for the crew, as the Coast Guard randomly boards vessels for security and at other times for inspections, so it wasn't likely to raise any red flags.

While the enforcement team were doing what they did, I took a moment to look around. In my earlier days in the Coast Guard as a petty officer, I'd conducted boardings and inspections on something like a billion cargo ships—no exaggeration. Well, maybe a little, but it sure felt like a billion—so I was as familiar with this type of vessel as I could be.

"Notice anything?" I said to Carter. She definitely hadn't been on a billion ships—like I had—so I wanted to see if she saw anything amiss.

"I see a long, mostly flat steel deck, pilot house in the stern, some 40-foot shipping containers stacked three high or so forward of the cargo hatches. We looked at the ships manifest before and this old girl hauls break bulk, so I would expect most of the cargo, in this case gravel, is down below in the holds." She shrugged and looked at me. "Tell me, oh master, what am I supposed to be seeing?" I could tell she wanted to bow.

"It's not what you're supposed to be seeing," I said, ignoring her, "more of a question of what you're not seeing. We can't get into the cargo holds as it's too dangerous, so for all we know, they could be hiding crates of guns or whatever underneath all the gravel. So, what we're looking for could be hidden in plain sight. We'd have to monitor every second of the offload, and we don't have time right now. We can ask customs to keep an eye out in the meantime. But what we can do right now is pop a few of these containers and see what's in them."

"Do you think they'd be that obvious to hide stuff in the containers?" Carter asked.

"Beats me. They have to move the guns and presumably drugs around somehow. Why don't we get the enforcement team to help pop a few random ones once they're done with their safety assessment, then we can at least say we did our due diligence. Why don't you take care of that while I walk the deck and I'll meet back up with you here," I looked at my watch, "in say, fifteen minutes."

I had a crew member shadow me as I walked around. I wasn't concerned he was following me, as he was just doing his job and making sure I didn't fall overboard or into a cargo hold. I didn't see anything weird and headed back to where Carter was.

"Anything?" I said.

She pointed to the open door of one of the containers. "See for yourself."

I borrowed a flashlight and shone it inside the can. I was met with the sight of twisted and rusty metal. "Scrap?"

"Yeah. According to the manifest, most of the containers are full of scrap. This is the third we've popped, and all three look the same. They ship it back here for recycling."

"Seems like a lot of effort for scrap," I said.

"You'd think so, but if this was coming from Cayman, there's nowhere else for it to go. You know, an island surrounded by water. If the ship's already on a scheduled route, the scrap gets a free ride and makes a few bucks. Better than dumping it in the ocean."

"Which I'm sure they never do." I'm sure they did. "All right, good job. Let's get the team here to pop a few more while we go and have a chat with the captain. You never know, we might get lucky and find some guns or something, although I doubt it."

I asked one of the deckhands to take us to the captain. The deckhand was a short Filipino, dressed in greasy coveralls. He had the barest whisper of a beard and only a rudimentary grasp of the English language, although it was far better than my Filipino. With a combination of smiles and hand gestures, he offered to take us up in the elevator to the bridge, but from experience, I knew the things were super slow and would have been a tight and uncomfortable squeeze for three. We'd all be crammed in, with sweaty sailor at the controls. That wasn't in my game plan, so we opted to take the long way via the stairs. We plodded up a mountain of steps, following the aroma of unwashed sailor until he finally motioned us into a small room with a large table.

"I get captain. Wait here," the deckhand said. He left Carter and me alone in the room.

"Welcome to the good life, Carter," I said, gesturing at the cramped room. She went to sit down at the table, but I shook my head and she stopped. "It'll undermine any authority you have if you're sitting. A lot of ship cultures already don't take women in positions of power well, so it's wise not to make it easier for them to ignore you."

"Roger that," she said, and we waited.

The captain entered the room shortly after, preceded by the rancid odor of dirty sailor. I think this was Sweaty Stink Number Five, a great classic, and added to the allure of pungent cigarette breath. I moved as far away in the tiny room as I could manage. It wasn't far enough. The captain was a swarthy man, about five-ten, looked as if he shaved once a trip, and changed his shirt on the same schedule.

After brief introductions, I came straight to the point. "Captain. What did you pick up in the Caymans?"

The captain shrugged and sat down, gesturing for us to do the same. I remained standing and was happy to see Carter doing the same, both of us leaning on the bulkhead wall. "Water, coffee, Coca-Cola?" he said, ignoring my question. His English was clipped but understandable.

We both shook our heads, and without looking, he rattled off something quick in a language I couldn't catch to a young cabin boy behind him, who nodded, and ran off quickly as if his life depended on it. Which it might. I repeated the question a little slower to get the captain's attention again.

"The manifest, it is here," he said, shoving some papers across the table. He tapped at a column with his nicotine-stained fingers. "Here, and here."

"Right," I said, noticing the yellow nicotine stains on his rat-a-tatting fingers.

"Is this a regular run? Cayman to Corpus?" Carter said.

The captain paused, refusing to look at Carter.

After enough time had passed to feel awkward, I said, "I believe my partner asked you a question?"

The captain dragged his eyes to Carter. "No. Is not regular," he said, stretching each syllable, making it sound like reg-ooh-lar.

Carter grimaced when he looked at her, no doubt anticipating what the captain was thinking. The cabin boy chose that moment to return with coffee for the captain and bottled water for us, which we hadn't asked for. He also placed a tin of English shortbread cookies in front of him on the table. The captain dismissed him with a wave of his hand and a curt command, and the cabin boy left in a hurry.

"What was the reason for this trip?" I said, eyeing the tin.

He shrugged again. "I go where cum-pan-e say. They say go here, I go here. They say go there, I go—"

"There. Got it, thanks," I said. I showed him a photo of Willis. "Do you recognize this man?"

I watched his face carefully as I slid the photo across the table. He barely glanced at it before shaking his head, busying himself with opening the tin of shortbread. I pulled out another photo and placed it on top.

"How about this man?"

This time, his composure slipped. The captain's hand trembled, betraying him, as he put the lid back on the shortbread and fumbled for a cigarette instead, shaking one loose from a Marlboro red soft pack. "No. Never seen."

I'd shown him a picture of Mr. Black. It was clear he knew who the man was. Also, obvious he was scared. I knew Black and Willis were getting their guns into the country somehow. These freighters seemed like a logical place. On a four-hundred-foot-something ship, though, there could be a thousand hiding places.

After a few more generic questions, I'd run out of anything else to ask. It was obvious Black scared him more than we did. I looked at Carter, but she subtly shook her head. Our best bet now was to watch the vessel and see where the cargo went after it docked. Once back on the deck, we liaised with the enforcement team, but they hadn't found anything interesting, so we made our way back down the gangway to the RB-M and back to port.

Back in the truck once again, we headed to the office, both deep in thought. I kept an eye out for anyone following us, but this time saw nothing suspicious. The traffic was light, and I took a circuitous route, braking at green traffic lights and speeding up at red ones to see if I could shake a tail loose. It was quiet.

We hadn't had much time to talk since we left the ship, so I asked, "What did you think of that whole evolution?"

"The captain was nice. I was thinking maybe when the ship docks, I could invite him out for a drink or two."

I smiled at the obvious humor. "Yeah, you should. I'm sure he'd be delighted. In all seriousness, though, you're going to find lots of people like him. I'm glad you kept your cool. It made the interview much easier."

"Sure. I did see something strange, though."

I tapped the brakes involuntarily. "What did I miss?"

She couldn't keep a straight face for long. "I saw you eyeing those shortbread cookies. You could hardly contain yourself." I was about to protest but finally gave up and shrugged. "What can I say? You caught me."

Back at the office, we split to grab some food. I was at my desk nibbling a ham sandwich I hadn't had a chance to eat at lunch, when the duty officer called.

"Sir, there's a Miss Lancaster from Lancaster, Lancaster and Mitchell here to see you." I looked at the clock on the wall. It was creeping into late afternoon.

I was surprised she was here after our less than auspicious meeting the day before, so I was curious about what she wanted. I hoped it wasn't to complain about the investigation. I told the duty officer to send her up. Carter wasn't back yet from her hunt for food, so I met Lancaster at the elevators by myself and escorted her to one of the interview rooms. I watched her while we walked. She wore a similar gray suit, but this time, she appeared mollified, less angry than I expected.

Inside the interview room, I closed the door and turned to her. "So, to what do I owe the pleasure, Miss Lancaster?"

She cleared her throat. "Mr. Dalton. It appears I owe you an apology."

"Really? To what end?" I asked.

"Can I sit?"

"Of course. Please do," I said, grabbing another chair from the corner of the room for myself.

Lancaster guided her chair to the table and delicately sat down, placing her briefcase on the table and opening it, pulling out a folder. I sat down across from her.

"I reviewed some of the applicable rules and regulations regarding marine investigations, and I have to say everything you did was perfectly in line," she said. "I appreciate you didn't evict me from the vessel, even though you could have done so."

Lancaster sounded contrite. Genuine. I was used to dealing with lawyers, but it was a surprise, a first I think, for a lawyer to apologize to me. Usually, they were pig-headed, so my appreciation for Lancaster went up a couple of notches.

"Well, thank you," I said. "Apology accepted. I can assure you I never have and never would do anything beyond the bounds of my authority. You have to admit, though, we do have pretty broad authority so I can understand why it confuses people. Real life isn't like TV."

"Yes, I know now. You can board any vessel at any time for any reason and take whatever you deem necessary to conduct your investigation."

I smiled. "You make it sound like we all wear jackboots. But yes, that about sums it up. Surely that wasn't the only reason you came here, though?"

"No." She opened the folder she'd pulled out, glanced at it as if to make sure she wasn't inadvertently giving me the wrong file, and pushed it over to me. "I thought, seeing as though I made a bit of an ass of myself, I could offer you an olive branch and show you these documents. I would rather cultivate relationships with law enforcement than abuse them."

"What's in here?" I asked, grabbing the folder.

"It's Mr. Willis's last will and testament. I know you're trying to fully investigate what happened, and I thought this might help. Our firm was retained as executor, as Mr. Willis did not have any living relatives and while I can't show you anything confidential without a subpoena, I can share the gist of it."

I leafed through the folder. Some papers were loose and appeared old. A lot had messy legalese penciled across the top, mostly indecipherable to me.

"Miss Lancaster, thanks for this. I can't tell you how much I appreciate it. I don't know what I'm looking at, though. Could you give it to me in a nutshell? In English?"

This time she smiled that cute, upturned smile I'd caught a glimmer of the first time I'd met her. It was nice to see on her face. "In Mr. Willis's last will dated June 5th, 2003, he bequeathed all his worldly possessions to his wife."

"Wait. 2003? That's what, almost two decades ago? He didn't have a more up to date will?"

Lancaster shook her head.

"Then that would make his wife Julia Rivas?"

"Julia Willis back then, but yes. The will is valid. Mrs. Rivas is the sole heir."

She hadn't mentioned that back at her house. "How much are we talking about?"

"Mr. Willis had approximately two point three million dollars in his checking account."

I stared at her. "Two point three million?" I repeated like an idiot.

She nodded. "Yes. But that's not all. He also had a house in San Antonio he left her, a market value of three million give or take, and a small beach condo in North Padre Island, valued at just under a million. Various other small accounts, but they're the biggest."

I added it up and mentally whistled. "So, he left his now ex-wife around six million dollars in cash and assets."

"Yes."

"And he never changed his will, even after he got divorced?"

"Correct again."

"Jesus, that's a bit of an oversight, wouldn't you say? Makes you wonder why he was working on a fishing vessel, doesn't it?"

"I did find it unusual, but I'm not the investigator. Maybe he enjoyed the sea?" She smiled at me again. I liked her more and more.

"Did he leave his business partners anything?" I asked.

"No, it doesn't look like it."

"Why would he leave his ex-wife all that money?" I said, trying to think it through. "They got divorced years ago from what she told me and haven't spoken in just as long. Are you sure this is his most up to date will?"

"I couldn't say why he left her the money, but this is his will, fully notarized at my office. There can be no question of its authenticity. And as the sole beneficiary, Mrs. Rivas almost certainly knows about the will."

I rubbed my face. This was becoming a long day. Still, I had to admit, this was promising. Really promising. Maybe it was even a lead. "All right. Thank you, Miss Lancaster, for the information. Can I get a copy of this?"

"It's yours."

THIRTEEN

Lancaster gathered her things from the desk, sliding the papers back into the briefcase, and we stood and shook hands. I escorted her back to the elevators, making small talk about the weather and other nonsense. I was vibrating with excitement and all but pushed her into the elevator when the doors dinged and opened. As soon as they closed, I hurried over to Carter's desk, where she was chowing down on some sort of enormous burrito.

"And you made fun of my cookie fetish," I said. "Get that down you or bring it with you and grab your bag. We need to go talk to Julia Rivas again. There's something she wasn't telling us." I filled her in on the conversation with the lawyer.

"Are you sure she knows about the will?" Carter said, around a mouthful of burrito.

"With that much money, it shouldn't have slipped her mind. Makes me wonder why Willis never changed it."

"Maybe he was still in love with her."

"Maybe. Or maybe he never expected to die so soon. It gives her motive, though. I don't care how loaded she looks, six million is a lot of fish."

I gunned the V8 out of the parking lot, and we set off for the short distance to her house. As we turned down her street, a gray sedan burst out of her driveway, barely made the turn and headed our way, slowing when it saw us.

"Is that the same car from before?" Carter said.

"It looks like it. He came out of Rivas's drive." I turned the visor down, lit up the blue lights, and turned the siren on. As a Coast Guard criminal investigator, I surely had arrest powers, but a traffic stop was a bit dubious. However, I felt I could verbalize why I was doing this, and if I'd made a mistake and tagged the wrong vehicle, I'd apologize profusely and wait for them to lodge a complaint.

The car slowed and stopped in the street a scant two hundred yards in front of us. Even squinting, I couldn't see inside the sedan because it was heavily tinted. I slowed the truck but continued rolling forward, silencing the siren but keeping the lights on. Luckily, there were no other cars around to get in the way.

"Carter, get your—"

The sedan punched it in reverse, now moving away from us, smoke billowing from the rapidly spinning tires. The acrid stench of burning rubber blew through the AC vents. I jammed my foot down on the gas, and the truck responded effortlessly, closing the gap.

Without slowing, the sedan executed a J-turn, going from reverse to forward with a barely discernible loss of speed, and was now hurtling away from us. It appeared we were correct it was the same car, and now I had all the authority I needed to pursue. The sedan screeched around the next corner, and I lost sight of it momentarily behind a high brick wall. I increased speed, hitting the siren again, and barreled after it around the blind corner.

"Hang on," I yelled at Carter.

The sedan had stopped as soon as it had gone around the corner and not having time to brake, I smashed into the back of it, airbags deploying in the truck with an explosive thump. I lurched forward into the seatbelt and then was immediately crushed into the back of the seat by the force of the airbags. My teeth mashed down on my tongue and the coppery bitterness of blood flooded my mouth. I fought off the airbag, trying to get it out of my face. I needed to see what was going on. I thought I heard the airbag go off again.

"What the fuck? Carter, you okay?"

Carter didn't respond. Shit.

The airbag exploded again. I was confused, but adrenaline kicked in, and I realized it wasn't the airbag that was still exploding.

"Carter, get down. We're taking fire." I pushed at her to get down, releasing her seat belt. She slid into the passenger well, unconscious. Shit. We needed to get out of here. The truck had stalled, so staying low in the seat, I pushed the starter, but nothing happened. Double shit.

Several shots pinged off the side of the truck and one hit the window, glass shattering into a patchwork of fragments but holding together. The glass wasn't bulletproof, but if we stayed low, the hefty engine block would provide some cover.

I crawled over to Carter's side, staying low, and pushed her door open wide, sliding over her and onto the ground. I pulled out my service weapon. I couldn't see who was shooting at us, but figured it was whoever had been driving the sedan. I left Carter on the floor of the truck, so she was protected and checked for any wounds, but didn't see anything obvious. Hopefully, it was the airbag that knocked her out.

I inched around the door and raised my head over the hood. A shot pinged off the engine block, and I ducked again, but now I had the general location of the shooter. I checked my weapon and returned fire, popping off three shots in rapid succession.

I heard a loud hiss from somewhere, and another shot clunked into the truck. Thank God we still didn't have that econobox. We'd never have survived the crash, let alone the gunfire. It would have gone straight through the thin metal.

I fired again, but this time ducked down low under the truck. No one fired back at me, and then I heard a car further up the street start up and peel out. I ran out after it in time to see the flicker of its brake lights as it rounded a corner.

"Shit." I fumbled my phone out of my shirt pocket and called the incident into the duty officer along with a description of the car I'd seen, but I hadn't had a chance to get the plate. I also asked them to call an ambulance for Carter.

I took a moment to evaluate any potential wounds, in particular focusing on her neck and head, searching for any sprains or knots. Finding nothing, I carefully pulled her out of the car and gently repositioned her on the ground, folding my jacket and placing it under her head. Her eyes opened and slowly came into focus.

"What, what happened?" she said.

"Hey sleepy. You missed all the fun, is all. Stay down all right? You've been in an accident. I think you're okay, but I called the EMTs to check you out just in case."

"What's going on?"

"Nothing much. We rear-ended the car we were following, and they were so pissed they decided to shoot at us. The ambulance should be here soon."

Her eyes widened, and she tried to get up. I gently restrained her with a hand on her shoulder. "Ambulance? I'm fine," she said. She attempted to get up again, but winced when she raised her head.

"You're not fine, and you're going to stay right there until you get checked out."

I could hear the ambulance approaching, the *wee-wah* of the siren getting louder, but then I noticed a sound like a high-pressure hiss getting louder. It started as quiet, but as bothersome as a mosquito whine, but rapidly formed into something loud and terrifying. I realized the sound had likely been there the entire time, but the gunfire had momentarily deafened me, and now my hearing was coming back, the hiss was more pronounced.

At about the same time it clicked in my head where I'd heard a similar sound before, a roaring like a plane taking off on full thrust slammed against my ears, and I felt a deep rumble in my ribs as they rattled together. The concussion wave rocked the truck on its wheels and blasted safety glass at us from the windows that hadn't been shot out. Car alarms up and down the street warbled and chirped.

"What the fuck was that?" Carter shouted.

"Stay down," I said, leaning over her so the debris from the car wouldn't hit her.

I stood up as soon as the shock wave passed and saw a huge funnel of fire and smoke hit the sky. It was coming from the direction of Mrs. Rivas's house.

"Stay here. Wait for the ambulance. Call for backup if you can. And a fire truck," I shouted over my shoulder. She nodded, still seeming dazed, sat up and put her back to the truck, drawing her gun.

I ran back around the way we'd come, sprinting as fast as I could. I turned into Mrs. Rivas's driveway, arms pumping, legs going. Fragments of burning and charred paper were falling around me, and I dodged them as best I could. I ran around a bend in the driveway, dodging a burning piano that must have gone up during the explosion. It had collapsed in a heap of sizzling wood and sonorous chimes. The adrenaline punched in an extra notch. I didn't have time to be startled, just ran around the thing and kept on going.

My steps faltered as I got closer and saw the house. I slowed and stopped. Where before a magnificent sprawl of decadence had stood, now there was only an enormous crater, with smoke and flames raging within. The front door was incongruously still intact, closed and upright, supported by part of the framework. The entire top floor appeared to have vaporized. The house was gone. Completely. There was no saving anyone or anything.

I raised my hand as another flare-up scorched the sky and I tried to shield my face from the brutal heat. I backed off as the hairs on my arm singed. Behind me, I could hear the wail of sirens coming up the driveway. Either Carter had got through to the fire department, or they were coming anyway. But it didn't matter. The house was gone. And so was Mrs. Rivas and anybody else that was inside. Fuck.

I moved out of the way as the fire department arrived so they could do their thing and looked for the guy in charge with the red fire helmet. It wasn't a guy, but a girl and I reported to her what I had seen and heard. She asked a few questions which I did my best to answer, and then I went to find Carter. She was sitting in the back of an ambulance with a blanket around her.

Carter had guessed what was up. "Mrs. Rivas?" she said.

I shook my head. There was nothing to say. Although the official cause of the fire would have to wait for the arson investigator's determination, I'd bet my hind teeth this wasn't an accident. Not with that sedan having been in the driveway.

"You okay?" I said.

She nodded. "Sore. No concussion, I was probably stunned by the airbags. If I remember right, I was holding on for dear life when we went round that corner. Anyway, the medics said I could go if I want."

"If you're sure?"

She nodded.

"Let's go then. We'll have to get a ride back to the office, as I don't think the truck's going anywhere. You sure you're okay?"

"Yeah. They said to take it easy for a bit. Might have a headache. If it gets worse call the doctor, etcetera, etcetera."

"You know. This is getting out of control," I said, trying not to grind my teeth. I helped her off the ambulance.

"Do you think it has anything to do with our case?" said Carter.

I snorted. "Sorry. Yeah, I do. It's all connected somehow. I think it might be time to pull in Black and have a little chat."

Before I could follow up on that, my phone rang. It was Paul. He said he was using an old payphone at a neighboring dock near the *Reel Lady*.

"Mr. Dalton? I don't know how much longer I can do this." He sounded scared.

"What's going on, Paul?"

"I don't know, sir. I think the guys are getting suspicious, they're looking at me funny like...like they know I told you something, like they don't trust me anymore—"

Paul was working himself up. "Paul, you need to get a handle, buddy. I understand this is pretty crazy for you—"

"Crazy? You call this crazy? You come aboard and tell me the captain was dumped from the boat while we were at sea. *This* boat. The one I'm on. That he was already dead. And then you tell me the rest of the crew are in on it. You know how easy it would be for them to dump me? And then you ask me to stay here, to act normal. Come on, Mr. Dalton."

"Paul. I get it, buddy. Listen, we're pulling Mr. Black in for questioning right now." Right after Paul hung up, and I made the call, at least. "I need you to hang tight, for a little longer. Can you do that for me? Can you hang tight just for a bit?"

I heard Paul sigh as if he had deflated like a week-old party balloon. He said something I didn't quite catch, and then he said, "Yeah, I guess."

"Okay, Paul. You do that for me, buddy, hang tight. I've gotta go but call me if you need anything. Anytime, remember?"

All I heard was a dial tone from the phone hanging up. I felt like such a shitheel. I hoped he was overreacting, but I needed him to come through for me. I needed a break in this case. I needed to figure out what was going on. How did Willis make all that money? Why did he give it all to his wife, and why did someone blow her up? Where would the money go now? Was it Batman? Where were all the guns? There were too many unanswered questions, not to mention who had trashed my boat and shot at us. It felt like forever ago I was hanging out on *Ghost*, getting bored. I was starting to miss those days.

I made the call to get Black. It didn't take long for agents to pick him up for us, but it gave me enough time to get back to the office and change out of my stinky and smoke-riddled clothes into something fresher. Carter was waiting for me outside the interview room and looked a lot better, the aspirin must have helped, and we went in together, a united front. We sat down across from Black, and I opened a folder on the desk, took out the photo we'd found on Willis's phone, and pushed it over to him so he could see it. He looked bored.

"Good evening, Mr. Black. In case you've forgotten my name is Special Agent Dalton, this is Special Agent Carter. Thank you for coming into the office this late in the day. Take a look at the photo, please. Recognize anyone?"

He snorted, the only concession to my welcome speech. He was sporting another foul velour jogging suit. This one was a deadly shade of bright orange and zipped to the top. The chubby fingers of his right hand, still clustered with gold rings, reached for the photo. He hesitated a moment before withdrawing quickly as if the picture was scalding hot.

"Nice picture. Where'd you get it?" he said, in his staccato clip.

"Do you recognize the people in the picture?"

"Can't say I do. Should I?"

I tapped at the photo. "So, you're telling me that's not you, Captain Willis and George. We found it on Willis's phone."

Black glanced at the photo again and then regarded me with a steady gaze. He shrugged. "I know those other men, of course. I know me. I just don't *recognize* them or me. In this photo, that is. Perhaps...yes, perhaps it is photoshopped? The things they can do with computers these days. It's almost like magic."

"And who would do that, and then put it on Willis's phone?"

"Who can tell? In business, one always has enemies. Some people are naturally envious of me."

I shoved a piece of paper across the desk. "You should be able to write their names down for me then. We'll be able to follow up with any complaints you may have about their conduct."

Black didn't move to take the paper. I pushed down a wave of frustration. I had to play this cool. I switched tactics.

"What can you tell me about Mr. Willis's will? Did you know he left his ex, Mrs. Rivas, all his money?"

He shrugged again. "Didn't know. Don't care. What Willis did with his money was his concern. He didn't tell me what to do with mine. I didn't tell him what to do with his. What am I in here for, anyway?"

"Just a few more questions, Mr. Black. Did you know Mrs. Rivas was murdered earlier today?"

"No. Now, much as I appreciate the good arm of the law, I have more important things to do. Perhaps you should be out there looking for her killer instead of bothering an innocent businessman like me."

There was a knock on the door and the duty officer poked his head in.

"Sorry to bother you, sir, but—" he said.

"Really, Mr. Dalton, I thought we had a better relationship," Lancaster said, as she pushed past the officer. "You should have notified me that my client was here."

I smiled tightly at her. She'd changed into a prim and tan pantsuit since the afternoon. I nodded at the officer that it was okay, and he closed the door. "Mr. Black is not under arrest, we just had a few questions."

"And now he's leaving. Mr. Black. Ready?"

"Of course, Miss Lancaster. I was just telling Mr. Dalton I didn't know anything useful."

Black pushed his bulk away from the table and tipped an imaginary hat to me, the gold on his fingers flashing in the stark light.

"Agents, I hope we don't meet again."

Lancaster escorted him out, glaring at me as the door closed.

I blew out a breath of frustration and slammed my fist down on the desk, rattling the metal.

"Dammit all to hell."

FOURTEEN

Where to turn? What to do? I was in turmoil, feeling angst driven. I knew, absolutely knew, that Black, George, Ricky, and Jimmy were all involved. Some more than others. I was reasonably sure Paul wasn't. I just didn't know how all the pieces fit together. What caused them to kill Willis and dump his body? Were they hoping it would look like an accident? Why was Rivas blown up? Were they trying to scare me by ransacking my boat and leaving that message, or was it misdirection to hide what they were looking for?

The thoughts spun through my head, round and round. I needed to focus on one element, follow the leads and rabbit trails, and either find conclusions or move on. But first, I needed my haven back, and I needed a place to rest. If my head wasn't in the game, I was of no use to anyone. *Ghost* may have been physically clean, but I felt its sanctity was blemished. It didn't feel like the old *Ghost* anymore. Something was missing. I'd said before I thought the previous owner might have been a shaman. It was time to put that theory to the test.

Good bartenders were always a wealth of knowledge, and Pete knew a guy that knew a guy. That guy put me in touch with a local shaman he knew, authentic, so he said. It was easy to find a crackerjack, advertising on Craigslist, Facebook Marketplace perhaps, or in the small print at the back of sketchy magazines, but someone who could really perform? That was much harder. I wanted that safe, secure feeling back on my boat, and I was willing to give it a shot.

I'd kept this part of my life separate from work. Telling the guys at work my boat had lost its mojo didn't fit the image of a law enforcement officer. Mainstream or no-stream was the only way. However, Carter had tagged along for the meeting. She said she'd never met a shaman, and I think it piqued her interest. I didn't mind having her with me, either. It was only a couple of days since I'd met Carter, but in that brief time together, I had learned there was a lot to like about her. Although new to the Guard, she could draw on more than I'd initially given her credit for, and despite our rocky beginning, we were working well together. I trusted her. She had my back.

"Listen," I said. "This, uh, isn't the most comfortable experience for me, but I'd appreciate it if you'd keep this between us, you know? I don't need to be Frank, the shaman lover or whatever, back at the office."

"Sure, Frank, sure," she said, her mouth forming a glimmer of a smile. "I won't say a word." I had the feeling the exact opposite was going to happen when we got back to the office.

We'd met the shaman at the T-heads where I moored *Ghost*. She was not what I was expecting. I was thinking it would be someone adorned with native robes or wearing a bearskin, maybe a long staff, but I realized how stupid that was. It wasn't Gandalf the Grey I was waiting for, and it wasn't likely a shaman would go walking around with a great big bear suit on, not in the heat of South Texas and not unless you wanted to get thrown in the nut bin. Instead, she was wearing a straightforward, off-white cotton suit. Her only adornment was a small brown leather satchel she carried over her shoulder, and although I'm awful with guessing ages, she looked somewhere around her early thirties. Maybe?

It threw me off when she walked right up to me and said, "You must be Dalton."

It took me a moment to transfer the mental image I had in my head of walking bear rugs with the person standing in front of me.

"I'm sorry," I said. "I'm not sure how to address you."

Her hair was flaxen and tied up simply in a ponytail. She smiled when she spoke, dimples appearing in the corners of her mouth.

"If we go all formal, you can call me Shaman Satinka, but I prefer Tinka. It's simpler. And cuter." More dimples.

She turned to Carter and took her hand in hers. "And you, my dear. What's your story? No, don't tell me." She paused for a moment and closed her eyes. That moment turned into a longer moment. I looked at Carter and she raised her eyebrows. I was about to intervene when Satinka's eyes fluttered open and she said, "I sense distress from you. Something else as well, something more...I sense protection."

She closed her eyes again. We didn't say anything. I scratched my nose and felt awkward while nothing seemed to happen.

After another minute, she said, "I feel someone from your past is looking out for you, someone close. Family? A sibling? Sister? No, a brother."

I got chills down the back of my neck. There was no way she could have known anything about Carter's brother. A tear slid down Carter's cheek, and she just nodded.

Satinka nodded back. "It is so." She smiled and, still holding Carter's hand, said, "I rarely get such clear images without my cards, but with you, my dear, your brother must be close." Satinka frowned, her forehead creasing. "This might sound trite, but there is a shadow in your aura. It will pass, but a change is coming for you." The frown deepened, and Satinka let go of Carter's hands. "I'm sorry, that's all I have."

"What do you mean, a shadow?" Carter said.

"There is nothing more. I wish I could give you definitive answers, but it's not always clear. I'm sorry." Satinka turned to me. "Mr. Dalton, I believe you need my services. What exactly is it you need me to do?"

"Shaman Satinka—"

"Just Tinka is fine."

"Tinka, then. This is going to sound stupid." When she didn't interrupt, I carried on. "Well, when I got my boat, I was told a yogi or shaman or someone blessed it, or something like that. Maybe it was a sales pitch, maybe not, but I've always felt weirdly calm and comfortable on board. Safe." I strained for the right words. "But more than a secure feeling, something, I don't know, other? It's always been like that—until yesterday. My boat was broken into. I knew the moment I stepped foot on her. The calm has gone, and well..."

"You would like me to replace the sanctity of your vessel?"

"Well, yes. If that's a thing?"

"All things are possible. Please, permit me to enter your vessel by myself so that I may draw upon the old auras."

She walked over to the *Ghost and* placed her hands on the superstructure for a moment, shook off her shoes and slipped barefoot aboard. I saw her disappear into the cabin.

"What do you think, Jess?" I asked.

"You know, that's the first time you've called me that."

"I'm sorry. I—"

"No, no. I like it. The only other person who ever called me Jess was my brother. Somehow, it feels right coming from you."

I took her hand in mine without thinking, then immediately dropped it. "Sorry. I just wanted to make sure you were okay. That was some pretty heavy stuff the shaman said."

"Oh boy. Yeah, that was a surprise. I didn't think shaman were psychic like that." Carter squeezed my shoulder. "Thank you for thinking about me. You know what, though? It does make me feel better. Perhaps my brother really is looking out for me from somewhere. He certainly made me get my life back together. Maybe he's my guardian angel." She shrugged.

"I think shamans come in all shapes and sizes. She wasn't what I was expecting, either. Maybe that's a good thing." I waved at my boat, changing the subject. "I wonder how long this takes."

Not one for standing around, I started pacing. I hoped Satinka could do something. When I glanced back at *Ghost*, I saw clouds of smoke billowing from the open hatch.

"What the..." I ran toward my boat, but then Satinka came out onto the stern deck. She waved me off.

"Not to worry," she shouted. "Give me a few more minutes."

I stopped where I was, not sure if I should listen to her. Carter came up to me and placed her hand on my shoulder again, this time letting it linger for a moment longer.

"Trust her. It'll be okay. I have a feeling."

"I hope you're right," I said.

A few minutes later the shaman calmly walked back toward us, carrying something that was still smoking.

"Sage." She held up the smoking bundle. "This is sage. I'm sorry if I alarmed you, it took more than usual. Sage is used to ward off unwelcome spirits and cleanse a place. There were many bad vibes from the people who did this to your boat. But I have replaced what you called your calm. I have also left some feathers above the sink. Do not remove them from your boat. If they fall, let it be of their own accord. The feathers create a natural form of protection. However, there is one thing." She paused for a moment and looked me in the eye. "The name of your home. Names are important, they hold meaning. The old name has been irreparably blemished, and it must be cast out for this cleansing to hold. You must choose a new name for her."

"What should I call her?"

"That is up to you. It will come. Go aboard, feel her."

I walked down to the old *Ghost*. She didn't look any different. The smoke had dissipated soon after Satinka left the cabin. I looked back. Carter urged me on. When I stepped forward, I almost stopped. It was as if I'd walked into a big fluffy blanket, like in those science fiction movies where the actor walks through a portal to another world. Something enveloped me, and a feeling of comfort entwined around my soul. I sat down in the stern, and the name came to me. Instantly. I think the old girl must have told me herself.

After a few minutes to soak it all in, I walked back up to Satinka and said, "*Serenity*."

"Then that shall be her name." Satinka turned to leave.

"Wait," I said. "Thank you. She feels like home again, maybe even better. What do I owe you?"

"Nothing. I do not charge for my services. I take blessings in that I helped you." She turned to leave again, but then stopped. "Perhaps, though…"

"Yes, anything."

"Take my arm, walk with me a ways."

"I won't be a minute," I said to Carter.

I walked arm-in-arm with Satinka for a minute until we were away from *Serenity*, and then we stopped. She turned to me and placed her hands on my shoulders and said, "Your friend. I feel a bond between the two of you."

I scoffed. "Who? Carter? I've only just met her."

"It doesn't matter. Your souls talk to each other; I can hear their happy chatter when you two are close. Do not ignore your inner self. She will need your help soon. Trust yourself."

She already had, but I didn't want to correct Tinka. "What do you mean?"

"As I said before. I don't always see everything clearly, but she will need you. It is your duty to her, to your souls."

I didn't know how to respond to that. Satinka left, perhaps leaving me with more questions than answers. I didn't believe in a lot of things, but I know she said stuff to Carter no one could have known. I filed it away in the file that said to think about when alone with a beer. On *Serenity*. I didn't know then, but I was to see Satinka again, however it wouldn't be for some time.

I walked back. "Jess. What are you doing with the rest of your night?"

"I don't have any plans."

"We've been going a million miles an hour on this case. I'm bushed. I think a bit of R and R would do us both some good. Perhaps a brief break will give us a fresh perspective. Would you do me the honor of letting me cook dinner for you aboard *Serenity*?"

She looked at me in the dwindling sunlight as the last rays caught her brown eyes, emphasizing tiny flecks of green.

"I'd be flattered," she said. She gasped when she came aboard. "Oh, Frank. Is this what it felt like before?"

"It's better now. I think the old gal is happy."

I settled Carter in the cockpit seats and poured her a glass of pinot grigio I took from the fridge, an old bottle I'd been saving for a special occasion.

"To *Serenity*," I said.

"To *Serenity*."

I went to work in the galley. I cooked my go-to meal, shrimp scampi. It was a family recipe an old friend had given me a long time ago, and one I could cook quickly and simply. Less than twenty minutes later, I brought two steaming plates out to the cockpit, set on trays. The sun had set, and a warm glow surrounded *Serenity*. The air felt clean and refreshing.

We sat down to eat. Carter took a bite. "Oh. My. God. This is freaking delicious," she said.

"You like it? I'm sorry, I didn't even ask if you were allergic to shrimp."

"No. No. This is simply amazing. Frank, you have hidden talents."

"Thanks." We ate in companionable silence, enjoying the view, lights flickering on in neighboring boats, the wink of red and green buoys reflecting off the water. I refreshed our glasses, shaking the last drop from the bottle.

"I've only poured two glasses. The bottle must have shrunk," I said.

I felt some of the pressure of the last two days slide off me. Carter giggled. It sounded girlish and womanly at the same time. I liked it. It sounded good on her.

"That's because your pours are absolutely massive, Frank."

The double entendre was on the tip of my tongue, but thankfully my filter engaged in time. Instead, I smiled and nodded.

After we finished eating, Carter scooted closer to me. "Do you have a blanket? I don't want to go inside, but it's getting chilly."

I hopped down the steps into the cabin and came back with two fluffy blankets.

"Here," I said, and wrapped one around her shoulders.

"Thank you." We sat next to each other and watched the stars come out. One shot across the horizon, leaving a short trail. I glanced over at Carter and made a silent wish.

"Make a wish," Carter said.

"I already did."

We sat in silence for a while, listening to the gentle splashing of the water and the occasional murmur of conversation coming from some of the other liveaboards. I was hoping for something like this the other night, but I'm glad it turned out the way it did, as this was by far and away a better experience. With a better person.

I didn't want to ruin the moment, but felt I had to take a shot. "Would you like a nightcap?" I asked.

Carter didn't say anything for a moment, lost in thought. "I should probably get going, Frank. I'm sure we have an early start tomorrow. It's been a beautiful night, though."

"Sure? I have some excellent bourbon."

Carter looked torn, while I waited hopefully, but finally, she said, "I bet you say that to all the girls."

"Actually? No."

She looked pleased. "How about a rain check? I really have to go. I need my beauty sleep."

She leaned over and gave me a gentle kiss on the cheek. "Thank you again for a super evening."

"Anytime, Jess."

I walked her back to her car, wistful but happy and content.

She leaned out of her car window and said, "Next time, I promise I'll take you up on that nightcap." She blew me a kiss and drove off, waving.

I walked back to the *Serenity*, cleaned up the dishes and settled down for the night. The night hadn't gone the way I wanted, but strangely enough, I was hopeful. I couldn't wait for that nightcap. Maybe all that soul-talking mumbo jumbo had some truth to it. Who knows? I couldn't fault what Tinka had done with *Ghost...Serenity* so maybe there was something there.

FIFTEEN

At the same time as the morning light started pouring through my cabin porthole on board *Serenity*, my phone angrily vibrated off the end of my side table and fell to the floor. I groggily picked it up without looking at who was calling.

"Dalton," I said.

"Special Agent Dalton?" said the voice on the other end of the line. "There's been an accident."

I shot out of bed, got dressed, and drove straight to the scene, a place I'd been to several times recently. Carter was there already. She looked pale.

"How bad is it?" I asked.

She didn't say anything. The look on her face told me all I needed to know.

I walked past the flashing lights of ambulances, the sirens long gone quiet. Passed the Reel Fish, Reel Quick sign, walked onto the deck of the *Reel Lady*, and saw a sheet covering part of what may have been the top of a torso. The rest of the body was firmly wedged under a gigantic crate. Scallops, judging by the words on the side. A massive crate of scallops had fallen from the rust-ridden crane. Fallen on what I was told was Paul. Poor, poor, Paul.

Paul hadn't known what he was getting himself into. I had. But I thought he'd be safe. Pitiable, foolish, stupid, naïve me. I knelt next to him. There was nothing the paramedics could have done. They were just waiting for us to release the scene so they could take him to the morgue.

I should have known. I should have pulled him out of there when he called me. Instead, I'd taken the night off, had dinner with Jessica, assumed everything was fine. Now he was dead.

While I beat myself up, Carter went around and started interviewing potential witnesses. I could see no one wanted to talk. No one had to. We all knew why it couldn't have been an accident. Sure, accidents do happen. The commercial fishing fleet is notorious for being supremely dangerous, but in this case, Paul was just another unfortunate who got in the way of the massive churning machine that was Batman Black. It hadn't mattered if he knew anything. It only mattered he might have known *something*, might have given the game away. Might have.

In all the worlds of *might haves* and *could have beens*, this was the one where Paul's story ended. Goddammit.

I shook myself out of my thoughts. I wasn't going to get the bastards like this, feeling sorry for myself. Instead, I felt myself turning angry. They wouldn't get away with this. I went in search of the crane operator.

I found him joking and laughing with Jimmy and Ricky, a steaming paper cup of coffee in his hand. I smacked the cup out of his hand and rammed him into the wall behind him, the metal shutters clanging and vibrating, coffee splattering the wall and sliding down.

I shouted at him, inches from his face, spittle flying from my mouth. "I know what you did. You're a fucking murderer. You worthless piece of shit."

The grin left his face, and he looked at his friends for backup, concerned I might do something worse than beat him. I don't know what I would have done next, probably nothing good. I was blinded by rage, rage for the innocent. I felt fury for Paul, who couldn't express his own, and I felt the unfairness of it all. But a hand on my shoulder and soft words in my ear stopped my assault.

"Frank! Leave him. He's not worth your career," Carter said.

I wanted to ignore her. I wanted to smash the laughing, stale-breathed mouth of the crane operator, but most of all, I wanted a release from my emotions. Pounding on his face would help. But I didn't give in. I didn't do it.

"We can do this the right way," she said, pulling at my arm. "We can put them behind bars and lose the key. But you can't hit him. Then you'll be off the case. You'll have lost, and they'll have won. Don't let them win, Frank. Let's do this together."

I let him go, giving him a final shove.

"Yeah, get lost," he said, trying to save face.

I ignored him. Carter was right. I was better than this. I'd do it the right way. I'd carve their empire apart one piece at a time. I'd do it for Willis and Rivas and Paul and all the other poor souls these fuckers had ever killed.

There was nothing useful for us here. I left with Carter, walking back through the warehouse. Big fat Black was there, sitting in his chair, an unlit fat cigar firmly clenched in his teeth, his massive jowls fighting for space on his face. His beady eyes encased in flesh watching us.

He couldn't resist saying to me as we passed, "Such a tragedy, Special Agents. Paul was such a nice boy. A good boy. Such a shame."

I wanted to kick him in the head. Instead, I said, "He was good. You got to him too late though, Black. He already spilled. I have a signed affidavit from him back in the office. It won't be long now before we're bringing you in again, but this time in cuffs. Enjoy the cigar."

I had the satisfaction of seeing his eyes widen in fear, like the crane operator. I didn't give him a chance to reply. I could feel his beady little pig eyes staring at our backs the entire way out and refused to give him the pleasure of turning around.

Since we were both in our personal vehicles, we'd agreed to meet at the park and ride where we first met, where Carter jumped into my car. We drove straight back to the underground lot, but I couldn't find an empty space where I usually parked, so I drove down a further two floors than usual. I wanted some space. Some space around me, around the car. We pulled into a spot where the overhead light hadn't been fixed in a week and stayed in the car. I felt the anger still burning inside me like burning coal.

"It's okay, Frank—"

"No. No, it's not, Jess. I should have protected him. He called me and thought he was in trouble, that they knew, but I convinced him to stay put. I needed him there. I should have known."

"No one could have known they'd drop a crate on his head. It wasn't your fault, Frank. You didn't do it. Look at me, dammit."

I turned and looked at her. She took my hand and held it firmly. "Avenge Paul, Frank. Let him be the last person these bastards kill. Let's figure out where the guns are coming from, where they're going. Let's nail them. Maybe Mark has something we can work with. Perhaps the ME has something else she can tell us. If you give up now, they've won, and Paul's death and everyone else's were in vain."

I pulled her hand away from mine and rubbed my face. She was right. I couldn't lose my head now. I felt a wave of gratitude for Carter wash over me. "Has anyone ever told you how beautiful you are?"

She rolled her eyes but smiled. "Not the right time, Frank."

"I mean it."

"Thank you. Come on, let's get to work."

I was about to open the door when something caught my eye. "Hold on, Jess. Don't open the door."

She looked where I was looking. "Is that…"

"Yeah. It is." I had a sick, weary feeling in my stomach after Paul. What caught my eye before we got out now made my stomach turn sour and boil. We'd sat in this dark corner of the lot long enough for anyone coming in not to notice us. The elevator at the end had pinged, the light coming on. That's what had caught my eye initially. Coming out of the elevator was Lewis, our Special Agent in Charge. A car had pulled in and parked near the elevator and getting out of it was George. Good old wraith-like George. I knew Lewis well enough to spot him from a distance. I spent lots of time trying to avoid him. The sharp-looking, black-tailored suit was a dead giveaway. George was hard to miss as well, being so tall and rail thin.

The burned-out light overhead shrouded us in darkness. I would have tried to take a video on my phone, but it was too dark, and I was too far away.

Lewis looked around and then handed George a folder. George flicked through it, never saying a word, and then took a bulging white envelope from a pocket and handed it over to Lewis. Much as I couldn't quite believe what my eyes were telling me, I'd bet my front teeth that the envelope was full of money.

"Fucking bastard," I said. "The SACs on the take."

"What do you think Lewis gave George?" Carter asked.

"I don't know. Fairly sure it's got something to do with our case, though."

"Shouldn't we go out there and confront them?"

"No. Not right now. It's too dangerous. And what if it's nothing? What if I'm wrong? No, we need to be sure before we confront him. Let's wait until they've gone and see if we can get the security footage for this level. Maybe the different angle will show something we missed."

We waited until it was clear and headed up to the office. I told Carter to keep this to herself for now. If the SAC was taking bribes, there was no knowing how many other people were involved. We were on our own for the time being. We couldn't trust anyone.

Carter had some calls to make, so I got Malone to show me how to review the security footage. I considered asking him to leave the room while I checked the footage but decided if anyone was on the take, Malone was the least likely. I know I'd told Carter not to trust anyone, but I felt since I'd known Malone a lot longer than Carter had, it was a risk I could take. And I might need his help.

On the monitor, I saw us drive into the underground lot and park. There was a time and date stamp on the bottom of the screen. It was a wide-angle shot and you could see us talking in the car, and then it cut straight to us walking to the elevator.

"That's not right," I said.

I reversed the footage and played it again. Maybe I'd accidentally hit fast-forward or something. The same thing happened. The footage went straight from us in the car to us going to the elevator.

"What is it you're looking for?" Mark said.

"I'm not sure. I must have screwed something up. The footage is missing a section. Are there any other cameras down there?"

"Just that one. Move over. Let me drive for a moment." Mark sat down and started typing, and then the footage appeared again. Exactly as it had twice before.

"See," I said. "What's wrong with it?"

"Wrong with it?" Mark frowned and tapped a few keys. "Nothing's wrong with it. It's all there."

"No, it's not right. There's a bit in the middle that's missing. Something happened between us sitting in the car and walking to the elevator. Like two or three minutes are missing."

Mark checked again and showed me the time stamp. "Look," he said. "The timestamp never alters. There's you in the car at 0942, and then at 0943 there's you and Carter going to the elevator."

"I'm telling you, Mark, that's not how it happened. Could someone have tampered with this?"

"I don't see how. It's in a secure system. Very few people have access to this, for just that reason."

I had a sinking feeling. "Who has access, Mark?"

"Well. I do, obviously. Otherwise, I couldn't have shown you this."

"Who else?"

"The SAC does. He has overall authority. It's his unit, after all."

"Could someone have tampered with it, without you knowing? Could they have altered the time stamp, erased some footage?"

Mark gave me a strange look. "What are you suggesting? I would never—"

"I know you wouldn't. I'm not saying you did, but is it possible?"

"It shouldn't be. If you're positive something's happened to this footage, I'll review it in my lab. Maybe I can figure something out."

"Do it. And Mark.," I lowered my voice, "don't tell anyone. Not even the SAC."

"I have to tell him if he asks—"

"Not even the SAC, Mark. Do you hear me?"

Mark stared at me for a moment as if I was off my rocker. Slowly, he nodded. "Yeah. I got it. What do I tell him?"

"If he asks, tell him to come and see me."

I walked out and went to find Carter. We needed a break in this case, needed some luck, something to bust it wide open. When I found Carter, she was hanging up the phone.

"We have it, Frank. We've got a piece of the puzzle."

Sixteen

Carter brought me up to speed from her phone call. "It appears a Medical Review Officer, a Doctor Keith Scott, down in Miami," Carter said, "was taking bribes in return for reporting positive drug tests on commercial mariners as negative."

"Sounds like more of a case for the sector guys, Jess. What does that have to do with this case?"

"Let me finish."

I sat down, waved her on, and looked around for my coffee cup.

"You're right, it is a sector case. Sector Miami is dealing with it and reviewing all of Scott's files to see which ones were altered. It's a laborious process, as he has files going back for years."

"Still not seeing the relevance here."

"Bear with me, all right? You know commercial mariners on inspected vessels have to take random drug tests, right?" I nodded. "Well, Scott was one of a handful of doctors from around the country qualified to make the final determination from a drug test on whether it was positive or not."

"Wouldn't a positive drug test always be positive?"

"Not necessarily. If you had a valid prescription and popped positive, Scott could override the positive result and inform the mariner's employer the test was negative. That would be perfectly legal. Scott, however, was taking some of those positive results and suggesting to the mariner that for a small fee, which ranged from a few hundred dollars to a few thousand, he could make the positive result a negative. There was no one to question his authority. He'd make a notation on the chain of custody form, notify the employer the test was negative, and the mariner would keep his job. This had been going on for years until someone wasn't happy with the excellent doctor's service and complained to the authorities. He's been raking in tons of cash, and there are untold hundreds of mariners out there in charge of vessels that have no business driving them."

I spotted my coffee cup on the far side of Carter's desk and reached for it. "Go on, I'm listening," I said.

"Miami is going through all of Scott's files, and whenever they find an altered report, they notify the nearest Coast Guard office where that mariner lives, so the local unit can follow up. One of those reports came to our sector on a Mr. Joe Deacon, and when they ran his name, they found he was a captain on one of Black's boats. This is where we come in."

"I was waiting."

She ignored me. "This boat is a large fish processing vessel. We're around three hundred feet long. They're required to be captained by a licensed mariner and have licensed crews. This guy, Deacon," Carter pulled a page from her notes, "has been a captain for eighteen years, with an otherwise clean record. He wants to make a deal."

"A deal for what?" I said.

"Well, he thinks he's looking at some jail time or at the very least, the loss of his license. You and I know he wouldn't go to jail for failing a drug test, but he doesn't know that. And besides, his license is worth a lot of money to him, if he loses that, he loses his job. Some of these guys pull down upward of two hundred thousand a year. Although his bank records suggest he's up shit creek."

"And you said he works on one of Black's boats?" I sipped at my coffee thoughtfully.

"Yeah. Like I said, a big one the, I can't even say the name with a straight face, the *Reel Thing*."

I scoffed. Terrible pun. "Where does Black come up with these God-awful names?" Carter rolled her eyes. "All right, so this mariner, what's his name, wants to make a deal?"

"Again, Joe Deacon is his name, and yes, he does. What do you think?"

I put down my coffee and folded my arms. "Truthfully, I'm hesitant, but only because it's not a criminal case, it's civil. But if he thinks he's in serious trouble, it might be worth having a chat with him. Maybe he knows something about Black's operations that could help us. But I still don't get why you're so excited. We have other leads that look like they may be of more value. Don't you think we should follow up on those first? Where does he live, anyway?"

"Out past Calallen, but you're missing the point, Frank."

She let me dangle for a second. I couldn't think what she was so excited about.

"The *Reel Thing* is a fish processing vessel, not a fishing boat," she said. "Regular fishing boats offload their catch to the *Reel Thing* and then continue fishing without going back to port. The *Reel Thing* stays out at sea and processes the fish. They're sometimes called factory ships for obvious reasons and have hundreds of workers preparing and storing the fish. When it's full, it'll head to port and offload everything, already packaged and boxed for transport to stores. Sometimes they even sail overseas."

I nodded. "Yeah. No. Still not getting it?"

"The *Reel Thing* is a fish process—"

"You said."

"Let me finish. No, better than that, you figure out the question you should be asking."

I should be asking why we were talking about fishing factory boats, but then somebody turned up the rheostat on the light bulb above my head, like an old cartoon, and I finally understood what Carter was talking about. I barely stopped my mouth from dropping open.

"The *Reel Thing* is basically a floating freezer," I said.

"Finally," she said. "He shoots, he scores. I was getting worried the Dalton everyone told me about was going to have to be out to pasture. Black owns the

Reel Lady and the *Reel Thing*. The two boats could have met up when they were out at sea. It's a perfect cover and explains how Willis could have been frozen."

I looked at Carter with new appreciation and thought how lucky I was to have her as a partner. I could kiss her. Still, I had to be certain we were on the right track. We didn't have time to be off on wild goose chases. "Why wouldn't the *Reel Thing* have dumped him themselves?" I said.

"I don't know. Maybe they couldn't. Maybe it would have been too obvious. Who knows? It's only a theory."

I shook my head, excited. "No, it's an excellent theory, Jess. I'm glad you stuck with it. I wouldn't have picked up on that. What I'm wondering is why Paul wouldn't have said anything about meeting this fish processor?" Thinking of Paul made some of my excitement fade. "It could have helped us. I don't know, maybe it could have helped save his life."

Carter put a hand on my shoulder. "You can't blame yourself, Frank, and you can't blame Paul. Could be he was asleep. He said he was down below a lot more on this trip than usual. Those other assholes didn't want him nosing around. Besides, if that was their routine, it wouldn't have struck Paul as unusual."

I slurped some coffee. It tasted like mud.

"You know that's yesterday's coffee, right?" Carter said.

I hadn't. It explained why it was so God-awful. And cold. I grimaced.

"Where's this mariner now?" I said, putting my mug down.

"He's at home. He knows we're coming."

"You think of everything, don't you? Well, let's get there then before this guy ends up dead, too."

We drove to Calallen. It was a small town on the outskirts of Corpus Christi, only notable because you had to pass through it to get to San Antonio. Nothing much was in Calallen, a few businesses, a couple of hotels, some houses, but mostly a dusty and flat, flat landscape. They say that in South Texas you can see your kids running away from home for a week, it was so flat. I didn't know about that, but I could believe it if I lived out here.

The captain's house was an unassuming ranch, set back from the road. It didn't look new, but had a recent coat of paint, and looked like it was well kept. There wasn't much in the way of grass, but what was there was trimmed neatly. As we drove down the driveway, dust billowed a mile behind us. An old barn stood in the back, the doors wide open. We pulled up to it, and a man, his neck almost perpendicular to his body, came out, shading his eyes with his hand and staring at us.

"You got this, Jess?" I said. It was her lead. It was only fair.

She didn't blink. "Yep."

We got out of the car and met him about halfway. He was wearing a pair of bib overalls and wiping his hands on a rag.

"Excuse me if I don't shake yer hands," he said, gesturing to the rag, "was working on an old tractor in the barn."

Carter nodded and said, "Sir, my name is Special Agent Carter. This is Special Agent Dalton. Are you Mr. Deacon?"

Deacon nodded. "Figured you must be the feds. Don't get many visitors around here. Yeah, that's me. I suppose you've come about the drug test results, then?"

"Something like that. Do you have somewhere we can sit down and talk?" Carter said.

He motioned us to an old picnic table. It was early afternoon, still a comfortable heat and deliciously warm, so it would be nice to sit outside. Carter and I sat on one side, Deacon on the other.

"Sir, do you have your merchant mariners' credential on you by any chance?" Carter said.

Deacon patted the top pocket of his overalls. "My license? As it happens, I do. Knew you'd be coming out, so I kept it with me."

He handed it to Carter, and she passed it to me. I flicked through it. The credential looked like a burgundy-colored passport, and inside it was a photograph of Deacon with his address, date of birth and other vitals. This one stated Mr. Deacon was a master of unlimited tonnage on ocean-going vessels. No restrictions, multiple endorsements of the usual kind. No wonder he wanted to make a deal. This credential was like gold in the world of mariners and would have taken years to obtain.

"Mr. Deacon—" Carter said.

"Sorry, Miss, to interrupt. I haven't been a mister for years." Deacon frowned. "Sounds weird. I usually go by Deke or captain."

"Of course. Captain, our partners down in Miami uncovered an illegal operation by a Doctor Scott. Instead of reporting positive drug tests to the authorities, he was selling clean drug test results. Your name came up."

Deacon nodded and looked down at his hands clasped on the table. "Yeah. I heard."

Carter leaned forward. "Normally, we wouldn't be having this chat. We would just issue a legal complaint and revoke your license. It'd be gone. For good. We could also look back at all the other drug tests you were required to take and see how many of those were positive, and how many fraudulent applications you filled out. Perhaps it turns out you don't even qualify to hold a master's credential. Perhaps it'll include some jail time."

Deacon's face paled. "No. No need for that. I was stupid. It was a onetime thing."

"In our experience, captain, opiate users don't generally have a onetime experience. That was what the test said, wasn't it, opiates? How much did it cost you to have Scott alter the report?"

Deacon sat hunched over, defeat written all over his face. "Too much." He rubbed his face with his hands and sighed. "What can I do? I can't lose my license. It's all I've got. Ever since my dear Rachael died, things haven't been going right. I need to work. I'm one payment short of losing all this." He gestured at the house.

"I'm sorry about that," Carter said, "But we can't ignore the issue. It's our job to ensure the waterways remain safe and to take unsafe mariners out of the picture."

Deacon raised his head. "I'm not unsafe. I've never had an accident, never used while I was underway. Surely, you've looked at my record. I don't have a blemish on it."

"Well, that's partly why we're making this house call." Carter let that comment sit there so Deacon could digest it. "We understand you work on a vessel owned by Mr. Black."

He looked at Carter, his expression suddenly blank.

"We're interested in what you might have to tell us about the operation Mr. Black is running," Carter said.

He tried to shrug casually, but it didn't fit the rest of his body language. "What's to tell? I run a fish processor. Can't say it's the most glamorous job, but it gets hard to keep a steady job, what with..."

'Right. I'm sure,' Carter said, as Deacon trailed off. "Here's the thing, though. This is how it's going to work. You tell us what you know about Mr. Black's operations, and we'll see what we can do about the drug charge."

"Can I keep my license?" Deacon said, eyeing the credential where I was keeping my hand on it.

"It sure would be a shame to lose this," I said, tapping it on the picnic table to emphasize my point. I could see Deacon's eyes following the up and down motion of my taps.

"Honestly?" Carter said, pulling his eyes back to her. "Maybe. That's as good as I can go right now." And then she threw him a nugget. "But based on what you tell us, if it's good, we can make a deal and you can go back to work. The other option is you lose your license and probably do some jail time. Depends on what you tell us."

Deacon thought for a minute, stood up and walked off. He lit up a smoke and started pacing, talking to himself.

Carter leaned toward me. "What's he doing?"

"It looks like he's weighing his options," I said. "Nice work, by the way."

She tried to suppress a smile and failed. "Do you think he'll bite?"

I looked at him, walking the same patch of dirt, kicking up dust. I shrugged. "Have to wait and see. Shouldn't be long. Let him walk it out. When he sits back down, don't say anything until he talks."

"Why?"

"It's like working in sales. The first person to speak usually loses the deal. Let it play out," I said. Carter looked skeptical, but nodded.

Deacon finished his smoke and flicked the butt toward the house. He pulled the pack out for another smoke but then paused, stared at the sky, and put it back in his pocket without lighting one. He slowly walked back to the table, and we waited while he sat down.

Deacon spoke first. Winner, winner, chicken dinner. "I don't know much. I've only been working for Black for a short time. What is it you want to know?"

This was the tricky part. What he told us depended on whether he was more scared of us and what we could do, or Black.

"Like I said, we want to know about Black's operation," Carter said.

"If...if I tell you what I know, you got to protect me from Black. He's a vicious SOB. If he ever finds out I told you anything he'll, well, let's just say I won't be worrying about that license no more."

Carter looked him in the eye. "We understand Mr. Black's reputation. We'll do what we can."

Deacon abruptly stood up. "No, that's not good enough. I need some sort of guarantee."

"Sit down, Cap'," I said. "Listen, if what you tell us is good enough, we aim to put Black and his crew down for quite some time. They won't be able to get to you."

"You don't know Black, if that's what you think. Locking him up won't stop his reach. You know he's connected, right?"

I made a decision. "Captain," I said, "why don't you stay put here for a minute, while me and Special Agent Carter confer? Maybe we can talk it through and make a deal."

Carter and I walked back to the truck.

"What do you have in mind, Frank?"

"Let's see what we can do for him. We need to find out what he knows. It might not be anything useful, but the guy's not going to say a word until we can offer him some sort of protection. Let me make a call to Tobias. He's in regular contact with the assistant district attorney, and he might be able to set something up. I'm not going to lie to Deacon, but maybe we can get him into witness protection or something." I hoped Smith wasn't working with Lewis, but I couldn't offer Deacon anything worthwhile myself.

I called Smith and gave him the rundown. He asked a few amplifying questions, and he said he'd call back in five minutes.

Smith was good to his word, and the call came through promptly. I put him on speakerphone so Carter could hear, and he told us if what Deacon said was enough to break the case open, we could have a US Marshal monitor Deacon. He wasn't going to offer him witness protection, but it was at least something. Hopefully, the marshal could keep an eye on him and keep him out of Black's way.

We headed back to Deacon, who looked like he'd smoked ten more cigarettes in the short time we'd been gone. His hands were shaking slightly, either from nerves or the nicotine overload. Probably a bit of both.

As I sat down, I made a show of looking around and said, "It's pretty quiet out here, captain. You must like the peace after the bustle of being on a ship. Been here long?"

The small talk helped relax him like I knew it would. "Yeah, I like it. Was my Poppa's house 'fore he died. Thought I'd be able to live out my retirement here."

"Maybe you still can. I spoke with our direct boss, the assistant special agent in charge, and he's prepared to provide a US Marshal for your protection, twenty-four-seven, on the condition what you tell us is actionable."

"What's that mean?" he said.

"It means if the information you tell us is good enough to lead to the arrest and subsequent conviction of Black, we can make a deal."

"Do I have a choice?" he said.

"Sure. We can walk away right now. We'll take your credential with us, of course. We can't have a drug addict running around at sea in charge of a vessel. After the boys down in Miami finish their investigation, we'll be back with cuffs for you." I was bluffing, and I felt a tiny bit sleazy, but Deacon might have what we needed to get to Black.

Deacon lit another smoke, the last of the pack. He let out a long, thin stream of smoke. "Not much of a choice."

I shrugged. "You tell us what you know, and we'll provide the protection you wanted. Although..."

Deacon looked hopeful. I met his eyes and leaned forward.

"You're an intelligent man, Deke. You know Black has his fat fingers in a lot of pots. It wouldn't surprise me if he already knows we've been talking to you," I said. "But he doesn't have any idea what you've already told us, so if we walk away from here with nothing, well, it might slip that you've been super helpful..." Even sleazier.

Deacon looked at me, coughed, spat on the floor. "That's a mighty dick move, Agent."

I shrugged. "It is what it is. It's cards on the table time, Deke. What'll it be?"

Deacon rubbed his face as if he was trying to wash away the cracks and crevices of his life, then stared at the ground.

After a moment, Carter prodded him. "Deke, tell us about the guns."

SEVENTEEN

He spilled the beans, not just a can of beans, but the whole damn enchilada. We set up a digital tape recorder on the table between us, so we could review it later if needed. It would also be evidence if this ever went to trial. Deacon told us how he would liaise with a freighter far, far offshore, out of US waters. There, they would transfer shipments of guns to the fish processor in waterproof crates and store them way down below in the refrigerated holds. Then they'd get covered with fish when Black's other fishing boats dropped off their catch. That way, if Customs or the Coast Guard ever boarded them, all they'd see if they checked the holds were massive mounds of wriggling fish. It was a neat idea. No one was going to search a fish hold full of fish. At some point, he'd get word the Coast Guard cutters were deployed elsewhere, and he'd use that window to offload the guns to one of his fishing boats to bring to shore, again buried in the fish hold underneath tons of fish.

"Hold on, Deke." I knew not to interrupt a witness when they were on a roll, but I needed an answer. "How did Black know the cutters were deployed somewhere else?"

"I dunno. He never told me. He always radioed and told me when to do it."

It had to be Lewis, damn him, giving the locations of our assets.

I let Deacon continue and he spilled his guts. "I didn't know they was guns, to begin with," he said. "I knew it was probably nothing legal. No one goes to that much trouble otherwise. But I don't ask no questions. That's the way Black likes it. No questions and no answers. If you work for him, you keep quiet. The pay was good, and I was happy for a while."

"What changed your mind?" Carter said.

"I'm not a crooked man. I've been at sea for years, but I needed the money, and the bank was looking at me hard to pay down the mortgage on this old place. That and the drug problem. I kept it clean on the boat like I said, but it was getting harder and harder and more expensive."

Now Deacon was talking, he looked more at ease. The way he talked, you could tell it was like he'd almost wanted to get caught somehow. It was just our lucky break it came in the way it did. That and Carter's good eye.

Deacon continued, "I could maybe turn a blind eye to those crates, but then we started getting these odd-shaped packages, maybe once every couple of months. They looked wrong, I think I knew what they was, but my mind didn't want to accept it. So, one night, I get a bee in my bonnet and start nosing around. No one's going to question the captain. I went down to the main reefer to see for myself. Don't ask me why, I never should have, and God help me, you have to believe me. I never had nothing to do with it."

He paused for a moment to shake out another smoke from a new pack. Hands shaking, it took him several tries to light it. When he had it good and going, he continued. "The package was hanging from a hook in the meat locker. I had to look. I knew, but didn't want to be right. Curiosity killed the cat, you know? Anyway, I slit open the package with my knife. It was all plastic on the outside, and underneath was some sort of muslin material. I cut at the top, a little slice, but it was enough to see."

When he paused for too long a moment, Carter prompted him. "And?"

Deacon shuddered. "And it was a face. A human face. Frozen. Looked like she'd been dead a while."

Carter did a double take, looked at me, said, "I'm sorry, did you say she?" Her eyes were serious and intense.

"Yeah." He shrugged. "P'raps I could have handled it better if it'd been a man, but it wasn't. It shook me up, right down to the bone, I tell you. I must have been in the freezer for a while, as all of a sudden, I felt cold to the core. I wrapped her up again, best I could so no one would notice, and went back to my cabin. No one saw me."

"What happened to her?" Carter said.

"Another boat came alongside the next day. Their crew came on board, knew where to go, and took her off themselves. I don't know what they did with her after that, I can only guess. They wouldn't let us out on deck when they did it, same as when they dropped her off. Imagine old Black thinks it's easier that way. Less explainin'."

The digital recorder took that moment to beep. I replaced the memory card with a fresh one, and Deacon took out another smoke and lit it with the end of the old one. I don't think Black had much to worry about. The way Deacon smoked, he'd probably die of lung cancer before too long.

"Was this the only time you took the delivery of bodies?" I asked.

Deacon looked crestfallen, as if his soul was telling us he was done. His face sunk into itself, dark rings under his eyes.

"No. There were others. Three or four at least."

"Did you ever look at the others?" Carter said.

"No. Never needed to. I knew what they was. One was enough."

We talked some more, wrapping up the details of when, where, and so on. I was disgusted and giddy at the same time. Disgusted with the callous way Black treated my fellow humans like so much flotsam to be jettisoned into the deep. How Black could pretend to be above it all, never getting his hands dirty, I didn't know. I was giddy. I could finally nail the son of a bitch. Giddy, I could exact justice for Paul, Rivas, and Willis. Even though Willis was up to no good, no one deserved to be dumped unceremoniously overboard. No funeral. No peace. Just like a piece of garbage in the waves.

We made good on our promise and a marshal showed up before we left. He was a big, hefty guy, and looked like he knew what he was doing. My last glimpse of

Deacon was in the rearview mirror as we drove away. He was still sitting at the picnic table, smoking, looking into space with a vacant stare. I didn't feel sorry for him, and I didn't feel so sleazy anymore. He could have come in at any time and told us what was going on. It was going to get a lot tougher for Black and his crew, though. Much tougher.

What I still didn't know was why the *Reel Lady* had dumped Willis and made it look like he slipped overboard. Surely, with the operation they had going, it would have been easy enough to make him disappear. Perhaps it had something to do with the millions Willis had squirreled away. Maybe Black thought he was going to get all that money. I bet it surprised him to find Rivas was getting it, but if he had her killed, how would Black get his greasy, pudgy fingers on all that loot? Although we'd broken the case open, there were still many questions that had to be answered.

More worrying for me was how the SAC was involved. It wasn't as if I could go up to Lewis and say, "Hi, sir. Hey, Carter and I were in the parking lot the other day, and we couldn't help but notice you gave George, who works for Black and is under suspicion of murder, a folder of something and he gave you a bulging envelope of what looked like cash? Oh, and by the way, are you giving Black information on the patrol schedules of our cutters?" What proof did we have now the surveillance feed was deleted? Shit. I wondered if anyone else in the department was involved. How deep did the treachery go? One thing was for sure, there was a lot of money floating around, so to speak.

The medical examiner called on our way back, and since we'd pass right by, we stopped in, even though it was getting late. Malone also called or rather texted a cryptic,

> must talk soon

I texted back

> be in shortly

He didn't reply.

"Frank, good to see you again," Hutchins said as we walked into the morgue. "And Jessica, is Frank treating you well?"

"He is, thanks," Carter said.

"What have you got, Doc?" I said.

"Come over here, and I'll show you."

We walked through to a different section of her lab, one I hadn't been in before. Where the business end of the morgue was all stainless steel, immaculate tile floors, fluorescent strip lights and the overwhelming scent of bleach, here were microscopes and books. This room was lit by several lamps shining onto haphazardly placed piles of notes, and it smelled better, less like formaldehyde and more like a research lab and fresh ozone.

"How do you know which pile is what?" I said, waving at the notes.

"Frank, dear. Don't you worry about me. Now then," she said, pulling over a stack of papers and gesturing us to sit on two stools. "When you were in here before, I told you I'd made an analysis of Mr. Willis's tissue samples and said he was frozen at some point before he was recovered from the water."

We both nodded. "That was a big help, Doc," I said.

She smiled. "Good. This should help some more. That was my preliminary finding, something quick to help your case. What I didn't know then is the frozen samples left a residue we could analyze. Most remarkable indeed. If I hadn't been looking closely, I might have missed it..."

"Come on, Doc. Don't leave us in suspense," I said.

She smiled again. "Quite simple, the residue comes from anhydrous ammonia."

"What's that?" Carter said.

"I can answer that," I said. "It's a chemical that's used for many things. Some fishing vessels use it as a refrigerant. It's also mixed with nitrogen to make ammonium nitrate, which is a fertilizer, and it's also a component of meth. Highly toxic if inhaled."

Hutchins gleamed. "Quite right, Frank. You are paying attention. It is used in fishing vessels, but it's not really a component of meth, though it is used in manufacturing meth. It's also used to make the explosive of choice for your homegrown terrorist. You mix ammonium nitrate and diesel together, and it can pack quite a punch. Commonly called ANFO. That's what McVeigh and his accomplice used in the Oklahoma City bombing, back in '95."

"But the key point is it's another link back to Black," I said, getting excited. "It solidifies that Willis could have been frozen on board one of his vessels, maybe even the *Reel Thing*. I don't suppose there's any way to match samples of anhydrous ammonia, is there?"

"Yes and no. It would require ion chromatography analysis. But you're unlikely to get a sample of anhydrous ammonia, I suspect you've forgotten your chemistry lessons. What's more likely is I can match the burns the anhydrous ammonia caused in the flesh of the different subjects."

I got up to leave.

"One more thing, before you hustle out of here. We have several Jane & John Does in here—"

I couldn't resist. "Cold cases?" I said.

"Shut up, Frank," Carter said. "Not funny, again."

"Sorry. Carry on, Doc."

"As I was saying," Hutchins said, "in the last year or so I've had several unidentified people in here. Seven, to be exact."

"Is that a lot?" Carter said.

"It's not as unusual as one might think. Corpus is a big city and, being so close to the Mexican border, we do get a lot of strays coming through here from time to time. We take samples before the bodies are cremated and store them for future reference. Mr. Willis's frozen sample matched all seven when I ran it through the database. They were all frozen at some point, all using anhydrous ammonia. All had similar burn marks from the ammonia."

"Didn't you know they were frozen before?" I asked.

"No. As I said we have so many unidentified people passing through. Standard procedure is to take the samples and close out the case. It wasn't something I invested a lot of time in, nor expect my staff to either. Nothing about the bodies appeared unusual, and they certainly didn't show signs of freezing when they came in. That wears off pretty quickly. It's almost dumb luck Mr. Willis was brought in so soon. But because this is a higher-priority case, I ran his samples through our database and got a hit. Seven hits."

"Seven dead people. All previously frozen. Anything else, Doc?"

"That's it, Frank," she said, standing up. "I'll keep you guys informed if I discover anything else. Goodbye Jessica, lovely to see you again. I can tell you look more comfortable."

"I am, thanks. Bye, Doc," Carter said.

As we walked out, I said, "Jess, it makes more sense now."

"What does?"

"Why we found Willis's body."

"How so?"

"Remember who it was that called in the missing captain over the radio?"

I gave her a moment to think and then she said, "Paul!"

"Yeah. Poor dumb Paul. He radioed in for help. He was never supposed to. The rest of the crew dumped Willis, but when Paul called the station, they had to pretend he'd fallen overboard and had to go through the motions of rescuing him. If they didn't look for him, it would be suspicious." I blew out a breath. "In the end, I think that's what made them kill Paul. He was a liability. They couldn't have him putting two and two together, or us, and the easiest way was for him to have an accident." I air quoted accident.

It made sense. They killed these people on land, or maybe another fishing boat transferred them to the fish tender, which froze them, then transferred them to another fishing boat for burial at sea. The bodies would make an excellent snack for a hungry shark, but if they washed up on shore, they'd be bloated, rotting, putrescent flesh. The ME would do a once over, and with no missing person's report or grieving relative, they'd be classed as a John or Jane Doe and cremated. Not unusual with all the coyotes transporting illegals across the border.

They probably didn't think twice about Paul being on board. Let him do his shift, keep him out of the way while they dumped the captain. They probably make a few trips like that, and then when the new crew finds out what's going on, it's too late. They're in too deep. Tell the authorities about us, and you'll end up the same way.

Willis had been dead the entire trip. I bet the crew were shitting bricks this whole time. If only I'd known. I knew there was something wrong, just couldn't place my finger on it. I cursed myself all the way back to the office for not seeing what was in front of me. I still felt responsible for not pulling Paul off the boat. If I'd known any of this, I would have gotten him off immediately. Twenty-twenty hindsight and all that. It spurred another question though. Who were all these people Black was disposing of?

We parked in the underground lot and entered the elevator. When the bell dinged, and the doors slid open on our floor, all hell was breaking loose.

Eighteen

When the elevator doors parted on our floor, there was a sea of federal agents in front of me. Nothing unusual in a federal building, except these agents didn't belong here. Their windbreaker jackets were emblazoned with the bold yellow logos of the Alcohol Tobacco and Firearms and Drug Enforcement Agencies. Officers were carrying cardboard boxes toward the freight elevator. I stopped one of them.

"What's going on?" I said. He shrugged and carried on to the elevator. I weaved my way through the cubicles to my desk. My locked file drawer wasn't locked so much anymore and hung open and empty.

"Hey," I shouted, to the room. "What the hell?"

Smith came up behind me and put his hand on my shoulder. "Frank, keep it down. Come into my office. You too, Carter."

I followed him in and slammed his door behind me, narrowly missing Carter and making the blinds shimmy.

"What's going on?" I said.

"Sit down."

Carter went to sit down but stood back up when I said, "No, I don't want to sit. I want to know why my desk is busted open and the ATF and DEA are here."

"If you sit down, I'll tell you," Smith said.

Smith waited. I got my anger under control, looked at Carter and nodded, and we both sat at the same time in the two chairs facing his desk. Smith perched himself on the edge of his desk. "The SAC called and ordered us to hand over everything to the ATF and DEA. He said based on all the new information you two have uncovered, this case had to be referred—"

I jumped up. "Bullshit! You can't do that, Tobias. We're about to bust this thing wide open—"

"That's not fair—" Carter said at the same time, standing up.

"Yes, I can do that. And don't interrupt. Either of you. And sit back down. Both of you." He glared at both of us until we did. "The SACs made his decision. It's done. The case was close to getting out of hand." Smith held up his hands in front of himself, trying to placate me. "Not with your work. It was getting too big for us. We're a small service with a narrow investigative focus. Gun running? Multiple deaths? All linked to Black's operations? This is beyond our mandate, so it was inevitable we'd hand it over. Listen, for what it's worth, you've both done some great work, and I know you've put in some long hours. Take some time off, relax a little, and I'll give you the next juicy case that comes in. Carter, this has been your first case. I'm sure you have a lot to process."

"You know this is still bullshit, Tobias. Lewis just wants to cover his..." I caught myself.

Smith looked at me to finish my sentence. When I didn't, he finally said, "Lewis wants to do what?"

Carter butted in to try to save me, "You can't pull us off this case, boss. We're so close to nailing that bastard, Black."

"You've been hanging out with Dalton for too long, Carter. Watch your language in my office. Now, Frank, I'll ask you again. Lewis wants to do what?"

I shared a meaningful look with Carter. I couldn't tell him. And it killed me I couldn't, but I didn't know whose side he was on, not for sure. It was certain, though, the SAC thought we were getting too close. He'd made a deal with the devil and was whisking away all our evidence. I wouldn't be surprised if a few of those boxes were going to conveniently get lost en route. Black sure had his fingers deep inside our organization.

"Nothing, Tobias. Nothing. Anything else?" I said.

Smith stared at me, probably mulling over whether he should press the issue, but he let it pass. "No. Nice work, though. I'm sure there'll be some arrests in due course, I'll make sure you both get credit for the assist. I'll let you know if they find anything out."

We stood and walked out, saying nothing else, and I closed the door behind me.

"Frank?" Carter said. I could see in her eyes she wasn't ready to give up.

"Hold on, Jess," I said quietly. "It's not over yet."

We walked over to the DOMEX office. Malone had his eyes pressed to a microscope, his hands prodding at something only he could see.

"Mark?" I said.

"Oh hi, Frank, Carter."

"What did you text me about?"

"Doesn't matter now. I was going to tell you the DEA were in here with their big Gestapo jackboots on trailing mud through the place. They took Willis's phone and all the evidence I had collected. I tried to tell you." Mark gave a little apologetic scrunch of his shoulders.

"Shit. So that's it then. No evidence, nowhere to go," I said.

"Well, not entirely," Malone said. "What they didn't know is I'd already cloned Willis's phone. The chip-off finally finished. When I saw them coming, I slipped the clone into my pocket. It's activated and working. You can read all the old texts and look at everything that was on the phone. Even the deleted stuff I recovered."

"You're an angel, Mark. I could kiss you." I reached over as if to do that, but he dodged me.

"Hey. Enough," he said, batting my arms away. "About the other thing you asked me to look into, you know, the thing." He winked at me, but the left side of his face scrunched up when he tried.

"I love you, Mark, but you'd make a lousy spy. It's okay. Carter knows."

"All right." Mark lowered his voice. "You were right about the camera footage. It was tampered with. I used the feed from the backup camera. Whoever deleted the main one didn't do a thorough job. That or they didn't know about it. I recovered the missing few minutes." He paused, obviously thinking through the ramifications. "Is that who I think it is in the feed?"

I nodded. "Best you forget what you saw, Mark."

His eyes widened. "I put the feed on this thumb drive for you," he said, handing over a small envelope he took from a pocket, his hand shaking. "I hope you know what you're doing, Frank. I...I'd rather not be further involved." Mark gave a little shrug. "I hope you understand."

"It's okay, Mark. I get it. Thanks for all your help." We shook hands like businessmen, and by the time I was at the door, his head was buried back in his microscope. What a guy.

Carter and I decided the best place to camp out and come up with a game plan was Pete's. A friendly face I trusted to bounce around ideas wouldn't hurt and neither would a beer or six. If we were supposed to be off the case, this would be a good cover.

Smith asked us where we were going on the way out. I told him we were going to celebrate working a good case and have a few beers, no harm no foul. The answer appeared to mollify him, and he went back to his office. Through the slats in his blinds, I saw him picking up the phone as we left. I hoped he wasn't crooked. He seemed like a decent guy.

"Come on, Jess. Let's get out of here."

We drove over in silence, still stewing over what had happened. When we got there, Carter greeted Pete like a long-lost buddy. He'd fixed the glass in his door since we'd last been in, and he told us he hadn't had any repeat visits from unsavory characters.

"Probably didn't like how he exited the bar," Pete said. "Headfirst."

"I thought you said you pushed him?" I said.

He waved his hand at me. "He left. That's all I care about."

Well, good riddance. That guy had messed up my boat. Pete got us a round of beers, and we sat in the booth at the back. Pete only has one booth. It's perpetually reserved, mostly for Pete. All the locals knew it was his, so they never bothered with it. Once in a while, a lost tourist would try to sit there, but it didn't last long. The rest of the bar had a few tables scattered haphazardly, but most of the actual seats surrounded the bar.

I filled him in on what had happened, including being taken off the case.

"By the way," I said. "Thanks for the shaman hookup. She made my boat better than new."

"The *Serenity* now, I hear?"

"Yeah. Word gets around, huh?"

"Only when my best customer does something different."

Pete got us another round of beers and tended bar for a while, seeing to his regulars.

"What do we do, Frank? Where do we go from here?" Carter said.

I scratched my chin and thought for a minute, taking a swig of my beer. "Honestly? I don't know. Nothing like this has ever happened to me before."

We sat in silence, both of us deep in thought. I couldn't think of a way out. I knew Black and his crew were smuggling guns. We had, or at least did have, until the Gestapo took my files, evidence from Deacon that linked Black to the weapons. We had testimony, again from Deacon, that he'd seen bodies on board the *Reel Thing*. That other fishing vessels transferred them on and off, all owned by Black. Add that to the evidence the ME had that proved all the bodies were previously frozen by a product used on fishing boats as a coolant. It all added up, but I still had a few gaps. I didn't know what had pissed Black off enough to kill Willis, or what the other poor saps had done, either. On the plus side, I had a working clone of Willis's phone, so perhaps I could do something with that.

Pete came back to the booth with the third round of beers just as ours were getting empty. I wasn't worried about driving as I could walk to the *Serenity,* and besides, I didn't have anywhere to go.

Instead of talking about the case, Pete reminisced. I think it was his way of offering advice in the roundabout bartender way.

"Remember when you first came to work for me, Frank?"

"Yeah. Long time ago now." I took a swig of beer.

"True, but you were all mixed up then. If I remember rightly, you were an angry man. Torn between serving your country, which was what you had joined for, and working for those numbskulls at your first unit."

"I remember," I said with a frown. "There was a trifecta of leadership bullshit. I can still remember their names as if it was yesterday, Chief Riedel, Petty Officer Charlie Baker, and Petty Officer Robin Man. It was hopeless. Everything I did was either wrong or not good enough. It wasn't just me, though, it was everyone in the department. They mentally and emotionally beat us down. I was ready to get out."

"Couldn't you have reported them up the chain?" Carter said. "I mean, you could have seen your CO. People get relieved of command all the time for climate issues."

I loved that she thought that. "Not back then," I said. "Things were different. That was an era we called the Old Guard when men were men and sheep were scared. Advancements and promotions, transfers, who was in and who was out, none of that was based on merit. It was all run by the good old boy network. If I'd gone over their heads and reported the shit they were doing up the chain of command, it would have been their word against mine."

"I haven't heard much about the Old Guard. I thought it was all a joke," Carter said. "They were serious?"

"Yeah. It was just the way it was back then. Thankfully, it's changed a lot these days, mostly for the better." I took another swig of my beer. "But I think the pendulum has swung too far the other way now, what with micro-aggression training and if you look the wrong way at somebody, they'll complain their feelings were hurt." I swirled the remaining beer in the bottle. "The good stuff, Jess, is you don't have to worry that a man would get promoted over you or paid more, and you definitely shouldn't have to worry about being sexually harassed.

That shit is right out, and I agree wholeheartedly, there's no place for it, and there never should have been. The Coast Guard does a much better job now than it ever did.

"What I don't like and it's hard to explain, but it sometimes feels as if they've taken the guts out of the Guard. We used to have fun at work. Now everyone's head is buried in a computer, or up each other's ass, too nervous to say boo. I mean, Jesus, with all the second-guessing and posturing, sometimes it feels like you need congressional approval to take a shit during work hours, for Christ's sake."

One of those rare moments in a bar happened just then, where everyone stopped talking at the same time, the music stopped, and it felt like I shouted the last few words for everyone to hear. A few of the patrons turned to stare, and then as if nothing had happened, the conversations started up again and the next song played on the jukebox. I sat there feeling justified and chagrined at the same time.

"You done?" Carter said after a while.

I nodded.

"Next, you'll be telling me they've repealed 'Don't Ask, Don't Tell,'" Pete said, breaking the ice.

We both stared at him and burst out laughing. "I hope you're not being serious, Pete," Carter said.

"What?" Pete said, and we both laughed again.

"Stop," I said, "you'll make me cry."

"You do know," Carter said, still chuckling, "they repealed, 'Don't Ask, Don't Tell,' like, I don't know, a thousand years ago? Next, you'll be telling me women are allowed to vote or something."

"Oh my God! Stop. I can't take it," I said.

"Listen," Pete said. "I was kidding. It is what it is. Times change. Perhaps it's time for you to move on, Frank. Let these youngsters like Jessica here take over." He smiled.

"I'm not that old, or that much older than Jess," I said. Carter looked like she was going to say something. "And don't tell me I'm deaf, either." Carter closed her mouth and smirked. I reached over with my empty beer, and we clinked bottles.

"It's great to fix the world's troubles with you, Pete, but it doesn't help our current situation." I sighed, bringing it back to reality. "I haven't got enough to go to above the SAC's head. All I've got on him is a few minutes of video, and all that shows is he gave something and got something in return. It's a smoking gun, but it doesn't prove anything."

"How about having our case reassigned?" Carter said. "Surely that means we were getting close to the truth?"

"Unfortunately, there's a million ways Lewis could play that out, too. He could easily say we were in over our heads—"

"That's bullshit, though," Carter said.

"Jess. I know it, you know it." I gestured at the bar. "The whole damn world probably knows it, but we don't have any proof. I'm surprised he picked the ATF and DEA to take our files. I'm assuming the files won't make it where they're supposed to go. For all we know, Lewis had them load the boxes into the back of his car." Frustration welled up in me and I slammed my empty bottle down on the table. Pete gave me a scathing look, but didn't say anything.

Carter sat back. "What then? We give up?"

"That's what I'm trying to tell you. I don't know," I said. "Look, I don't mean to get angry. I'm frustrated. I'm sure you are too. We need a change of pace. Pete, I never work well on an empty stomach. Any chance you could rustle up a ham sandwich or something?"

"Sure. Jessica?"

"I don't suppose you have a big fat juicy burger back there somewhere, do you?"

"I don't usually serve burgers, but for you? I'll see what I can do. I might have something in the back of the freezer."

"Thanks, Pete. 'Nother beer when you get a chance?" I said.

"What am I, a bartender?" Pete said. He grinned and loped off into the nether regions of the bar.

We shelved the case and chatted for a while, Carter and me. I asked how her mom was doing, she said she had good days and bad days. I asked what her favorite color was. It was purple. And I asked if she wanted kids, yes six. I snorted beer out of my nose.

"Six?"

"Yes. No. I don't know. Perhaps it has something to do with losing my brother. I want a big family."

She told me she didn't have anyone serious in her life right now. She asked about me, and I said I wasn't good with relationships. Always seemed to find the wrong person. I said I wanted someone I could talk to, someone I could share my thoughts with. Someone I could trust.

Perhaps the beer had gotten to me when I said, "Someone like you."

Pete chose that moment to come back, saving Carter from having to say anything and from me making more of an ass of myself. I couldn't tell if my comment intrigued her or scared her. "Ham sandwich for you, and the best burger I could find in the freezer for you. Oh, and a couple more beers. Bon appétit!"

Around a mouthful of ham sandwich, I said, "Pete. Any bright ideas? You've been in that scullery for long enough to have written the Magna Carta."

"Slaving over the hot plate, you mean? Maybe I do, slide over." Pete sat down next to Carter. "Logically, you should do what your ASAC, Smith said. You should rest, watch a movie, have a few beers, which you're doing very well on, by the way, and go back to work tomorrow. File this one away and hope to God the ATF and DEA don't screw it up."

"And not logically?" I asked.

"Not logically, which is probably what you're going to do anyway, is you should pursue the case. Quietly. If you're right about Lewis taking bribes, then he probably got the case transferred 'cos you were getting too close. He was probably paid by Black to keep you out of it. All of this is supposition, of course, and I'll deny everything if anyone asks."

I nodded. "Of course. Go on."

Pete scratched his chin. I could almost hear the rasp of hand on bristles. "You were warned away. They trashed your boat, left you cryptic messages. Got rid of Rivas. Shot at you. And you *still* didn't get the message. So Black probably ordered him to relieve you. I doubt he wanted to kill you. That would have drawn way too much heat, and Lewis wouldn't have been able to give the case away, too much visibility from up high, media too. It's not every day a Coastie gets killed. Would've been big news."

"It certainly felt like they were trying to kill us," Carter grumbled.

"Didn't actually hit you, though, did they?"

"Not with a bullet," Carter said with a grimace, rubbing her head.

"I suppose you could be right," I said. Pete raised an eyebrow. "Okay. Okay. You *are* right. But that still doesn't help us."

"Doesn't it?" Pete asked. This time, it was my turn for the questioning look. "I'm not going to rehash your whole case again. I think you've done that enough yourselves. But I believe you're missing something that's staring you right in the face. Why was Rivas killed?"

"But we've talked about that. We don't know," Carter said.

"How's the burger, by the way?" Pete said.

"Perfect, thanks."

"And my ham sandwich is great too. Thanks for asking," I added.

"I don't need to ask you," Pete said. "All you ever eat is ham sandwiches. And get distracted by random questions when you should be paying attention."

"Huh?" I said with a mouthful of sandwich.

Pete rolled his eyes. "Listen, I think you should follow up on Rivas, follow the money trail. Why did Willis leave her all his money? They got divorced years ago, and from what you tell me, it's not like she needed the money. You said the fire marshal was investigating?"

I nodded.

"Well, he's probably not in the—you're off the case—loop. So, my suggestion is to talk to him or her and find out if they know anything. Maybe the cause of the fire will lead you somewhere. Do you even know if Rivas is dead? What if she wasn't in the house when it exploded?"

I stopped chewing and put my sandwich down. "Son of a bitch. I didn't think to check if she was even there. I just assumed...No one could have survived that. I was there. It was a raging inferno. We've been so busy..."

"It's okay, Frank, she probably is toasty barbecue, but you need to follow up all the loose ends you can. Especially if you can talk to people quietly. But don't do it tonight. You've had too much to drink. One last piece of advice, do what Smith said. Take it easy. Relax. Come up with a game plan. And first thing tomorrow, act like nothing's up, and go about your business sharply."

I shook Pete's hand. I felt a bit like a dumbass. How could I have missed something like that? I was in such a rush to keep moving forward I wasn't thinking clearly.

"Right. First thing," I said.

Pete left us to go about his bartender duties.

As soon as Pete was out of earshot, Carter said, "Frank? What you were saying before?"

"Before what?"

"Before Pete came back with the food. You were saying something about how you wanted someone to talk to..."

Uh oh. I looked down at my empty plate. "It's nothing, Jess. Forget it. Just the beer talking is all."

"I don't believe that." I looked up and Carter met my gaze. "I think...I think I would like to get to know you better. We do everything you said you wanted out of someone. We talk, I'm funny."

"You're funny?"

Carter grinned. "Yes. You're not, you just think you are. I feel like we connected. Even Doc Hutchins said so."

"I don't know about the ME, but the shaman thought our souls were connected."

"You never told me," she said.

"Must have slipped my mind." Really, it was the other stuff she'd said about Carter being in trouble and me saving her. That was what I didn't want to tell her. Why make someone worry unnecessarily? "What do you propose?" I asked.

"One small baby step at a time. Why don't we go for a walk, shake loose this burger and those beers. I must have put on ten pounds while I sat here for the last two hours, and then maybe you can take me to a movie or something."

I was excited to see if she liked the same genre of movies I did, but it was the, 'or something,' that got my caveman brain excited. "I'd like that very much, Miss Carter. Barkeep? Check please." Pete ignored me, and I threw some money down on the table. I knew he didn't want anything from me, but it felt the right thing to do.

We caught a cab to the local theater. It was showing re-runs, and we watched *The Finest Hour*. It was based on a true story set in the 1950s, about a group of Coasties at a Coast Guard station on Cape Cod in Massachusetts. I thought it was very apropos. An oil tanker had split in two on one of the worst winter nights, with a massive Nor'easter approaching. Against all odds the crew had gone out and rescued everyone on board, far offshore. Like any movie, some liberties were taken, but it wasn't bad, and it was what we needed. I'd bought popcorn that we shared, and we messed around, acting like schoolchildren on a field trip. After the movie, we caught another cab back to the *Serenity*, and I offered Carter an evening cocktail.

"There you are," I said, handing her the drink. "Something special I made up."

"What is it?"

"Try it."

Carter took a sip. "Oh my gosh. Bubbles. This is excellent, Frank. What is it?"

"It's called a French 75. It's made from champagne and gin. I didn't really invent it, though."

"It's great. I don't care who made it up. I normally don't like gin, but this is fantastic."

We toasted ourselves and to a new day tomorrow, clinking glasses, sparks of optimism finally heading our way. We had a couple more drinks, watched the sunset from the cockpit, and then Carter asked me for a blanket.

"Just bring one this time."

I did. A big one we could both use. My back was against the bulkhead, and Carter snuggled up to me, making my caveman brain lurch into gear again.

"This is breathtaking here, Frank. I can see why you would want to live on board."

"Did I ever tell you how I got her? It's quite an interesting story," I said.

"I'm sure it is. But I have another story I think needs to be told."

She twisted in my arms and ever so delicately kissed me on the lips. I couldn't tell if the stars were coming out in the night sky or if I saw stars in my head. I kissed her back, savoring the tang of the gin mingling with the faint perfume of her lipstick.

"Let's go inside," she said, "and continue this story in private."

NINETEEN

I n the morning, I woke up early, made coffee and a small breakfast, and
brought it into bed. I stood watching Jessica sleep for a second, her chest rising
and falling with her gentle breath. It was so different from the feeling I had a few
nights ago when I had to lie to get that other woman to leave. I'm not normally
one for such a quick turnaround, but there was just something about Jess that
I hoped this turned out well. I woke her, and after she had freshened up in the
head, she returned to bed, where we ate breakfast and drank strong dark coffee.

We agreed to meet back at the office. She needed to change her clothes and
shower at home. She kissed me goodbye. I showered, changed, and drove to work.
It was a glorious morning, deliciously warm, and the light seemed to glow all
around me. I felt buoyed and happy, unlike I'd ever felt before. If nothing good
came out of this utterly sordid Black investigation, I'd at least found Carter. And
if I was to die today, I could make peace with the world, a happy man.

But for me, peace was to be a conceptual endeavor. Something that bald
professors with bleached goatees and snappy bow ties would wax philosophical
about on late-night TV. How such-and-such Armpit Country was at war again,
and the poor civilians were caught in the middle, screaming and crying, begging
the stoic reporters on the other side of the camera for help, except they've been
down that path before and know it's of no use. No, peace was something that
never lasted long, and I should have remembered what the shaman said, as storm

clouds were brewing in the mists overhead. She'd warned me that trouble was coming, but her warning was the furthest thing from my mind.

I drove to work oblivious.

Happy for the moment, but oblivious.

Smith was waiting for me. "Frank, you must have taken my advice to get some rest. You're looking relaxed," he said, as I walked into the office. It was quiet this time. No marauding Federales.

You have no idea, pal. "I did, Tobias, thanks. Felt good." *Reel Good*. See? I can make funny jokes.

"Have you seen Carter? I wanted to reassign her to another case. Let her work with a few other folks. Get a feel for how each shop works."

Well, shit. "I think she should be in soon, but I figured I'd show her how we input some of the casework, filing, and so on. Thought now the exciting stuff is over, I'd show her the real side of detective work, case reports and paperwork."

Smith laughed. "You're a hard taskmaster, Frank. Okay, I'll give you a couple of days. Is that enough?"

I looked thoughtful for a second. "Yeah, that should be fine. Thanks."

"No problem. Let me know when you cut her loose."

"Yeah, sure thing, Tobias."

After Smith walked off, I rifled through what was left in my desk drawer and found an old business card for the fire marshal. I casually glanced around on the pretense of stretching before I called the number and made sure no one was near me. I dialed the digits with the eraser end of a pencil, and he picked up on the third ring. We gossiped for a while about old investigations, and then I asked him about Rivas. He told me some interesting things about her fire and said we should be able to catch the arson investigator if we got out there soon.

I changed into coveralls, and I was about to grab the keys to a G-ride when a meaty hand landed on my shoulder.

"Frank, going somewhere?" Lewis asked from behind me. "New case so soon? I thought Smith would cut you a break."

I turned and put my game face on. "Mr. Lewis, didn't see you there. What brings you downtown?"

"Oh, just doing the rounds. Say, no hard feelings taking you and, err..." He looked at me for help.

"Carter, sir," I said.

"Right, Carter. No hard feelings taking you two off the case, then?"

I felt a wave of anger and pushed it down under a fake smile. "Me? No, sir." I couldn't resist poking the bear a little, even though I knew I probably shouldn't. "I thought we were getting close to finally taking Black's operation down, though. I don't see why we had to turn everything over, at least like that. You know they came in here and cleaned us out? Didn't wait for me to brief them or tell them what was important or not. It felt a little like the evil feds the media always portrays, not like sister agencies. You know all jackboots and *eins, zwei, drei*. They even broke into my desk files. Now why do you think they would do such a thing when all they had to do was ask me for the key?"

Lewis's face tried contorting into an expression of concern, but it made him look like an afternoon soap actor rather than someone who cared. "Is that the way it happened? Sorry, Frank. I didn't think they'd be quite so harsh. I'll have a word with their commander. See if we can't get the miscommunication sorted out. That's not the kind of interdepartmental relationship we want to foster."

He sure could talk the talk. I'd bet my bottom dollar that was exactly how he wanted things to happen.

Fishing, I said, "Say, sir, I had some private files in my desk drawer, you know, medical information, that sort of stuff. Any chance I could go down there and retrieve it?"

Lewis looked at me thoughtfully. "Let me see what I can do, Frank. I'll put a call in. If you let me know what exactly is missing, I'll let them know and get it sent back up here. That's probably the easiest way, better than wasting your time in their rabbit warren. Now, where did you say you were going?"

"Oh, gonna tie up some loose ends on some old cases down in the basement. Didn't want to get my clothes all dirty, you know? Thought I'd show Carter how to do some real investigative work. Do some filing."

Lewis looked pleased. "Good to hear it. Let me know about those files of yours when you have a chance and I'll get them for...I'll get someone to bring them back over."

He walked down the corridor smiling and shaking hands with the other agents, occasionally stopping and saying a few words as he made his way to Smith's office as if he was a freaking movie star. Bastard. He didn't want me anywhere near those files. Just one more nail in the coffin, old man, one more nail.

Carter had come in while I was watching Lewis and I'd told her to change into coveralls too. Fire sites were usually stinky and dirty. We left quickly before anyone else stopped us, and before anyone else soured my morning glow.

We arrived at Rivas's house, or at least what was left of it. The door still stood, but little else did. I introduced me and Carter, and the arson investigator said his name was James London. "But call me Jim."

London gave us Tyvek booties to cover our shoes so we wouldn't trash them or contaminate the scene, and he offered us face masks for the stench.

"Although they don't help much," he said. "If you follow me, and tread carefully by the way, as it's still pretty sketch, I'll point out anything relevant."

We made our way through the wreckage. Some of it was still damp from the fire department, putting out the fire, even several days later. It smelled like an old campfire, but worse. Gradually we worked toward what would have been the epicenter of the fire, treading carefully like he said, and talking. If I looked closely, I could identify some pieces of furniture and appliances, but not much else.

"So, this was what you'd call extreme fire behavior, most unusual for a house fire," London said.

"Aren't all fires extreme?" I said.

I looked at Carter, who rolled her eyes. "I think you need to keep it simple for us, Jim," she said. "I could show you ten different ways to subdue a perp, but fires? Not usually in our fire lane, so to speak." I smirked. Now who's making bad jokes?

"Of course. Extreme fire behavior is simply a fire that can't be put out with the usual methods, due in this case to a high rate of spread, meaning the fire was almost everywhere at once and especially intense. We had to call the local marine unit and borrow some A triple F, which is a type of foam they use in boat fires. I won't bore you with what it stands for, but we had to use that in conjunction with water. Kind of layering." London gestured with his hands. "The back of the house here, where the kitchen used to be, was the head of the fire, the side with the fastest spread."

"So, you're saying this was where it started?" I said, looking at what he said was the remains of the kitchen. If you'd asked me what this room was without being told, I would have had a hard job telling you.

He nodded. "Yes. Usually, on an incident, I would hesitate to say what the definitive cause was so soon, but I can tell you, in this case, it was arson. A natural fire wouldn't have moved like this and left so much devastation so quickly, with no one noticing."

"What could've caused it?" Carter said.

"We've sent evidence out for analysis, to confirm my theory, but you can follow the burn line back here to the kitchen, and if you shine your lights over there," he pointed at a large lumpy object, "you can see the old granite kitchen counter. It stood up to the intense heat, only cracking in a few places, and luckily stayed more or less intact. If it had been Corian or tile or whatever, the counter would have disintegrated, and we might never have figured it out." He retrieved a handkerchief and wiped the moisture from his forehead. "On the counter, we found the remains of a drip coffee maker. That was the ignition point."

"What was? The coffee maker? Wouldn't you expect to see a coffee maker in the kitchen? How could that be arson?" I said.

"Because it wasn't being used to make coffee, it was used to make a super-heated fire, one that can literally...burn a house down. We were lucky enough of the coffee maker remained to identify it, but once we had, and the ignition point matched, the rest was easy. The way it works is like this. The arsonist puts granulated chlorine into the carafe, which is the same regular chlorine you'd use for a pool, right?" He looked at us for confirmation. We both nodded. "You then pour regular dot three brake fluid, like you'd use in a car, which is polyethylene glycol, into the reservoir on top. It's stable for as long as the two chemicals remain apart, but when the coffee maker is turned on, and the brake fluid drips onto the chlorine, it creates an intense smoke and heat and within seconds shoots out a flame ten to fifteen feet high. When it went off, it would have caught all these cabinets and taken off from there. It looks as if someone also left the gas oven on and ajar, lending itself to a further explosion. I've read your initial report, Frank, and the gas explosion was what you guys heard and felt."

I whistled. It was crazy to think the rumble I'd felt a street over was caused by a coffee maker. "How do you guys ever figure this stuff out?"

London smiled and perked up some, a little gleam appearing in his eye. "Some of its experience. You follow a certified fire investigator around on some fires for training. Some of its classroom stuff, learning how things burn, and a lot of bookwork and homework. But the fun part for me at least, I'm a hands-on guy, was the practical experience. You get to set stuff on fire and see how it burns, and you also try to figure out from staged fires where the ignition point is and so on. The old coffee maker trick isn't common, but you can find a few idiots on YouTube who have made them, so it's not a secret. You should watch one of them. It's quite impressive."

"Yeah, no thanks. I've seen the effects close up."

"So, you like to burn stuff, huh?" Carter said.

"I think every arson investigator likes to burn stuff," London said. "We prefer to stay on the right side of the law and an arsonist doesn't."

"How would the arsonist escape?" I said, "If your coffee maker goes boom so quick?"

"Well, that's the marvel of modern coffee makers. They have timers. In effect, you're making a bomb and can set the timer to go off whenever you want. In this case, from what you've told me about running into the culprit, it would have been a short timer, a matter of minutes. Long enough for him or her to get away, but not long enough for anyone to discover the gas was on, and the coffee was going to taste burned."

Another joker. I resisted the urge to roll my eyes. "So, he would have had to have gained access to the house somehow?" I said.

"I don't suppose the security footage survived, did it?" Carter said.

"No. But as it happens, the feed went into the cloud. Mrs. Rivas had quite a high-tech house all around. We've been able to retrieve part of it before the cameras burned up."

"I'd like to see that, and get a copy if I can?" I said.

"Of course. I have it on my laptop in the truck. I can show you when we leave here. And of course," London said in passing as we walked back to what remained of the front of the house, "You'll probably want to talk to Mrs. Rivas as well. She's been nothing but helpful."

"Wait. What? She's alive?" Carter and I said together. Man, Pete was good.

"Well, yes. Didn't you know? Your Special Agent in Charge called yesterday, expressing his thankfulness that she was okay."

I felt chills down the back of my neck. "As this is an arson investigation and Mrs. Rivas was the target..."

"Yes, of course. We have that covered. She's under the protection of an armed fire marshal in a private room at the hospital. At least until we figure out she's not in any danger."

I didn't realize I'd been holding my breath. I exhaled and said, "How did she escape? How bad is she?"

"She has some smoke inhalation and a few burns, but remarkably, she's pulled through quite well. She had a panic room upstairs. By the time the fire was raging, she said she didn't have enough time to escape, so she ran to her panic room and secured the door. What with the video feed and communications burned out, and the fact she didn't have time to get her cell phone, we didn't know she was in there for quite some time. She's super lucky, as that part of the floor is one area that didn't collapse. The room wouldn't have saved her if that had happened."

I could have jumped in the air. It was about to get even better. Outside, we reviewed London's laptop video of the security footage and got a good idea of who entered her house. It looked like the perp was wearing some sort of repair company coveralls, and Jeeves, may God have mercy on his soul, let him in, presumably to do repairs on something in the kitchen.

We thanked London for his time, stripped out of our coveralls, bagged them so they didn't stink up the car with that burned house smell, and headed to the hospital. Time for a chat with Mrs. Rivas.

TWENTY

Things were finally coming together. We had conclusive testimony from Deacon, footage of Lewis receiving a bribe, and footage from the arson.

I knew time was running out before Lewis and Smith would become suspicious we weren't following up on old cases and filing shit like I'd said, but we had a little wiggle room.

I high-fived Jessica in the truck. She was just as excited as I was as we pulled up.

"I think we're finally getting somewhere, Jess. They took all our old evidence, but now we've got something else."

"It feels like they're getting sloppy, rushing to try to cover evidence."

"It does, doesn't it? Good thing we've got Deacon and Rivas under protection."

The nurse on duty in the hospital was hesitant until I showed her our badges, and then she was delighted to help. She called ahead to the fire marshal to expect us, so I was confident the security was as tight as it could be. Still, I didn't know who to trust, so I stayed on guard.

The elevator took us to the fifth floor, and when it dinged, we exited and walked down a long, sparkling corridor reeking of Pine-Sol. It was an interesting juxtaposition from the dank smell of burned house. I kept my eyes on a swivel, ready in case a janitor was an assassin. I think I watch too much television sometimes.

The fire marshal watched us come down the corridor and checked our IDs when we got close. He let us in after knocking on the door and confirming with Mrs. Rivas that she was awake and presentable.

The room was private. A large picture window on the far wall let in most of the light, and she was propped up in a standard-issue hospital bed. After what Jim London had said, I thought she'd look a little better, and I was shocked by her appearance, but tried not to show it. Bandages were wrapped around her hands and the left side of her face, presumably from the burns. Her once beautiful hair was gone, too. It looked painful, and I'm sure it was. She truly was lucky to be alive. All sorts of machines were beeping, and a glance told me her blood pressure and heartbeat were low, probably because of the morphine they were giving her for pain.

She tried smiling when she saw us, but then immediately grimaced.

"Mrs. Rivas, I'm so terribly sorry. I thought the worst when I saw your house. I was there, I tried to get in, but the flames..." I said.

Julia Rivas spoke in a soft, raspy voice. It looked like it hurt when she talked, and we moved closer so she wouldn't have to strain.

"...told you, call me Julia. And thank you for trying to help," she said.

"Julia," Carter said. "I know this was awful, but do you know why someone would set your house on fire?"

I saw the look on her face. She wanted to tell us, only something was holding her back. I could see the inner struggle play out on her face, and then she relaxed, overcoming her inner demons.

She nodded and winced. "Maybe. I didn't want to say anything before. I was anxious if I did, that bastard Black may do something to me. I guess I should have come clean. Freddie came to me last week," she stopped talking and closed her eyes. I looked at Carter and shrugged, feeling awkward. I'm not a fan of hospital rooms.

"Take your time," Carter said.

Rivas's eyes fluttered open. "Sorry," she said. "It's the drugs. Where was I...Oh, yes. Freddie was agitated. I hadn't seen him for years, and there he was, on my front porch." As she spoke, her voice gained clarity. "He was acting bashfully. He knew I'd remarried, but said he needed to talk to me urgently. I took him into the library, and he sat where you did, Special Agent, when you came to see me."

I shivered. Almost as if I had been sitting in Willis's ghost's shadow. "Frank, remember," I said.

She tried out a half smile. "He told me he thought Black was turning against him," Rivas said. "He'd found out Black had taken out life insurance on him for two million dollars. He didn't know how he'd done it without his permission. He thought there was probably someone at the insurance company he'd paid off. He said he thought Black might try to kill him and claim the insurance money...Do you mind handing me that cup of water, please?"

I handed it to her and helped her drink from the flexible straw. When she was done, I put it back on the table.

"Thank you. Freddie had a lot of money, and he said he had no one to give it to. He'd never bothered to change his will from when we were married, and I was the sole beneficiary of all his assets. He told me if something happened to him, he wanted to give it all to me for putting up with all his years of bullshit and for breaking my heart. His words, not mine. Of course, when Freddie said he had lots of money, he never told me how much. I thought it was maybe a few thousand at most."

"Why didn't you tell us about this when we visited, Julia?" I asked.

"Honestly, I...I didn't want to get involved at the time. I knew deep down Freddie's death probably wasn't an accident. I didn't want to do anything that would get back to Black. He has a long reach. I would have come down to your office and told you my suspicions, eventually. In fact, I was getting ready to leave the house when...this happened."

"Right," I said, not sure whether to believe she was on the way to our office or not. "Do you have any ideas who the man in coveralls was that your butler let in?"

She looked sad and closed her eyes. "Poor Roberts. They tell me it would have happened so fast he didn't suffer." She opened her eyes, full of tears. "Is that true, do you think?"

"I'm sure it is, Julia," Carter said. "It happened quickly. Did you get a glimpse of the person who did it?"

"No. I was upstairs. Roberts always deals with the front door. If it was important, he would have come up and announced the visitor, as he did with you two, so when he didn't come up, I assumed it was a delivery or workman."

"Was there a problem in your kitchen?" I asked. "Something that wasn't working?"

"I don't recall, to be honest. I'm not much of a cook, Roberts used to do..." She trailed off, lost in thought.

A big, brutish nurse with a no-nonsense look on her face came in and told us it was time to leave. I'd asked about all I could think of and a glance at Carter said she had as well. We said our goodbyes, and the nurse followed us out. Outside the room, the nurse's demeanor softened, and she told us the prognosis was good and assured me Mrs. Rivas was in the best hands.

I was happy Julia was going to be okay and sad Roberts had perished. It was a horrible way to go, but forgive me please for appearing callous. I was elated we were closing in on Black and his crew.

We now had a motive. Willis must have had a falling out with Black, and knowing he had taken a life insurance policy out on him behind his back, he knew his life was probably on a limited timeline. In a last fuck you to Black, he'd given all his money to Rivas, as I'm sure Black was hoping he'd be able to snag it somehow as well. Unwittingly, when Paul called the Coast Guard, he'd also helped them legitimize their operation. When they were just going to report Willis as missing at sea, they now had a timeline of a rescue, verified by the Coast Guard, that they could give to the insurance company. A drowned and dead Willis was icing on the cake.

What they couldn't have known, though, is our crack medical examiner figured out he was dead before they dumped him, and as they say on supermarket fish labels—has been previously frozen.

What we needed to do now was figure out if we had enough to make it stick. Finding some actual guns would be good, or better yet, finding the place where they froze the bodies. It may have been on the *Reel Thing*, which had conveniently disappeared, or it may have been somewhere local. I was sure they had it all set up in one place. It would be too hazardous for them to move that kind of operation around. If we could find it, there was sure to be some trace evidence or DNA we could find. That would be the final nail in the coffin. I couldn't help but wonder if the ATF et al. had done anything with the case or whether it was going to be buried deep inside some underground government vault. I wasn't big on conspiracy theories, but I did work for the government, and there were certainly some nefarious things going on. I wondered how long the SAC had been on the take. What his reasons were? He certainly earned an awful lot of money, much more than me. Perhaps it would be worth digging into his finances.

On that thought, Carter suggested we head back to the office. Maybe I could get Malone to check the SAC out? I knew he was nervous about what was going on, and I didn't want to see him get in trouble. I'd see how it went.

As soon as the door to the elevator opened, I was out and went straight into Malone's domain. He was busy with some contraption, and his hands were stuck inside sealed rubber gloves inserted into the side of a clear cabinet. I could see he was manipulating valves, and a sudden cloud of smoke filled up the small space.

"Hey, Mark. Watcha doing?" I said.

"Oh. Frank. You want to know?" Malone looked hopeful.

"Of course." Not really.

He grinned like a puppy, pulled his hands out of the gloves, and wiped them on his lab smock. "It's quite fascinating. I placed a piece of evidence in the cabinet from a case and the smoke inside—I won't get technical for you. It's a sort of vaporized glue—sticks to any residual oil from fingerprints. Then I dust the evidence using fingerprint powder, and if there are any fingerprints, the powder will stick to the glue. If we get any prints, I can run them through CODIS to see if we get a hit. It works way better than the traditional methods and is admissible in court."

"That's cool," I said, peering into the cabinet. I couldn't see anything. "Couldn't you dust for prints at the scene?"

"You could. However, this method is usually used when we don't get any hits on scene. It's more…" Malone rubbed his chin. "It's better at picking up faint fingerprints that otherwise would be missed. You must have watched CSI at some point. That's one thing they got right."

I looked suitably impressed for his benefit and then moved closer to him and lowered my voice. "What I was wondering is if you could help me out with something?"

"I'm not going to get in trouble, am I? I told you before I couldn't do that." He looked around me, out the door, as if expecting to see someone watching us. I almost looked too.

"No. Of course not. But I do need you to keep this on the down low."

"It's always something with you. Does it have anything to do with the case you and Carter were kicked off?"

"Indirectly. Look, Mark, I'll be honest. There's a leak in the department. I aim to plug it. I don't know who else to turn to. No one else has the technical skills to help me out. I came to you. I don't think you're the leak—"

"Never."

"That's what I thought. See? I came to the right person, after all."

Malone looked me over. "I'm not going to fall for your obvious flattery, Dalton. What is it you want?"

I told him as much as I could about my suspicions without giving away the whole enchilada, and then what I wanted him to do.

"You want me to what?" he said.

"Keep your voice down." I looked out of the office this time. No one was paying any attention. "I need you to search the SAC's online finances. I know it's unorthodox, but if you don't find anything, no one's going to be the wiser. It's important. Follow the money, right? Can you do it?"

Malone looked pained. "I know how. I trust you, Frank." He let out a weary breath. "Okay. I'll do it."

"Thanks, buddy." I slapped him on the shoulder. "Call me when you get something—anything. Don't leave me any post-it notes." He didn't look happy, but he nodded.

I grabbed a coffee from the break room, sniffing it suspiciously to make sure it wasn't old, when a bright red beetroot stomped through the door.

"Dalton!" Lewis screamed. "I gave you a direct order to leave that case alone." Spittle was flying from Lewis's mouth. People in the bullpen outside turned to look at him. "You're a fucking idiot. You hear me? A fucking idiot. I can't be responsible for the consequences of your actions—"

"Mr. Lewis!" Smith hurried over. "Perhaps this conversation would be better had in my office, sir?"

Lewis looked at Smith. Looked at me. He suddenly realized people were staring and strode across the room to Smith's office.

Smith looked at me. I hadn't said a word, and the coffee cup was still raised to my nose. I slowly lowered the mug.

"You too," he said.

I followed them. The SAC paced back and forth in the office, ignoring me. Smith sat down behind his desk after he closed the door.

"Mr. Lewis, I—" I said.

"You will stand at attention when you are addressing a superior officer, Special Agent Dalton."

Surprised? You betcha. I didn't move, momentarily frozen in mid-step. As a CGIS agent, although I was still on active duty, we didn't do the whole standing at attention, saluting, military stuff. I was kind of sideways from that, you know, and to have Lewis yell at me was one thing, but to demand I stand at attention? Yeah, I was surprised.

"Did you hear me, Dalton?" Lewis said, his face still a dangerous shade of stroke-red.

I still had the coffee mug in my hand and slowly put it down on the corner of Smith's desk and came to attention. Chest out, stomach in, shoulders back, head up, eyes in the boat, arms straight at my sides, hands closed, feet six inches apart. Man, this felt weird. "Yes, sir!"

Lewis circled me twice, looking as though he was trying to calm down. I kept my eyes straight ahead, not blinking. He stopped right behind me and spoke into my ear.

"Do you understand what you have done, Dalton?" Lewis said quietly.

"No, sir." I'd done lots of things. I wasn't exactly sure which one he was referring to.

"I can't protect you anymore, Dalton. I'm not going to have this on my conscience. I ordered you off this case. Why did you disobey me? Speak, Dalton."

"Mr. Lewis, sir, I didn't disobey you. I was following up some leads on some old—"

"Bullshit!" Lewis walked around to face me. He was now a softer shade of pink. I didn't think I'd have to get the defibrillator out just yet.

"Smith," Lewis said, not looking at him but still giving me the proverbial eyeball. "You told Dalton here to back off. Am I correct?"

"Yes, sir," Smith said. "We had a conversation right here."

Turning back to me, Lewis said, "Imagine my surprise then, when I got a call from an old buddy of mine, Jim London. He was concerned you didn't know Mrs. Rivas was still alive and wanted to make sure there hadn't been a breakdown in communications. I assured him everything was okay, and you'd probably just missed my call."

Ruh-roh, Raggy. "Thank you, sir," I said.

"Thank you be damned." Lewis moved to a chair along the wall and sat down heavily, burying his head in his hands. He didn't say anything. If I was a psychologist, I might say he was splitting. I risked a glance at Smith. He looked alarmed but tried to hide it. I couldn't tell if it was because of the SAC's breakdown, or if it was because I'd gone behind his back.

Lewis straightened himself in the chair, his face now down from the alarming stroke-red to an equally alarming pale, pasty and sweaty. His voice, when he spoke, was weary and modulated.

"You disobeyed a direct order. Your conduct was unbecoming of an officer. I'm placing you on administrative leave until a formal investigation under Article 134 of the Uniform Code of Military Justice can be conducted. You are to leave this building immediately and not return until this shit show has been resolved one way or another. Are we clear?"

I stood ramrod still. The blood drained from my face. I felt weak. Lewis had pounced on me before I could get to him. I felt sure, given enough time, I could counter this, but for now, he had me. I glanced at Smith for support.

"Don't look at him," Lewis said. "I asked you a question, Dalton. Are we clear?"

"Permission to speak, sir?" I said.

Lewis waved me to go ahead. "What is it?"

"Carter, sir. She had nothing to do with it. I want to be clear this was all my direction. She was following my orders, following along. She's new. This would ruin her career."

"Do you see her in here with you?" Lewis snapped. "No, of course you don't. Don't try my patience, Dalton. I'll consider your statement. I—" He paused for a moment, and a slow smile appeared on his lips. "Are you admitting the charges? I'll go easy on Carter if you do. We can clean this up quickly. Minimum of fuss. You're what? Seventeen, eighteen, years in?"

I clenched my jaw, my teeth grinding, and spat out, "Yes, sir. Almost twenty."

"Excellent. Plead guilty to the charges. Carter will be reassigned somewhere far away from here, Guam maybe, but she'll keep her job, and I'll let you keep your retirement, but you'll be done in the Guard."

I felt like I was back at my first unit, as a junior petty officer. I was being bamboozled. I'd lose my career, my job, my life. Everything. Everything that I'd worked for. And this bastard would get away with it all. If this plays out, I'll expose him.

And then I thought of Carter. She was just starting her life, her career. If I took the fall, she'd be okay, and with that final thought the decision was easy.

"I have your word?" I said.

Lewis nodded. "As an officer and a gentleman, you have my word that Carter will be looked after. ASAC Smith will be a witness." I didn't think Lewis's word was worth anything as an officer or a gentleman.

"Sir," Smith said, silent until now. "This is highly irregular, you can't just—"

Lewis stood up. His face now instantly purple. "I'm the commanding goddamn officer of this unit, and I can do any goddamn thing I damn well please. Is that clear? If it's not, you can follow him out the door too."

This guy was off his rocker.

"No, sir. I mean yes, it's clear, sir." Smith looked apologetically at me. I didn't blame him. If he spoke up again, Lewis would just give him the boot too. But the fact he tried meant something. Perhaps I could trust him after all.

"Your answer now, Dalton. I don't have all day." Lewis folded his arms.

I felt even weaker. "Yes, sir. I admit the charges."

Lewis smiled a tight smile, almost a grimace. "Very well, Dalton." He turned to look at the ASAC. "You heard that, Smith. He admits to all the charges. You'll type up a report for me to sign along with Dalton's resignation letter. Have it on my desk by close of business today." He turned back to me. "Your badge and gun. Put them on the ASAC's desk."

My heart sank lower. I had no choice but to do as he said. As I placed my badge on the desk, it felt like a small piece of my soul was ripped away and shredded. Inwardly, I was cursing his mother for ever having had sex with his father. I was impotent right now like I wished his dad had been, but there was nothing else I could do right now.

I left without another word. Walking like a zombie. Devoid of life. An automaton. All thoughts of the case, of Julia, of Willis and Paul and George, fled my mind. I didn't hear Jessica calling my name. I didn't hear Lewis ordering her into Smith's office. I don't remember getting in my car. I don't remember the drive home. I was in a haze. The world was passing me by, but I wasn't in it. I was a passenger in life at this moment. On autopilot.

I sat on the back deck of *Serenity,* cracked the first of many beers, and just drank.

Twenty-One

I was flat on my back, on the back deck of *Serenity*. It was dark. I had an awful taste in my mouth. Beer bottles clinked as I tried to move. Carter stood above me, looking concerned.

"Jesus, Frank. How much did you drink?" she said.

"Mmmmffff." Was all I could say.

"Here, take this. Drink it."

Carter propped my head up with her hand to help me drink, and a million small explosions bounced around in my skull behind my eyes. She forced three pills into my mouth, and blessed, refreshing, cool water, nectar of the gods, washed them down.

"Aspirin. It'll make you feel better," she said, to my unasked question.

There was some clanking as Carter cleaned up. It sounded like she was throwing bottles and cans into a steel garbage can with all her might. I squinted but only saw her carefully placing empties into a white garbage bag.

"Noisy," I mumbled.

"Yeah." She placed a pillow under my head. "Wait until the aspirin kicks in. You'll feel better."

I felt my world spinning. Was the boat moving? Were we underway? Where were we going? I didn't remember casting off. The stars above were spinning. I attempted to stand, falling down the steps to the lounge in my hurry and lunging for the head. I vomited the vomit of many beers and no food. It felt as if my stomach was turning inside out, purged. I vomited the angst, the anger. The shame and fear. It all came out and was flushed away.

I sat back, sweaty and exhausted, but feeling oddly cleansed, somehow fresher. Jessica came in holding her nose, disavowing me of the fresher aspect and turned the shower on. When it was steaming hot, she ordered me to strip off and get in. The burning water surged over my head and aching body. I stayed under the spray until my water tank ran cold. Jessica held a towel out for me. She'd cleaned the toilet.

"You didn't have to," I said.

"I know. Don't be stupid. I made coffee. And toast. You need more aspirin. You probably threw up the ones I gave you. Get dressed and come out when you're ready."

I padded into my cabin wrapped in the towel. She'd even laid out clothes for me. How did I get so lucky?

A moment later out on deck, all cleaned up, with my darkest shades on to ward off the evil brightness of night sky, she handed me the toast and coffee. I'd already washed the aspirin down with a mouthful of tap water. I carefully eased myself down to the deck seats.

"I don't think you'll need those sunglasses. It's night. How do you feel?" Carter said.

"Much better, thanks to you. My headache's nearly gone. I think throwing up was probably the best thing." I looked around. "I'll keep the sunglasses on for a few minutes, I think. The dock lights are still quite bright tonight. At least we're not underway anymore."

"What?"

"Never mind. Thanks, Jess. Again." I looked out over the water. "How much did I drink?"

"Too much."

"Yeah. I'm so sorry, Jess. For everything. Dragging you into this shit show. I wasn't myself yesterday. What happened to you after I left?"

"Lewis called me in and told me you'd been relieved. I'm the one that's sorry, Frank."

"Did he..." I started again. "Did he..."

"No. Nothing happened. Well, nothing bad. He yelled at me some and assigned me to Fredericks. Told me to thank my lucky stars, and he'd keep an eye on my future performance. What did he say to you?"

I took a breath. It was still raw. "He accused me of disobeying a direct order. I was relieved of duty while he books me and an investigation into my behavior is conducted."

"That's such bullshit, Frank. He can't do that."

"He can. He did. I'm just glad you're okay. Fredericks isn't bad."

Carter grimaced. "Fredericks is an annoying twat. All we did for the rest of the day was sit and input data into a computer. He wouldn't let me go until well after hours. I came here as quickly as I could, Frank. He can't get away with this, can he? The SAC, I mean, not Fredericks."

I thought about how defeated I'd felt yesterday, hearing the news. All I could do was feel sorry for myself. But now I'd sobered up...I shrugged. "He has so far, but no. I did what I had to do, but I'm not going to stop. I can't let this one sit. He's crooked, Jess. If nothing else, his manic tirade just proves he was trying to cover something up. It was a complete and utter overreaction." I looked at the sky for a minute, pleasant now it wasn't swirling, and took off my sunglasses. "What did the others say in the office?"

"No one said anything to me. I'm still pretty new there, remember? I could see them talking, though. Quietly, in corners. I think you'll have support if you need it. Apart from Fredericks, though. He seemed like a wet blanket."

"Yeah. He is a little. He's solid, though, just unimaginative. Don't hold it against him. He's got a ton of kids. I'm sure he doesn't want to get pulled into something like this. Don't blame him."

She shook her head. "What'll we do, Frank?"

"We? Nothing. Me, I'm going to carry on. I need to track those guns down and find that freezer. I asked Mark before I left to run a check on the SAC's finances.

What I need you to do is to be careful and go to work as normal. I don't want anyone thinking you're anything but a loyal worker doing her job. No one at work knows about our relationship. No one can."

Carter put her hand on my own. "I can't let you do this by yourself."

"You can, and you will. I don't need you to screw up your career, too. Besides, I might need you to support me soon when I'm out of a job." I tried a smile on for size. "Let me talk to Pete. I think I know how to proceed. Just act normal, as best you can. I promise I'll call you when there's anything worth knowing."

She nodded. "I don't like pretending nothing's wrong. I'm not a good actor, but I'll do it."

We shared a blanket and sat in companionable silence for a while. Despite the coffee, I was getting tired, and we finally called it a night. We were both too emotional to do much else besides sleep, and I dozed off with Carter holding me in her arms. It felt nice.

I woke several times through the night, restless, sure I could hear something, but nothing ever happened. In the morning, Jessica was already gone. She left me a note next to the fresh coffee she'd made saying she had gone to work early, and she'd be in touch. I was a fortunate man to have found someone as special as Jessica.

It was early, but I knew Pete would be up, prepping for the day's crowd, so I walked over to his bar and banged on the bar's steel back door. While I waited, I had to wave off the occasional fly that got me confused with the nearby garbage. I sniffed myself but couldn't detect any odor, so I didn't think it was me. I had showered again, after all.

Pete finally wrenched open the big door, the hinges squealing in protest.

"You could use some WD-40 on those bad boys," I said.

"You look like hell. Come in." He left the door open, and I followed, letting the door screech back in place, and sliding the deadbolt home.

"To what do I owe this early morning pleasure?" Pete said, nodding at a stool. "Coffee?"

"Please," I said, and sat.

Pete poured from a carafe and handed me a steaming mug of coffee.

"I'm in a spot of trouble, brother," I said.

"Figured this wasn't just a social visit so early. What gives?"

I told him what had happened after we had left here the last time. I glossed over my relationship with Jessica, but Pete was savvy enough to pick up on it.

"Hot damn," he said. "I knew you too would be good together. But that's not all, is it?"

"No. Not by a long shot."

I told him how we'd found proof the fire was arson, that we'd seen the culprit on London's video. I outlined all the evidence I had against Lewis, and I told him he was right about Rivas being alive, which made him smile and nod in what he thought looked like a wise way. I finished by telling him how I'd been relieved of duty, the deal I'd made to protect Jess, and how she'd found me last night.

"She's going to be okay, though?" Pete asked. "You think Lewis will honor your deal?"

"I don't know. If it keeps me out, he may, but I don't trust him for obvious reasons. I think Jess will be okay for the time being." I hoped. I also hoped this was what the shaman was talking about and not something more serious. "I'd like to believe Smith is a straight shooter, that he'll look after her. I think he was genuinely shocked at Lewis's behavior. He looked it. He tried to speak up for me. Lewis shot him down and threatened his career too." I took a sip of coffee, blowing the steam away. "I've been thinking some. For Lewis to flip out like that, he has to be under a lot of pressure."

"Maybe Black is turning the screws a little tighter. Now he's in the bag, it wouldn't be difficult. Particularly with that George fella at his beck and call."

We talked it over some more, three mugs worth, and then Pete said, "I might know someone who could help. Many people pass through this bar. I have a monthly visit from an old colleague. You don't know him. He was a little before your time. He's a retired admiral, went into the security business. Does a lot of contract work for the government. From what I understand, and reading between the lines, he still has a lot of connections, some bigwigs in the government at Homeland Security. He might be able to help."

I grinned. "Thanks, buddy. I was hoping you might know someone."

Pete nodded. "Yeah. You know, though, what the SAC did. He can't legally do that. It was beyond his authority. Oh sure, he can book you, but when it comes to the court-martial, any lawyer worth their salt should be able to get you out."

"I figured. You know what, though? For all the years I've put into the service, all the long days and nights away from home, this brought me right back to my first unit and those shitbags that ran roughshod over me and everyone else. The Old Guard, back from the dead. I thought the times had changed. I thought that sort of bullshit was long gone."

Pete shook his head. "You know it's gone. This SAC of yours is running a different game. You can't compare the two situations."

I sighed. "Maybe you're right. I think after all this wraps up, I might pack it all in. Take that trip on *Serenity* I'm always talking about. Go hang out in the Bahamas somewhere."

"And take Jessica with you?"

I honestly hadn't thought about it, so I did now. "Sure. If she'll come. I think she would. For a time anyway."

"Even if you quit, she still has commitments, you know. You can't run off into the sunset forever."

"I know, I know. Just an idle thought."

My pocket vibrated. I reached down to pull out my phone.

"Who's that?" Pete said.

"It's a text from Mark Malone. You know, the tech guy I told you about who's checking out Lewis for me? He wants to meet soon." I stood up and put the phone away. "Thanks for your help, Pete. I've gotta go. Maybe this is the lead I need."

We shook hands. "Be careful," he said. He hesitated, in thought for a second. "You said you had to hand in your piece. Do you need a spare?"

It was good of him to offer. "No. I've got my backup in an ankle holster. I'll be careful. Thanks again."

I drove straight to a bakery down Fifth Street where Malone said he wanted to meet. I couldn't ever remember coming here before, as it wasn't close to the office, which was probably the point. The little bell on the bakery door tinkled as I pulled it open, and I was immediately assaulted by the heavenly goodness of freshly roasted coffee and baked muffins. Mark wasn't there yet, and though I was floating to the gills with coffee, I figured one more couldn't hurt. I ordered a large coffee with skim milk, gotta watch that figure, and scoped out a secluded seat in the corner where I could still see the door.

The gigantic flat-screen television on the wall in front of me had the volume turned low, but I could read the subtitles. It was some sort of TMZ show, probably a rerun, but I was just getting engrossed in the ongoing dispute between the queen of pop Taylor Swift and her arch nemesis Katy Perry when Malone walked in. If only I could have the same problems those two had. What a world we live in, where news is a petty argument between two pop singers.

"Thanks for coming," Malone said. He seemed nervous, which wasn't unusual for him.

"Sure. Can I get you a coffee?"

"No, I'm good."

Malone sat and took out a sheaf of papers he'd stashed under his jacket. He looked around before handing them over.

"It's okay," I said. "I've been here a while. We don't know anyone." Besides watching TMZ, I had actually been doing my job.

His eyes continued to dart around the bakery. "Sure," he said. My assurances didn't seem to make him any more comfortable, and he continued to fidget.

"You okay?" I said.

"No. I feel sick. I think I'm coming down with something. Excuse me." Millennials. Dragons behind every tree.

Malone dashed off in the direction of the bathroom, and I took a moment to look through the papers he'd brought me. A lot of it was random banking nonsense, but Malone had highlighted several entries. Besides the SAC's regular pay on the first and fifteenth of every month, he also had a wire transfer of fifteen thousand dollars. Every month. Like clockwork. I whistled to myself at the figure and continued to flick through the pages. It looked like this had been going on for a long, long time. I couldn't begin to grasp how bad this was. There wasn't any legitimate reason he'd be getting that much money every month, it was what? an extra hundred and eighty thousand a year? If it had been an inheritance or something, we'd all have known. It would have shown up on his security clearance. If you have too much money, they'll discharge you. He seemed to have gotten around that problem somehow. There was also a regular withdrawal to another bank. I didn't know what the code meant, but Mark had scribbled in the margin. He'd tracked the withdrawals to a matching account in Lichtenstein. A so-called offshore account, in a land-locked country. Everyone knows about Switzerland being the capital of unmarked secret accounts, but Lichtenstein is also another, sometimes better, option.

Fuuuuuck meeee. He must have…I couldn't fathom the figure. I was sure it was small peanuts for a guy like Black to have the local commanding officer of the Coast Guard Investigative Service in his pocket…But shit, it was riches to the likes of me. It made me wonder whether Lewis's buddies in the ATF and DEA were also on the take. It would go a long way to explaining how they'd grabbed all my stuff. It would also explain how they could put the kibosh on any follow-up investigation. This was getting bigger than I had ever imagined. No wonder they didn't want me snooping around. It had probably made them all super nervous, which was why I'd been ordered off the case and they'd secured my files. When Carter and I carried on the investigation, it must have flipped their lids.

With my hands tied virtually behind my back, I would have to tread carefully. If they found out I hadn't given up, I might suffer more than just those consequences Lewis had threatened me with. Surely, they wouldn't try to kill me? I was a law enforcement officer. Would they?

I was lost in thought, so it was a while before I realized Malone was spending a long time in the bathroom. I collected the papers, threw the dregs of my coffee out and went to the bathroom to check on him.

"Mark? You in here?" The bathroom wasn't large but had three stalls. "Mark?" I banged on the door of the only closed stall. "Mark?" The door swung inwards as I knocked, stopping partway. I looked down and saw a foot blocking the door. I pushed it open as far as I could. Malone was sitting propped up on the toilet seat, his pants around his ankles, feet sticking out at an odd angle, loose like they weren't connected to his body. His head lolled in such a way it could only mean it was broken. I knew without checking he was dead.

"Shit." I pulled out my phone and dialed 911 for an ambulance. I hung up when they asked me who I was. I felt Malone's neck, knowing it was useless, but I had to check. There was no pulse.

It didn't look like he'd struggled. There was nothing else I could do. While I was engrossed in the papers at the table, he'd been in here having his life stolen from him. Some special agent I was. Then I remembered my badge was gone, and I got angry.

Fury and sadness rose in me. I backed out of the stool and kicked the next stool door as hard as I could. It rattled on its hinges and slammed backward. I wanted to scream and shout, but knew I couldn't. I couldn't afford to be in here with him when the EMTs came. I didn't need the hassle, the questions from the cops. Why were you meeting him, Mr. Dalton? What did the two of you discuss? You say you're a special agent. Where's your badge? Your boss says you were fired…I didn't need them to know anything. I went back to the stool and searched Malone, looking for any evidence he may not have given me. I didn't find anything.

I opened the door to the bathroom a crack and poked my head out. No one was about, and I let myself out the back door of the bakery just as the sirens were approaching. I'd parked around the corner, and I walked back to the car. I had the strongest urge to smoke, a feeling I hadn't had in years. Now I wish I smoked again. I needed the distraction. What a fucking waste. Malone was an innocent. Once again, like Paul, someone trying to do me a favor had ended up on the list of the dead. Perhaps I should leave, like they all wanted, let it lie. At least this way people would stop dying.

I was running out of time. I could feel the hempen noose that was swaying in the wind, tightening around my neck. Like a pirate waiting to feel the tug and snap as you dropped to your death.

I had to work under the assumption whoever had offed Malone had probably seen me, which meant Black knew I was up to something. The other thing that would catch up with me sooner or later was the video feed from the bakery security cameras. The cops would take one look at that and put a BOLO out for my arrest as a person of interest. A be on the lookout was all I needed to add the proverbial nail in my coffin, but at least it'd take them a little time to figure out who I was. I couldn't be associated with this place. Hopefully, the cameras were on the blink, but that wasn't something I could take for granted.

I was tired of playing defense, seemingly always playing catch-up. I needed to stop this scratched record that kept repeating the same verse and go on the offensive. I needed to shake up Black, to stop this senseless slaughter of people.

I saw a Stripes gas station ahead on the other side of the road and crossed over. I broke down and bought a pack of smokes. The first drag was long and glorious, the nicotine giving me a head rush, making me lightheaded. I smoked about half of it on the way back to the car and then ground it out. I gave the rest of the pack to a passing bum. This wasn't a habit I needed to pick up again.

I bent over, leaned on my car, and coughed my guts up. Perhaps not my brightest move, smoking, when the night before I'd been hung over. I got in my car and drove. Where to, I wasn't sure at the moment, I just needed to move. I had a feeling my subconscious would direct me where I needed to go.

I texted. Yeah, I text and drive, so shoot me. I needed to know Jessica was okay. She got back to me saying she was stepping out for some lunch, and would I want to join her? I replied that I would, but couldn't risk being seen together right now. We agreed to meet at Pete's after work and swap developments. I didn't tell her about Malone. I didn't want her to worry. She'd find out soon enough.

I dropped the phone on the passenger seat and carried on, driving listlessly. My subconscious hadn't come through for me, as I still didn't have any clue as to where to go. I took back control, engaged my brain, and drove up to North Padre Island, accessing the beach by the Holiday Inn. The sand was always hard-packed and ideal to drive on. I parked facing the Gulf and rolled the windows down to listen to the surf.

I must have dozed off without realizing, as the sun had moved across the horizon a bit when my phone rang with an incoming call. I picked it up off the seat, my eyes blurry, and glanced at it. Smith, the phone said. What could he want?

"Dalton," I said.

"Frank, where are you? You need to come into the shop. Now." Shit. Surely, they hadn't tracked me to Malone this quickly?

"What's up, Tobias? I thought I was expressly forbidden."

Even over the phone, I could tell he wasn't interested in games. "Something's come up, so I'm expressly telling you to get your ass down here."

They knew. Shit. "Listen, Tobias, I can explain everything. I didn't want to wait around for the cops, you know?"

"What in the hell are you talking about? Never mind, I don't want to know. Come into the office. Now."

"Yes, sir." I hung up the phone, feeling grim. My time was up.

I drove off the beach, looking in the rearview at the waves with longing. I drove down South Padre Island Driveway at speed and got back to the office within a short time. I looked in Smith's office, but he wasn't there.

"If you're looking for the ASAC, he's in the CP," another agent said, and I turned in the direction of the command post. "Hey Frank," he said, and I turned back. "We're with you, man." He held his fist up in solidarity.

"Thanks." I nodded at him. At least there was one person on my side. I can't lie. It did make me feel a little warmer. I walked down two flights of stairs, preferring to kill a little more time, and entered the code on the door of the command post. I don't know why we bother, as it's always 1790, wherever you go.

Inside the command post, it looked like hell. Video streams were playing on all the monitors, papers were strewn all over the large conference room-sized table, and several nautical charts, I like to call them water maps, as it pisses off the boatswains, were tacked to the wall. I found Smith talking with a bunch of guys from the enforcement shop. They looked like they were prepped for business. Bulletproof vests emblazoned with US Coast Guard on them. Rifles and riot helmets ready to go.

"What's going on?" I asked, somewhat bewildered. "Is this all for me? Bit of overkill, no?"

"Sit down, Frank," Smith said, ignoring my question.

I pulled out a chair and sat. He pulled out another chair and sat in front of me. He looked serious. I was in some deep shit.

And then he made my world spin. "As of forty-two minutes ago, Special Agent Carter's been missing."

TWENTY-TWO

I blinked, not understanding, not wanting to understand. Wasn't I here because of Malone? They had to be wrong. "What do you mean, missing?" I finally said. "She just texted me, saying she was going out to lunch."

"She did go out to lunch, but that was two hours ago," Smith said.

I glanced at the large twenty-four-hour wall clock on the wall. I'd misplaced some of the afternoon during my sojourn to the beach.

Smith continued. "Frank, she was on her way back to the office when it happened—"

"When what happened? I don't understand. What's going on?"

"I'm trying to tell you, Frank. She was stopped at a traffic light. A late model minivan pulled up alongside her car. We've pulled the footage from the traffic cam across the street. It happened quickly. The door to the minivan slid open, and two men wearing baseball caps pulled low, and bandannas over their faces, smashed her window, opened her door and pulled her out and into the van. The surveillance gets patchy after that, but we're looking."

"No, no, no. That can't be right. We were going to see each other tonight. I..."

"I get it, Frank. Listen, it's not all bad news. We got a lucky break early on. One of our guys was monitoring the police scanner and heard the description of her car, sitting abandoned at the light. That's how we got on this so quickly. If it's any consolation, she didn't go easy. She fought back, Frank. She wasn't a pushover.

Looks like she got a couple of good licks in before they hit her over the head. Knocked her out. I'm sorry. I know you two were getting close."

I was numb. "There must be some mistake. It must be someone else."

"There's no mistake, Frank. Listen, I called you in to give you the courtesy before you saw it on the news. I also want to run the CCTV by you to see if you recognized anyone in the footage."

I struggled to pull myself together. We got up and walked over to one of the large screen monitors. Smith asked the tech sitting in front of it to play the loop. The scene played out in front of me like he'd said. I could see her stop at the light, and moments later, the minivan pulled up right next to her. Even though I knew the outcome, I was rooting for Jess when she punched one of the guys. As she did, it dislodged his bandanna, and I saw George's creepy features look into the camera.

"George," I said.

"What was that?" Smith said. "Did you say, George?"

I looked at him, feeling my face freeze with anger. "Yeah. George. He works for Black. He was probably the one who shot at us. And the SAC..."

"The SAC what?"

I didn't say anything.

"If you know something, anything, you have to tell us, Frank. The enforcement guys are ready to roll. They just need to know where to go. You know we look after our own."

I looked over at the group of well-armed professional Coasties. I had faith in these guys and gals. They knew what they were doing, and I wanted to protect Carter.

"I don't know where Black would be, and I don't have any idea where they could have taken Carter. We've been looking for their operating base. All I know is it's not where their fishing vessels are." I shook my head. "I have no idea where it is."

"Kidnapping one of our own is fucking stupid," Smith said, angry himself. "They must know we'd pull out all the stops to get her back. Black isn't thinking this through, unless ... you must have been getting close, Frank. You must have scared them. This has to be a stalling tactic, a diversion." He started pacing. "Think, man, think. Where could they have taken her?"

"I am thinking, Tobias," I snapped, standing up. "I don't know. Don't you think I'd tell you if I did? I'd like nothing more than to see that fat bastard obliterated from the face of the earth."

One of the enforcement team broke away from his people and came toward us.

"Frank, this is Senior Chief Montoya. He's a maritime enforcement expert," Smith said. "Senior, this is Special Agent Dalton, Carter's partner. Any news?"

"We're ready to roll, sir," Montoya said, nodding to me. "Until we have better intel, we're going to search the fishing docks around where the *Reel Lady* moors up. See if we can come up with anything. I don't like to keep my people standing around. They'll start breaking things. It's a bit like managing bulls in a china shop."

"Senior," I said. "You won't find anything at the docks. Black isn't going to be somewhere so obvious. He'll be holed up with his gang, somewhere we haven't located yet."

"That's probably true, sir, but we have to start somewhere. What if she is there? We'd look pretty stupid if we didn't try."

I shrugged, knowing it would be useless, but not having anything better to offer. "Sure."

The enforcement group, wrapped with Kevlar, left the command post. "We'll be on tactical channel twenty-two charlie," Montoya said and followed his group.

Montoya seemed like a good man. His reputation was solid. I couldn't think of anyone better to conduct the operation. Still, I wanted to be out there, to find and save Jessica. It frustrated and angered me that I was helpless.

Smith looked around the command post. "Come with me," he said. I followed him to a side office that looked like it hadn't been used in a while. "Close the door behind you," he said. The room smelled stale. I knocked the dust off a dull orange plastic chair and sat down. Smith didn't bother with the dust and sat down on another orange chair, sliding it over to me, so we were face to face.

I could tell he was looking at me, but I stared at the floor.

"What?" I said, not looking up.

He inhaled, held it for a count of three, and let it out. "I wanted to apologize for Lewis's behavior," he began. "It was inappropriate and uncalled for. There's procedure and protocol, and he didn't follow either. In his defense, though, you disobeyed his direct order to back off the case. You were also not entirely honest with me, either. That's something we're going to have to address between us in due course. But," I looked up for the first time, and we locked eyes. "I've known you a long time, Frank. I know we're not social buddies, but I thought we had an understanding, a good working relationship. This isn't normal behavior from you, either. If the SAC orders you off a case, and I tell you too, that should be the end of it. There's a chain of command for a reason. You're not privy to everything that's going on. That's why we make the decisions. What's got your goat with this case? I know something's going on. Lewis's behavior is odd, and the numbers aren't adding up. Murder, gun running, people being frozen, and now this with Carter." Smith stood up abruptly, knocking the chair backward. He paced in the small space. A plume of dust followed his movements. I could see the bags under his eyes. He was more tired than usual.

"Dammit, Frank," he said, facing me again. "What I saw yesterday, I've never seen in my entire career. I've known the SAC for a long time. He has an excellent reputation. Everyone likes him, but he flipped his lid. That's not normal behavior for anyone, let alone him. Even if you did outright disobey him, it's an administrative thing. He didn't even ask you why you did what you did. But I'm asking. I want to know why Frank. I want to know the truth. And we're not leaving this room until you spill your guts. All of it."

He came back over, righted the chair and sat down again. I needed a moment to think, difficult, while he was staring at me. I could feel the tension in the room, and if I'd had a knife, I could've sliced it six ways. I silently weighed my options. He could be grilling me to figure out how much I knew. I didn't know if he was that good of an actor. If Black's operation was crumbling, he could be under orders to find out what I knew. He could be in league with Lewis. Could be taking bribes. Was I next to disappear? Would I end up in some storage freezer in some God-forsaken place, hanging on a hook while the life slowly leached out of me? Is that what was happening to Jessica while we sat around with our thumbs up our asses?

On the other hand, he could just be a puzzled man. Wondering what was going on like he said. If so, he could be a powerful ally. He could help me. I could tell him about Lewis's finances. I absently fingered the files that were still stuffed inside my shirt. I should tell him about Malone. Poor Mark. I didn't know what to do.

My world had gone from wondering if I should sling my hook for a vacation in the Bahamas to almost being kicked out of the Guard. My newfound soul mate was alone and frightened somewhere with that fat freak. And a litany of dead and injured people was littering the landscape. All in a few days. I pinched my nose, stifling a sneeze, the stale air and dust drying out my sinuses. I made my decision.

"There's something you need to know," I said, taking a breath. "Mark Malone has been murdered."

I told him of my meeting with Malone at the coffee shop and why I'd run. I said Malone was working on a project for me and didn't want anyone to see us meeting. I told him I thought it must have been an inside tip that led to someone following him. Someone had to have seen me talking with Malone before we left or had seen what he was working on. I didn't know if Malone had saved a copy of his work on one of our servers. He was fastidious in his professionalism, so it was possible. It was also possible, thinking it through now, that someone could have accessed said server and figured it out. Someone with access, someone like Lewis. Maybe. Malone was pretty savvy with tech. I'm not sure it would have been that easy.

Smith looked shocked but took it in stride, his professionalism and training taking over. We could mourn Malone's loss later.

"Frank, I'll take what you told me at face value. I have no reason to disbelieve you, and until proven otherwise, I have your back. I'll make a call to the local authorities in case that video feed comes to light. Tell them you were working undercover. They'll probably still want to talk to you, but we can arrange it on our terms rather than theirs. I can get you some space. I need to know what Malone was working on for you, though."

And that was the clincher. If Smith was working with Lewis, this is where they'd get me. I probably wouldn't go down for Malone's death, but it sure would be a good way to get me out of the picture for a while. A special agent on administrative leave tormented with his loss of identity, his badge and gun gone. Yes, we know officers. He left here saying some bad things about revenge and payback. That's why we took his weapon from him. No, he's never been like that before. Yes, he and Mark argued before he left. Why yes, of course, he knew where Mark took his morning coffee. Mark was always very routine. I can't believe it, but I guess he must have flipped out. So sad, we never saw it coming.

And then I'd probably meet with a tragic accident while in lock up. Maybe I'd hang myself with the belt and shoelaces they conveniently forgot to take from me.

I wanted to trust Smith. I needed someone that had my back. I didn't want to be the only one holding these secrets. If something happened to me, there was no evidence, nothing that couldn't just disappear or be explained away.

"Frank? What was Mark working on?"

Fuck it. I made my decision. I started, so I might as well spill it all. "Mark was looking into the SAC's finances for me—"

"What. What in the hell for?"

"If you'd let me finish, I was about to tell you." I gave him a scathing look. "Me and Carter found some information and we've seen some activities that cannot be explained away. Lewis is dirty, and he's on the take."

"That's not possible. I've known him years," he said, raising his voice.

I held up my hand and was about to reply when a phone chirped loudly. It wasn't mine. I always have mine on vibrate. It kept chirping, the acoustics in the small room making it sound louder than it probably was. I looked at Smith, annoyed when he didn't answer it.

"You going to answer that?" he said.

I looked at him with surprise. "It's not mine."

"It is. It's coming from your pocket."

I pulled out my phone and showed him. "Look. No texts, the last call was from you."

The phone chirped again. I patted my pockets again and slowly pulled another phone out. Shit. I'd completely forgotten I'd been carrying around the clone of Willis's phone with me. It was that phone that was chirping. I clicked on the text message that had come through. As I read it, I chilled, my resolve hardened, and I felt rage. The message said,

> you know who this is. We have your girl. If you want her back in one piece, you'll hand over all the evidence.

Another text came through, and I clicked on that one. It was a photo. A picture of Jessica, standing on tip-toes, tied up with her hands over her head, secured to a beam. She had a gag in her mouth and looked terrified. Another text.

> Meet in one hour. Come alone.

What followed was the meeting's location.

Smith had been patient, letting me read the texts, but his frustration came through. "Come on, Frank. Put the phone down. Texting isn't appropriate right now."

I felt awful. I was going to run out on him. I was going to leave him hanging. I thought he was on my side, but not after I did this.

"Don't hate me, Tobias, but I have to leave," I said, reaching for the door. "Listen, take a long hard look at Lewis."

Smith followed me and put his hand out, stopping the door from opening. "Frank! Don't do this. You need to tell me what's going on. I can't protect you if you don't let me help."

I yanked on the door. "Like how you protected Carter?" It was a low blow, and I could see it in his face. I felt awful, but it had the desired effect. His arm fell from the door, and it gave me the chance to bolt.

I went straight to my car, half-expecting Smith to have the security guard stop me, but I drove out unmolested.

I looked at my watch. I had time before the meeting to gather a few things from my safe aboard *Serenity*, and I needed to bring Pete up to date. At least one person needed to know what the hell I was doing, especially if I didn't come back. I needed some insurance. As I drove home, I kept a lively eye on my mirrors. I didn't need to be followed or ambushed. This was the last time I was going to get careless. I felt my resolve harden and a tentative plan formed. It could work. I hoped it did.

After grabbing my things and talking with Pete, I drove to the meeting. It was to be at an obscure, abandoned airstrip in Aransas Pass. I thought of Jessica. Her sweet caress, her laugh, the way she touched the tip of her nose when she was thinking, the lock of hair that kept falling across her eyes no matter what she did with it. I thought of our long conversations on the deck of the *Serenity*, her eagerness to learn. How she liked to listen, how she could point out the obvious problems with my logic.

I missed her with a yearning that made my heart ache. So help me God, if they've harmed one tiny little hair on her head, I'll destroy them all. Vengeance may be some omnipotent being's prerogative, but I would invoke my right of free will. I would make them all burn in hell.

Rachel Platten's *Fight Song* came on the radio, and I turned it up. I thought it was appropriate for my mood. It could have been Queen's *Fat Bottomed Girls*, so at least I had that going for me.

Jessica would have laughed at my music selection, and that made me smile too, imagining her fake halfhearted scorn.

I slowed down as I neared the airstrip. I could see a gate had been wedged open, and I nudged the car through the gap. This place was far from any main roads, so there was no fear of any security or police happening along. I followed the road straight to an old hangar. The roof was wind-damaged, partly ripped off and missing. An old dilapidated sign, peppered with shotgun holes, announced this was the Aransas Commercial Strip and Hangar Number Two. I couldn't see any sign of Hangar Number One. Maybe that had blown away along with the roof, or perhaps it had never existed at all, the number two moniker making the airport sound bigger than it was.

I stepped out of the car and held on tightly to the envelope of evidence I had brought with me. It wasn't much. Lewis had made sure of that. It was unnaturally silent, the heat radiating off the blacktop of the runway and making it feel hotter than it was. The faint whiff of jet fuel still permeated the air. The sun scorched the landscape and played with tumbleweeds as I walked into the hangar.

My eyes didn't take long to adjust to the semi-shade of the hangar as the missing part of the roof let in plenty of light, and I saw Black sitting in a big brown leather armchair about halfway inside. The chair looked like the same one he had at the fishing warehouse. Maybe he took it with him everywhere. Wheel me over to the hangar, George. I have some kidnapping business to attend to.

Externally, I kept my expression neutral, but internally, I was on fire. I wanted to shoot him, punch him, scratch his eyes out in a girly way, piss on him—

"Special agent. Stop right there," Black said.

I did, reining in my anger. Not yet.

"I'm glad you followed directions and came alone. It makes things simpler. As I'm sure you must have guessed," Black said, indicating the upper walkway around the hangar, "I didn't come alone. My associates have you well covered, and I imagine you're also aware I have a supply of world-class weaponry at my disposal, so don't try anything cute. Just so we're on the same page, right from the beginning. If you fuck up in here, you won't see your lover again. I suggest you pay attention and listen carefully."

"Where is she? If you've hurt her—"

"She's perfectly fine. Although...I can't guarantee her safety forever. The boys do like to play rough now and again, and I can only stop them from having fun for a little while." His fat body wrapped in a neon green jogging suit jiggled up and down as he laughed. "I believe you have something for me?"

"What assurances do I have you'll let her go if I give you this?" I said, waving the envelope.

"Absolutely none. But if you don't give me that envelope, you'll die right where you're standing. And I'll take it, anyway."

I kept my rage in check. "I might have come alone, but I didn't leave unprepared. If I don't make it back in two hours—"

His fat slithered over his body as he barked a laugh again. "Yes. Yes. Yes. And you've left written instructions in a particular file to be opened if you don't return, blah, blah, blah. You amuse me, Special Agent. You must be very special. Special in the head, no? What? Do you think we don't know about your friend Pete? Or perhaps you left a copy with your Assistant Special Agent in Charge, Tobias Smith? Could you have placed copies oh so carefully and reverently inside the safe, you think no one but you knows about in your stupid boat? Men can be killed. Fires can be started. Boats can be sunk." He pulled out a butane lighter and carefully lit a cigar, the smoke wafting upward on his first puff. "Come now. I am not a patient man."

"You'll never get away with this." I stepped closer. "You can't kidnap a federal agent and expect to get away with it."

"You sound like a broken record, agent. You forgot to mention all the murders I've gotten away with. Come now, I've been playing this game a lot longer than you. Do you not think I have an escape plan? This game was getting tiresome, anyway. If you'd given me a few more weeks, we would never have had to have this conversation."

"Where do you think you're going to hide from me on this planet? I'll hunt you down, you egotistical cockfuck. There's nowhere you can hide."

"You're absurd. Perhaps you really are special? Special in the head. Do you think I'm going to tell you all my plans like a sad actor in a two-bit James Bond knockoff? Tie you up and expect the lasers and sharks to get you while I walk off into the sunset? Don't be stupid. No, you brought all this upon yourself, Dalton. You were supposed to back off. Don't you Coast Guard people know how to follow orders?"

"So, Lewis is on your payroll," I said.

"Is that a question or a statement? Either way, I'm not answering, and you're trying my patience. Enough. Bring the envelope to me. Now."

I walked a few steps closer.

"Far enough," Black said. "Throw it from there."

I gave him an evil grin. "What makes you think I won't put a bullet in your eye right now and skull fuck you? Carter could be dead already. I've nothing to lose."

"Oh, but you do," Black said, with a sick smile of his own. "What if she is alive? What then? You'd be killing her and yourself. You'd never know. And then think of the good Frank Dalton name. Was he crooked? Did he murder that tech guy? Maybe he set fire to that bitch Rivas's house? Whatever good you've done in your career, it'll all boil down to a media frenzy of bullshit. You'll be analyzed, chewed up and spit out. Your name will be nothing but dirt, and Carter will be right there with you."

For a moment I didn't blink, didn't move. And then I threw myself down to the ground and rolled quickly, coming up with my weapon drawn. Before Black could move, I put a bullet through his forehead, brain matter exploding out in an arc. Black-clad operatives rappelled down ropes that appeared through holes in the broken roof, machine guns chattering, bad guys falling to the ground.

I wish. Of course, none of that happened. I'd thought maybe, just maybe, I'd have some options, could figure something out. I was used to improvising, but there was no cover in this wide-open space. No stash of secret weapons. No small thermonuclear bomb designed for one and concealed in the envelope. No laser watches or cigarette darts.

No, this was real life, and just as real life sometimes is, this was an entirely stinky shit show. Whatever grand plan I had was just that, a grand plan. Nothing I could execute. Fuck it all to hell and back.

I threw the envelope down on the ground and kicked it over. "Helen Back," I said.

"What was that?"

"Nothing. Just a girl I used to run with." Jessica would have liked that. Or probably would have groaned. I felt a stab of pain, wondering if she was okay. "What now? You've got what you want."

"Quite. Now, you leave."

"And then what? What about Carter?" I said.

"All in good time. You still have that traitor Willis's phone?"

I nodded and tapped my pants pocket.

"Good, keep it close at hand. We'll be in touch with where you can collect Carter. Goodbye, Special Agent. It was entertaining, but there are things I must attend to. A few loose ends to tie up, as it were."

"And I walk out? Just like that?"

"Of course. We're not barbarians, just entrepreneurs. And I have business to attend to. Goodbye."

Black didn't move. I turned and started walking out, to light, to sanctuary. I glanced up at the walkway and saw a few shadows shaped like men. I expected a shot in the back of the head before I made it to the sunlight.

Twenty-Three

I left the hangar without dying. I walked to the car and let out a long breath. Black now knew everything I did about the case. Sure, I'd made copies, but he was spot on with where I'd put them. I shouldn't have been so obvious. It was evident Black had eyes on us all along.

I got in my car, scorching myself on the sun-heated pleather seats, and slammed the steering wheel over and over with the palm of my hand. I rammed the car into gear and peeled out. I thought about waiting and following Black, but it was so flat he'd see a tail for miles. And I still thought he might come through and let me know where Jess was. I hoped. And that was all I had at the moment. I couldn't jeopardize that, which was why I'd come by myself and not clued anyone else in.

My phone vibrated as I was back on the road. A text from Smith. It said the enforcement guys had turned up a blank. There were a few fishing vessels there, but nothing was going on. I knew that as his crew was here. He also told me to call him. I was relieved he hadn't cut me out of the loop, especially after the way I'd left. I didn't respond, though. I knew where Black was, but if I told Smith he'd send the troops, and if by some wild fluke, we did catch Black, I couldn't see him suddenly spilling the beans. He still had the upper hand. Temporarily though, I hoped. I knew taking Black in should have been a priority, but as slimy as the fuck was, my priority was now finding Jess.

I was running out of leads. I screamed in frustration. At a traffic light, the young woman who pulled up next to me glanced over and immediately looked away. She took off as soon as the light changed, no doubt wanting to put some distance between her and the crazy guy. The guy in the car behind me leaned on his horn, so I rolled the window down, stuck my left arm out and gave him a thumbs-down, slowly moving on. The thumbs-down momentarily calmed me enough to stop feeling sorry for myself and start thinking again. If you've ever been fighting road rage, instead of flipping someone off, which they'd expect, catch their eye in the mirror and, starting with a thumbs-up, slowly turn it upside down to a thumbs-down. It's incredibly therapeutic, especially when you catch sight of their confused face.

I called Pete and told him to watch his back. He said not to worry. The place was buttoned up tight. I asked him to keep an eye on my boat, and he said he had it covered, whatever that meant.

I ran through the options in my head. It didn't take long, as I didn't have any. As I crossed the bridge back into Corpus, I saw the sign for Calallen and decided to give Deacon another go-around, as that was about the only thing I could do. This was a guy that had worked for Black. Maybe he knew of a hidey-hole where Carter could be. It was worth a shot. I didn't have much else.

The flat landscape of Calallen fit my mood perfectly, and it didn't take long to get there. Halfway down Deacon's dusty driveway, a US Marshal's car blocked the way. The marshal got out of his car, hand on his sidearm, and walked cautiously toward me. I turned the engine off, rolled down my window, and placed my hands on the steering wheel. Didn't need to get shot. As he edged closer, I saw it was the same guy from before. I didn't have my badge anymore, so I showed him my military ID.

"Where's your badge?"

"Must be in my other jacket," I said, patting my pockets.

He gave my ID the once over, looking from its picture to my face and back again. After making me sweat for a moment, he handed it back to me without another word and walked to his car. I wondered if he was going to let me through, but his car started, and he backed it out of the way. He eyeballed me as I drove past, and then I saw him in my rearview mirror move the vehicle back into place, blocking the driveway again.

Deacon looked as if he hadn't moved since Carter and I had left him. I'm sure he had, but a large pile of smokes lay piled up on the floor next to the picnic table, and he was still staring off into space, a vacant look on his face.

I sat down. Deacon didn't move. I snapped my fingers to get his attention, even though I was right in front of him. His eyes slowly focused on me.

"Agent." He nodded at me.

"Deke. How've you been?"

He shrugged. "Just waiting for Black to come get me."

I froze. Was he coming here? "What do you mean?"

"Black always gets his way. Expect he'll send someone to take me out. I know how he works," Deacon said. He seemed resigned to the fact that this would be the way his life ended.

I relaxed a fraction. "I wouldn't worry about him. From what I hear, he's probably leaving the country. His operation is compromised. He has no out, except to leave. I doubt he's concerned with you."

"Maybe. Maybe not. You never worked for him, did you?"

I shook my head. "Deke, you remember that nice lady I had with me the last time we visited?"

He nodded and lit another smoke.

"Black has her. She's been kidnapped."

Deacon internalized this new piece of information for a moment and said, "Told you there was no escaping. She's probably dead."

"Cut the self-pity, man," I snapped. "She's not dead, and neither are you. I need to know where they have her stashed. Where did you guys hold hostages for Black? Rack your brains, Deke. You could help save her."

Deacon took a long drag on his smoke, letting the ash fall on the table to join the large heap already there.

"She's probably on a boat. Black owns lots of them. Take one out to sea. Safest place there is. You'd know if anyone was comin' near you."

"What boat, Deke? What boat would they use?"

He shrugged again. "Don't know. If it was me, I'd use a big one. Black only has two biguns. One I worked on and her sister ship. What I—"

Deacon didn't finish his sentence, nor would he ever. His head exploded, splattering me with blood and chunks of brain matter. I heard the report a moment later echoing from the tree line. I dove for cover under the table, pulled my piece from my ankle holster and returned fire in the direction the shot came from, although I couldn't see anyone. I looked behind me for more protection and bolted to the side of the house, weaving and staying low as I ran. The marshal got out of his car, and I waved him down. He was no dummy and used his car door as a shield.

There were no more shots. I knelt down low and peeked around the side of the house. I saw Deacon slumped over the table but could see nothing behind him. I shot into the trees, anyway.

Nobody returned fire. I saw the marshal on the radio and signaled I was moving out. I ran to the shed we'd seen Deacon come out of on that first trip. Still no shots. I peeked around. Nothing. I didn't feel safe running across open ground to the tree line. I'd leave that to the crime scene people. The shooter had accomplished his goal and Deacon was gone. Black was cleaning up. No loose ends. Guess Deke was right, after all. Shit and double shit.

I got back in my car and turned around. The marshal tried to stop me, saying he needed me to wait to give a statement. I told him I didn't have time and to call the ASAC if he needed me. He wasn't happy, but he had to deal with Deacon's body before he could deal with me. He moved his car out of the way. I spun out of the dust bowl.

Another one dead. Had Black no respect for humanity? No, stupid question. He felt above the law. He operated so far above us mere mortals, he thought he was unreachable. But, thanks to Deacon's last words, I had another clue, a starting place. Two ships. Two ships where Jessica might be. I needed help on this one. I called the office and told Smith I was coming in.

Smith cursed at me when I told him Deacon was dead. "This is becoming a habit, Frank." I gave him the details of what he'd told me so we could start on a plan.

I took the back door to the office so I wouldn't bump into anyone I didn't want to and took a moment to use the head. I needed a pee. While I was washing my hands after some blessed relief, I caught my reflection in the mirror above the sink and was startled to see pieces of Deacon still on my face. I gagged and scrubbed him off and down the drain as best I could. I dried off with some paper towels and headed for the stairs. I took a moment longer to change out of my blood-sprayed clothes, threw on some coveralls and headed for Smith's office. It was way past time I filled him in on Lewis. Turns out, no one had seen him since he'd balled me out and he wasn't answering his phone.

It was a long conversation with Smith. He listened well and made a few notes, his initial disbelief turning to resignation and then anger. I gave him copies I'd made of the video feed from the underground lot, the copies of the bank statements, all the stuff Malone had helped me retrieve.

"I don't know if there are any more informants in the department," I said. "That's why I've been playing this close to my chest. It wouldn't surprise me to know Black's got his fingers into more than one person."

"Is that why you didn't…wait…are you saying you didn't trust me?" Smith said, half joking. When I didn't reply, he said, "Seriously? Me?"

I shrugged. "Don't take it personally, Tobias. I didn't know who to trust. I knew I could trust Carter. And Mark. That was it. I didn't know who else was in on it. Black's reach seems to be everywhere."

"Very well. For what it's worth, I'll put my personal opinions of how you handled it behind me, so we can move on."

"Much appreciated."

"I wasn't completely idle while you've been gone, either. What you said about Lewis before you left got me to thinking, and I had a few agents I trust implicitly, quietly do some digging into Lewis. I'll fill you in later. By the way, no one's seen Lewis since yesterday, but I'll send agents to his house and pick him up if he's there. It's time we had some answers."

I breathed a long sigh of relief. "Thank you. I'm sorry I ever doubted you."

Smith smiled. A smile big enough to say he'd forgive me, not quite big enough to say he'd forget anytime soon. "Here, I think you might need these," he said, handing over something I didn't want to lose again.

It was liberating to get my badge and gun back. It felt like a part of me was home again, which made me wonder if I was too wrapped up, identifying with the job. I didn't want the job to define me, but perhaps it did. I shook that thought off. Introspection could come later. Jess was still missing.

"We'd better get over to the CP," he looked at his watch. "Montoya's briefing should start soon."

Acting on the intelligence Deacon had given us about Carter possibly being on one of the larger of Black's vessels, we pulled up each vessel's automatic identification system. The AIS allowed us to track each vessel, one was a no-go as it was on its way to Asia, no doubt to dump off a full load of fish, and besides it had left port about a week ago, so there was no way she was going to be on that one. The other vessel was about eighty miles offshore. Not so far.

Senior Chief Montoya had pulled up the vessel's blueprints and had them up on the large screen when we walked into the command post. The Coast Guard kept blueprints of all large US flagged ships in its database, the first stroke of luck we'd had in a while.

"Just in time, sir," Montoya said. "I was about to start the brief."

Smith nodded. This was Montoya's show now. He continued. "We're going to take the two new stealth helos. They're regular Coast Guard sixty-fives that have been retrofitted and equipped for covert ops. They have a sniper station and fifty cals mounted, and we'll be able to execute vertical insertions. They also aren't bright orange." He waited for the requisite smiles and continued. "One helo will hover over the stern deck, and that team of six will secure the engine room, then check the cargo spaces. The other helo, which I'll be on with another team, will hover over the bridge and secure that, the radio room and the cabin spaces. We plan to take off at dusk, putting us on scene when it's fully dark. We'll make two passes at a distance with night vision, and if there are any armed unfriendlies, we'll take them down first. Any questions?"

"I want to be on your helo, senior," I said.

Montoya hesitated for a second and said, "We can talk about that in private after the brief is over, sir. Any other questions?" Montoya looked around the room. "Very well. Wheels up in one hour. Get some rest."

After everyone had filed out of the room, I approached Montoya with my question again.

Montoya eyed me. It made me think I may have missed a spot of Deacon.

"Absolutely not, sir," he said firmly. "You're not trained for this sort of counterinsurgency op. We need to rappel quickly and quietly. I know you want to be there, but you'll hold us back, impede our mission. No offense, sir, but I don't have time to be your babysitter."

I bristled, but realized he was right. I never had dropped out of a helicopter on a piece of string. Now wasn't the time to try. If I was on the mission and screwed up, I'd never forgive myself.

Montoya could see I was agitated and threw me a bone. "Sir, if it's any consolation, we'll have live streaming of the whole evolution from our helmet cams. We'll have tactical comms set up in here so you can hear what's going on."

"Thanks, senior," I said. He turned to walk away. "Senior, one more thing."

"Yes, sir."

"This boat. Some of the people on board are just going to be fishermen doing their job. They're not all going to be bad guys."

"Understood, sir. We have that under control."

"Thank you. I didn't mean to step on your toes," I said.

"No offense taken, sir. If she's there, we'll get her back." I hoped he was right.

TWENTY-FOUR

While I waited for them to get on scene, I went in search of coffee and found a half pot of old coffee. I contemplated making a fresh pot, but couldn't muster the enthusiasm. What I wanted was something stronger, but this was all I was going to have. The coffee was cold, so I shoved it in the microwave for a minute. I added powdered creamer I found. We couldn't seem to keep milk fresh. I tasted the coffee, and yep, it sucked ass. But it was coffee, and I needed something. My hands trembled slightly as I picked it up.

Smith came and joined me. "We'll get her, Frank. We have to."

I nodded, unsure of what to say.

"Listen, it's rough on all of us, having one of our own taken, and especially with what happened to Mark. It's...it's not something we're used to. She'll be okay." He tried to console me by patting my shoulder.

"Are you telling me or hoping?" I said, shrugging him off. I wasn't in the mood. "I hope she's okay, too, but I don't see why Black would keep her alive. He's killed nearly everyone else. Why would he keep her alive?"

"He's killed a lot of people, you're right, but he hasn't killed any federal officers."

"What about Mark?" I said.

"He was one of us, of course he was, but he wasn't an agent. I think that's the difference. Mark was a civilian working in the department."

"That's an asshole comment, you know," I said.

Smith held up his hands placatingly. "I'm grasping at straws here, Frank. Just trying to come up with reasons, a theory. I don't know for sure, but it's the only thing that makes sense to me." His voice was strained. I knew he was struggling. I relaxed a little. "Come on," he said. "Let's get back. They should be getting on-scene right about now."

I followed him into the command post. The video feed was starting to come online, and the radios crackled with static, manned on our end by an operations specialist petty officer, who sat at a wide desk with various radios, the regular VHF radios all boats have so he could talk with them, an HF, a high-frequency radio for longer distances, although this was being mostly replaced with satellite phones these days, and he had some other equipment I wasn't completely familiar with.

"Radio check. Montoya One, to base," crackled one of the radios.

The operations specialist reached over and flicked a switch. "Montoya One, base. Read you five by five."

"Base, roger, have you loud and clear also. Out," came the reply. Out, signifying there was nothing further to say. I hated films that ended radio communications with over and out. Over meant it was the other person's turn to reply, so over and out was in effect saying, hey you can reply but don't as I've ended the conversation already. Stupid. No one does that in real life.

Smith and I watched the unnatural green glow of night vision optics flicker to life on the screen, split into twelve quadrants so we could watch each team member individually. It was eerie, a little like looking over someone's shoulder who was playing a first-person shooter, only this game had genuine consequences, and there were no extra lives. Underneath each section on the screen was a designator for each person, so we would know who was talking.

Sometime later, the radio crackled to life again. "Base, Montoya One. Target acquired."

"Montoya One, base. Understood."

Six Coasties fast roped down the lines extending from the hovering helicopter to the ship below and quickly spread out and made for cover. I don't think you need to ask me if we knew how to do this before 9/11. So much has changed since.

No sooner than their feet had hit the deck, the helo moved out of the way and the next helo swooped in low and the same evolution happened with six more tactical Coasties fast roping down to the deck. Each team wore black tactical gear, but with the night vision goggles on each member and the feed on the screens here, we could easily see what was going on.

They cleared the ship as quickly and methodically as they could, but she was a large vessel. On board was a small crew of eleven that ran the machinery and navigation, but down below there were another fifty scared-looking individuals, hired expressly to process and package fish. It took a while, and all the time I was pacing and biting my nails.

At one point, Montoya took off his camera and looked into it so we could see his face on the screen. I'd already guessed what he was going to say. "Sorry, sir. No sign of her." It was a nice gesture, but it didn't help the tight feeling in my stomach. "We've searched the vessel with neg res. She's not on board. The crew look like regular fisherman. There are no weapons on board, nothing out of place. Sir, I don't think she was ever here."

Two ships. Two fishing tenders. Our only clues before Deacon died. His dying breath was all but worthless now. One ship we've searched, the other on the way to Asia.

It wasn't long before the agents Smith had sent to bring Lewis in for questioning reported he wasn't home. They said the front door was unlocked. I'm sure it wasn't, and I smiled inside, knowing they would have forced entry. They conducted a brief search and discovered a messy bedroom, and it looked like some clothes were missing from his closet and drawers. It seemed as if he'd hurriedly packed for a trip out of town. There was no sign of a struggle, so we had to assume he was tipped off and made a quick escape. With the amount of money he had, he could probably get safe passage out of the country from many sources, if not Black himself.

Smith called the assistant district attorney and, after some quick explanations and promises to fill him in full later, had a bench warrant issued by a friendly judge for Lewis's arrest. He also got a court order to freeze his accounts. The offshore bank accounts were a little more problematic, but we had our liaison team working that angle with Lichtenstein. We put out a BOLO on Lewis and alerted the Port Authority and TSA, which would cover his possible escape routes. Customs and Border Patrol were notified, and his passport was flagged. He wouldn't get far, and he definitely wouldn't be able to leave the country.

What I got out of all that was a little redemption. If Lewis was in any way innocent, he wouldn't have run. Technically, he was still in charge and could have easily blustered his way through any accusations. At least until the evidence piled up. But running sure made him look guilty to everyone else. With no easy access to money and no legal way out of the country, we were hoping to keep him somewhat contained.

Smith filled me in on what his agents had uncovered and with what I'd added, it had all clicked into place.

"The association with Black appears to have started years ago like we thought, when Lewis was a junior grade lieutenant," Smith said, "before he crossed over and became an agent. It's a mite convoluted so stay with me. I'll try to cut out the fluff."

"Please do. Can we grab some coffee first? I'm running on fumes."

We walked back to the galley and this time, I decided it warranted a fresh pot. I made sure there wasn't any brake fluid or chlorine in the pot before I hit the button. And while that was doing its thing, we sat in the deserted galley and Smith started his story.

"Back then, Lewis was in charge of fisheries enforcement, and Black's operation was in its fledgling status. Black had control of a fleet of thirty or so fishing vessels, homeported in Palacios, a couple of hours up the coast. Each of these fishing vessels was required by law to operate on a quota system. This was supposed to protect the oceans from overfishing of any one species."

I got up to check on the coffee. It wasn't ready yet, so I leaned back on the counter.

"When the fishing boat had filled their allotted quota, even if the hold wasn't full, they had to head to port to offload. You can imagine this led to some disgruntled fisherman and loss of livelihood."

I nodded. The coffee maker finally beeped. I poured myself a big steaming mug and added some powdered creamer. "Want some?"

"Sure. Black. I don't like that powdered stuff."

"Don't blame you. Here," and I put a mug in front of him and sat back down.

"Where was I? Oh, yes, anyway, what Black was doing was this. If you have a quota to catch a plentiful fish, let's say red snapper. What Black was doing was calling everything his boats caught as red snapper, whatever it was. Tilefish, grouper, yellowfin, whatever, it was all logged as red snapper."

I took a sip of coffee, blowing the steam. "Isn't there a system to prevent that?"

"Of course there is. You have to report the catch to NOAA and the wholesaler of the catch has to report what he gets. There are random spot inspections, Coast Guard boarding's, and so on. It's supposed to prevent the overfishing of species that aren't so prevalent."

"Okay. I'm with you, but I don't see how this involves Lewis, though," I said.

"I'm getting to that. For all his other foibles, Black isn't stupid. He got around all those checks and balances by owning the wholesaler, which, might I add, is also illegal. His captains loved this system of Black's because they could stay out and fish for days until their holds were full. No more coming back half empty because the quota had been reached. When they offloaded at Black's wholesaler, he'd pay the captains at the red snapper rate, which was more than they would get for a quota and then he'd turn around and sell whatever the real species of fish were for full price to a fish broker, usually for cash. He made millions doing this. He even had a TSA agent paid off so he could fly the cash out of the country."

He took a swig of coffee. "And this is where that young lieutenant comes in. We never would have figured this out, but the investigative work you and Carter have done put us on the right track," a pang went through my heart at the mention of

Jess, "and it wasn't too difficult with the other agents working on it to get to the truth. As you know, the Coast Guard does random fishery boarding's and verifies at sea that the catch is good, within quotas and so on."

I nodded. "I think I know where this is going."

"Good, I won't get into the weeds then. So, Lewis was the commander of a small cutter that did boarding's. He'd purposely avoid boarding any of Black's boats, and Black would pay him a stipend. If another cutter was on patrol and he couldn't warn Black in time and one of his boats was boarded, when Lewis got ashore, he'd doctor the boarding reports to make everything look kosher. We believe that's how Lewis got involved initially. It probably didn't happen overnight. You know we don't make much money, especially junior Coasties. Maybe Lewis had a gambling debt or was maxed on credit. Who knows? Those are the details we'll run down later."

I shrugged. "It happens."

"Anyway, by the time Black moved into the more profitable gunrunning business, Lewis was already used to the wealthy lifestyle and just sunk deeper. Once in, it's hard to get out. Maybe Lewis didn't want to. Maybe he was scared he'd end up as fish food. Once Black has his hooks in you, pun intended, it's tough to get out."

"Man, I can't believe no one's caught up to him until now. It's been years."

"Every time we get close to Black, as you know, the informant seems to get cold feet or disappears. Like I said, Black's smart. Until now. He made a mistake with Willis, and it was enough for us to get a foot in the door." He hesitated and I could see he was deliberating if he should tell me something or not.

"Go on," I said. "I can take it."

"I like you, Frank. But you have to admit, until a few days ago, you had one foot out the door. Lewis knew this, which was why he assigned you, I think, assuming you'd do a half-assed job. He knew Carter's rep too and figured you'd be pissed enough you'd want to get done with the case and rid of her as quick as you could. It backfired on him, of course."

I sipped my coffee and mulled over what he'd said. It rubbed me the wrong way, but I had to admit, he was probably right. I *was* thinking about packing it all in. But that felt like a lifetime ago now. Almost like a different person.

"I hope you can see that's changed now," I said.

"I know it has. You're like the old Frank Dalton." He slumped in his chair and yawned.

"Tobias," I said. He looked up at me, bleary-eyed. "You should go home, get some rest."

"No. No, I can't. I...I failed her, Frank. It was on my watch. I failed." He looked down at his hands.

"Hey," I said. He looked up. "No one could have predicted what that nutter was going to do. I mean, Jesus, this all happened in the space of a few days."

"I hear what you're saying. Thanks. But ultimately, it's still my responsibility...No, I can't leave. I'm going to use the ready room here and rack out. If anything happens...you should go, though."

I weighed the pros and cons of staying here. I was tired, too. Honestly, there wasn't anything I could do. We were in a holding pattern, circling the same strip of ocean over and over, waiting for something, anything, to appear so we could change course.

"I'm going to go home, get a fresh change of clothes," I said. "Maybe I'll think of something. If anything happens, call me."

"You know I will. Likewise?"

"Sure."

I headed out and headed home to *Serenity*. I needed to change. I'd washed my face as best I could and changed out of my Deacon encrusted clothes into coveralls, but still, I needed to shower.

I ran the water hot, scalding, trying to sear the skin off my body, to feel pain, to lose myself for a moment. When the water ran cold, I got out and toweled off, moving to the bed. It seemed like weeks since Jessica had been here, helping me get dressed, making love.

Everywhere my eyes touched reminded me of her. A hairbrush, an item of clothing carelessly left in a corner. I spiraled into despair, my heart banging against my ribs, feeling lightheaded. I couldn't afford the self-pity. I couldn't afford the emotion. It was crippling. I sat down and took some deep breaths, centering myself. The emotions would have to stay deep down for now. I needed a clear head and control. I closed my eyes and pushed the last lingering thoughts of *what if's* and *what could be's* out with every exhalation, breathing in positivity and focus with every inhalation. I could do this.

Twenty-Five

A few minutes more of deep breathing and I had myself under control. I dressed and walked over to Pete's. I didn't need a drink, but I needed the company. Anything was better than sitting around worrying about Jessica.

As I pushed open the door, I saw the bar was more crowded than usual, bar stools all occupied. I stood on the precipice, unsure. I'd called earlier to let Pete know I was coming, and he told me he had someone I should meet. I wanted to talk to Pete but wasn't sure if I could do crowds. Thankfully, Pete spotted me and motioned me to the back, where the sole booth was. Decision made.

I walked over and saw an older gentleman already there. He was sitting with remarkable posture, an amber-colored liquor in front of him with no ice. Probably bourbon or whiskey. Pete introduced us.

"Admiral? This is Special Agent Frank Dalton. Frank, this is Admiral Jones, the man I was telling you about," Pete said.

We shook hands. He had a firm grip and dry hands. I looked at him and immediately felt I could trust him. He had steely gray eyes and a prominent nose. Although older in years, he still had a full head of hair, black but heavily streaked with silver, cut in a tight buzz. If I didn't know who he was, he would be easy to peg as ex-military or law enforcement.

"Pleased to meet you, Frank," he said, "I haven't been an admiral to any that care about that sort of thing for a few years now. And I've told you before, Pete, call me Robert."

Pete shrugged. "Old habits die hard, sir," he said.

Jones nodded. "Please sit, both of you."

We squeezed into the booth and got comfortable. I abstained from a drink when Pete offered. Jones leaned toward me.

"Pete has told me about your particular predicament, Frank. Are there any new developments?"

If it was anyone other than Pete that had been telling people about my situation, I would have been annoyed, but I trusted him, and in my world that meant I could trust the admiral. I went ahead and told him about the recent deaths and brought him up to speed.

"And we've alerted the relevant authorities to be on the lookout for Lewis," I said.

Jones looked pained and swilled the whiskey around in his glass. He'd been patient while I narrated the story, limiting his questions to a few succinct points. He looked at me thoughtfully.

"You know, I knew your SAC. I didn't know him well mind, but the Guard is so small you either know someone or know someone who knows someone. I was in the latter group. I'd heard some rumblings a few years ago before I got out of the service, but nothing anywhere near like this, like what you told me. It fills me with a deep sadness someone could bring such discredit upon the Coast Guard. It seems almost impossible that he's gotten away with it for so long."

You're telling me. "We're conducting an internal review. There's a possibility Lewis wasn't the only one. It looks like he's been on Black's payroll for many years."

Jones sat back and looked lost in his thoughts. I took that opportunity, made my excuses and went to use the head. When I came back, it was evident Pete and Jones had been talking.

"Frank, the admiral wants to make you an offer. I think you should consider it carefully before you answer."

"I'm sure Pete has mentioned," Jones said, as I sat back down. "I now run a security firm. I have at my disposal a well-trained, elite team, made up of various ex-special forces members. All hold top-secret clearances, and all of them have been tried and tested in the field. I work primarily with the DOD, but sometimes we're called on to perform operations that, shall we say, couldn't be seen to be handled by our government."

I nodded, unsure of where this was going. Pete slid out to get me another glass of water and to sling a few drinks for patrons. He probably didn't want to hear all of this, either.

"I'm deeply concerned your unit has been compromised," Jones said. "From what you and Pete have told me, and from what I could find out at short notice, you may be right that you have more than one mole. It strikes me as odd in this day and age of modern technology, counterterrorism, and so on, that Black could remain in the wind. He must have had or still have some outside help. What I'm proposing to you is you consider using my team for an extraction should you find actionable intelligence on where your Carter may be. Naturally, we would keep this in-house and would need your assurance there would be no interference from the Coast Guard. That's unacceptable and nonnegotiable."

I wasn't so sure about that last part. "So, you're asking me to keep this quiet?"

Jones nodded. "I know it's a hard decision. But if it were to come out that I was granting a favor, it wouldn't look good. And, it especially wouldn't look good if we have to take out a few of these cretins. Should the Coast Guard show up, they'd be forced to try to take my men into custody. That wouldn't go down well, and I don't want to be put in that position. So. It has to be this way, and with a potential mole still in your department somewhere, we can't afford to tip Black off. It's up to you how you play it later, but you cannot mention us. We weren't there."

The offer was tempting. But risky. "And if it should go wrong?"

Jones shrugged. "We still weren't there. But we don't lose. And my team doesn't have a mole."

Ouch. I leaned forward, meeting Jones' steely gray eyes. "Why are you doing this for me?"

"I'm not," he said evenly. "I'm doing it as a favor to Pete. I owe him one. I'm also doing it for your agent. The Coast Guard was good to me. I want to help in any way I can."

I didn't respond, thinking. Jones stood up to leave and put a hand in his pocket. "Here," he said. "This is my card. Call me if you need assistance. You merely have to tell me you're in, and I can have my operative's mobile within minutes. I'll put them on standby now, just in case."

I took the card. On it was a name and a number. Maybe this was an option. If... "One more question, sir. If and when I call you, I want to be in on the operation. I want to be there when we rescue her."

Jones looked thoughtful. "I can't answer that. I'll not have the operation jeopardized by a love-sick puppy."

It was Montoya all over again. "Now hold on a—"

Jones held up his hand. "But I will put your request to my operations chief. It'll be a go, or no go, from him. That's as far as I'm prepared to stretch."

There wasn't much I could do. Damn. "Very well."

We shook hands, and Jones left, walking with the same posture as he had sat, upright and assured. I knew I could trust him, but I still wasn't sure his team was the best option. It almost felt like I was hiring someone from *The Expendables.* Pete came back while I was still sitting in the booth, mulling the conversation over. The bar had emptied some while we were talking, and he wasn't as busy.

"Are you sure I can't get you a drink?" Pete said. "One shot of something. It might help you sleep."

"No thanks. Listen, I'm going to get going. And buddy," I gave Pete a big hug, wrapping my arms around him. "Thank you. For everything."

He slapped me on the back. "Always."

I walked back to *Serenity.* I wasn't tired, wasn't sure what I was going to do. I was at a dead end in the hunt for Jessica and it was killing me. I was hoping that doing something normal would let my subconscious pick up on a clue my active mind may have overlooked or dismissed. Something to calm me.

I eventually hit the rack. It was a restless night. I kept imagining what was happening to Jessica. It wasn't anything good. I awoke early, before first light. I wasn't going to get any more sleep. I knew I couldn't go back to normal, not until Jessica was found. I obsessively checked my phone while I was making coffee, getting dressed, taking a shower. I was paranoid I'd miss a call or text, or my reception or Wi-Fi would suddenly stop working.

I couldn't delay any longer and went to work. Smith looked like hell. He hadn't shaved. His clothes looked rumpled.

"Anything?" I said.

He shook his head. "Nothing. Except for this fax that showed up right before you walked in," he said, hiding a smile and handing it to me.

I took it. "What is it...?" And then I started to read. It was a departmental fax from Doc Hutchins. She'd faxed over the preliminary results from some fibers she'd taken from the Jane and John Does in the morgue. She'd also written she'd emailed, under secure password-protected files, the full results.

I went to log onto a computer and look at the results, but Tobias stopped me. "Here," he said, "I already got them."

I took the sheaf of papers from him, looked for somewhere to sit down and fell heavily with a bone-numbing weariness into the nearest chair. I scanned the several sheets of paper, trying to work around the doctoral terms.

"This is good?" I said, not completely understanding.

"Yes, it's good, Frank. It means we have something we can work with. After I saw this email, I walked over to Mark's assistant in DOMEX. I told him this was a top priority."

"What did he find out?"

"We know where she is, Frank. We know."

When I let go of my breath, I realized I'd been holding it in. My stomach flipped, and a glimmer of hope raced through me. We knew where she was.

It was going to be a close thing. Thanks to the work of Doc Hutchins, we had a break in the case, a huge break. The fibers she found were so small they couldn't be seen with the naked eye, but they were taken from scrapings under the fingernails and various other parts of the body that held onto transferred particulate. The fibers had been sent to a forensic lab, but because of their backlog, and the fact they were labeled as Jane and John Does, there was no rush on the analysis. The results had shown up in an unassuming email to the ME, without a follow-up phone call. As soon as she realized what it could mean, she'd sent over the fax, the secure email to us and followed up with a phone call to Tobias to ensure he had them.

DOMEX had linked those samples with the ones we'd brought back from the freighter we had boarded a few days ago in Ingleside, *The Bold Endeavor*. I should have known. It made perfect sense now. Deacon had said *two* ships. Here we were assuming he was talking about the two fish tenders like the one Deke worked on, because we were so wrapped up in the knowledge that they could freeze fish...and people. What idiots. But again, with hindsight. The *Bold Endeavor* could carry frozen products in refrigerated containers and would do so all the time, back and forth to the Caymans. It had been staring me in the face the whole time.

We were going to divert the *Glorious* to board the vessel as they were the nearest CG asset, but they still wouldn't intercept for about thirty-two hours.

That amount of time was an eternity. I imagined, or rather tried not to imagine, what could happen to Jess in thirty-two hours. I needed to get there now, not a day and a half later. All I could think of was that she was holding out hope, minute after minute, and we weren't there. And waiting for the *Glorious* was like waiting for a slow boat to China.

The other issue was, and this was hard to say, but I didn't know if the *Glorious* could handle a situation like this. It wasn't a normal boarding, it was a suspected terrorist, gun runner, drug smuggler, and kidnapper.

"Tobias, don't we have anything quicker? Or can't we get, I don't know, a Navy ship or something? Can't we fly Montoya's team down there? What about a SEAL team? Isn't that what they do?"

"I'm working on trying to get some more assets down there, Frank. I know the *Glorious* isn't the fastest, but she'll get there. I've already tried to get Montoya's team down there, but it's a no-go. And I doubt we'll get the authorization to send a SEAL team in. It's another sovereign nation's vessel. They won't mount an op with the limited intel we have."

"But will the *Glorious* get there in time?"

"I hope so, Frank. I hope so."

With that thought, I slipped away and called Admiral Jones and gave him the word. His team would take off in a company jet and land in the Caymans. From there, they would use a high-speed launch to intercept the freighter. The timing shouldn't be an issue. If everyone kept the same course and speed, the admiral's group should be there and gone practically a whole day before the *Glorious* even showed up.

I asked the admiral if I could go. He said his team was willing to let me accompany them on the jet and the small boat, but when they boarded the freighter, they wanted me to stay put until they secured the ship. We were expecting to take some heavy fire on this one, what with Black in the arms trade. I told him that was okay with me.

I'd agreed to any restrictions they imposed just so I could get there, but I wasn't going to stay put. The tricky thing was convincing Smith I was going to disappear for a couple of days without him wondering why. I felt awful lying to him, especially after all the work he'd done to expose Lewis, but Jess was forefront in my thoughts. He knew I'd want to know what was going on and the only way I could do that, short of getting on the cutter, which wasn't going to happen, was to be in the command post.

I had to come up with something convincing, something where he wouldn't be suspicious.

"Tobias. Where's the *Glorious* going after they rescue Jessica?" I said.

"They'll head for St. Thomas. It's the closest US port. We can get Carter back on a flight from there quicker than any other way."

And there I had it. "I'm flying down to St. Thomas then. I want to be there when she gets in."

"Frank, be reasonable. What if she isn't on the vessel?" He looked at me. I gave him my best beseeching Boy Scout look. "Oh, what the hell. Go. Let me know when you get there. We'll get some orders cut to cover expenses."

"Thanks, Tobias." That solved my immediate problem, but once we had Jessica, I'd have to figure out how I suddenly happened to be on the freighter. I put that thought out of my mind for now and got myself out to the private section of Corpus Christi airport where I was to meet the admiral's people.

The Lear jet had seating for twelve, plus pilot and co-pilot. There were ten operatives. I made eleven. I sat in the back by myself. Apparently, after the initial meet and greet, everybody had their way of prepping for a mission and that didn't involve me. I was good with that. It gave me a chance to think things over. These guys were in an entirely different class from our enforcement guys. It was no disrespect to our guys, but the ones on this plane were just different. They looked like they'd all seen a lot of action. The weapons they carried seemed to be more of a personal choice than issued gear. They did all have one thing in common though. They all wore black, even their faces were blacked out, and when the cabin lights were dimmed after takeoff, I could have sworn the plane was empty. No noise, no light, no reflections, no flash of skin to give them away. It was eerie.

TWENTY-SIX

When we touched down, I lifted my head with a start as the wheels hit the runway. Drool had oozed down my chin, and I swiped at my face with my hand. I hadn't realized I'd fallen asleep. With the restless night, the stress, the dark, and the constant white noise, uninterrupted without annoying announcements to put up your tray table, I had dozed off.

I worked the crick out of my neck and looked at my watch. We'd been in the air for around three hours. Grand Cayman has one international airport, but we'd landed on the other side of the island in a disused but well-kept private runway. I took a deep breath, levered myself out of the seat and followed the silent troops down the stairway and off the plane.

On the rough tarmac, I took a last look behind me at the jet, hoping I'd see it again soon. Up ahead were two dark vans and one of the guys pointed me to the second van, so I got in that one. I sat in the back again, out of the way. The less they thought I was a hindrance, the more they'd forget I was tagging along. At least, that was my plan. I could tell from the glances a couple of them gave me, they'd have sooner dropped me out of the plane and picked me up again on the way back, but they had their orders like everyone else.

We drove to a secure facility co-opted by the admiral's company. It was still dark, but I could just make out the narrow road, palm trees dotted along the side of the single-lane road. The driver was pushing the speed limit but somehow able to see perfectly well, always dodging potholes, well most of them, it was an island. Once through the facility security checkpoint, we made a beeline for the dock. Bright lights lit up two boats, both about forty-five feet in length.

The boats were already prepped and running, the coxswains ready at the helm. I was silently motioned to one of the two vessels. They looked like the Coast Guard's 45 RB-M, except these were all black, and were painted with some sort of goop I imagined reduced radar reflection.

The coxswain of my boat introduced himself. At least this guy was talking to me. Maybe he hadn't gotten the memo. It was a bit of a relief after so long without words. I didn't like to be wrapped up in my head that long. Especially now.

"Special agent?" he said. "My name is Foster. The admiral said to make sure you were kept in the loop."

"Good evening, Foster, on a night like this, you should call me Frank."

"Sure thing, Frank. On a night that's not like this, do I still call you Frank?"

I liked this guy. "It'll work," I smiled. "What's your story?"

"The name's Aaron. Don't you worry, sir. I know where you're coming from. I used to be in the Guard before I got out. I was a boatswain's mate second class. I've been working for the admiral ever since, well, for the last few years, anyway." Foster didn't look a day over thirty, so he must have signed up at an early age. He continued, "So you know, we've been keeping tabs on both the vessels of interest, the freighter and the *Glorious*. The freighter has slowed some, which makes our trip out a little longer, but the *Glorious* will still be quite some time before they show up. We'll be long gone."

I felt a small thrill of excitement and trepidation. We almost had them. "Let's get them," I said. Foster leaned out of the cabin window and shouted to his crew. "Clear line one."

"Line one, aye. Line clear," came the reply from the crewmember forward.

"Clear line four," Foster shouted.

"Line four, aye. Line clear. All lines clear," the crewmember at the stern said.

Foster gunned the engines, the Rolls Royce jet drives responded immediately, burbling smoothly, and he set an intercept course for the freighter. Our ETA was about two hours at twenty-seven knots, the cruising speed for this Coast Guard Response Boat clone. Maybe it was one originally. I was glad of the efficiency of the boat, crew, and the operatives who were now slumped down in the cabin chairs.

I walked out to the well deck, careful to avoid the warm sea spray. I didn't feel like getting wet right now. For what it was worth, it was a beautiful night. The speed of the boat blew away the Caribbean humidity, and the moon was waning, which would be good for the op. I saw a shooting star and made a wish, similar to the one I'd made that night with Jessica. Funny how that felt so long ago.

I didn't know what to expect. I had no idea what condition we'd find Jessica in, but we had a medic on the team for immediate triage. I hadn't yet come up with a plausible reason why I would be here and not in St. Thomas. Hopefully, it would come to me. I was both nervous and excited about what was coming. Excited I could finally see Jess again, nervous we might be too late.

After a brief reverie, Foster called me in. "Sir, we're picking up the *Bold Endeavor* on the radar. She's cruising at about six knots, so the boarding should be seamless."

"About that," I said. "This isn't my usual game, but I'm assuming they're not going to just lower the gangway or a Jacob's ladder and welcome us aboard. How do we get on?"

"That's those guy's problem," he said, gesturing to the operatives. "I just drive the boat. What I've usually seen, though, is we'll make a wide turn and come up from their stern. Lookouts on vessels usually look out to see where they're going, not what's coming up behind them. Their radar shouldn't pick us up either. We'll look like background clutter as the boats have been coated with anti-reflective paint. What we'll do is come up close. If there are any unfriendlies on the stern, we'll take them out, and then use a pneumatic grappling hook with an attached line. There are usually plenty of places on the stern the hook can grab onto, and then they climb aboard. I understand you'll be staying with the boat, so we back off until we get the all-clear."

"Yeah. I'm not okay with that plan, though. I want to get on the freighter."

Foster looked at me. "I don't know about that, sir. You'd have to clear it through Wardwell, the lead tactical guy. Did you talk to him?"

"No, not yet. I'll have to do that," I said. Fat chance. I was getting on that boat one way or another.

"He's sitting behind us, but better hurry. Okay, contact in two minutes," Foster announced. When I turned around to look at the guys, expecting them to still be shaking off sleep, or still slumped over, they surprised me as they were all standing on the well deck, weapons ready. I hadn't heard them move, nor even the door opening.

I walked out with them, making a show of looking for Wardwell, and was gradually able to make out the shape of the freighter ahead in the darkness. They were running with all the proper complement of lights on, so they weren't trying to hide. Or maybe they were trying to look innocent. The lead boat slowed speed to match the speed of the freighter and we matched that, staying back about two hundred feet.

I saw a man-sized shape on the deck of the *Bold Endeavor*, clearly carrying some sort of automatic rifle and I was about to shout a warning to the lead boat somehow, but the figure crumpled and pitched into the sea. They obviously didn't need my help.

I couldn't see exactly what was going on. They hadn't offered me any night vision goggles. I was, however, well-armed and had the foresight to bring my Kevlar vest with me.

In short order, the guys from the first boat made it on board. The plan was for them to find cover until everyone was on board.

I knew satellite images showing us the heat signatures of all those aboard were beamed directly to Wardwell, but it wouldn't show us if someone was deep inside a hold, or in the bilges, possible places Jessica could be imprisoned.

Our boat moved into position. One... two... three... on board. I positioned myself in the last spot. Everyone was too focused on the boat to notice. "I'll untie the grappling line for you once you're aboard, so we can clear out," I said to the fifth guy.

He nodded. Four on board, five on board, and as soon as he reached the freighter, I launched myself up the line as quickly as I possibly could. Luckily, each team member was finding cover and paid me no mind. I came over the stern onto the deck, keeping as silent as I could. Number five saw me and violently gestured for me to get back. I shrugged, ignored him and found cover. I saw him press a finger to his throat mike, no doubt telling Wardwell what I'd done.

I didn't care. I wouldn't put anyone's life in danger, but I needed to be here. I let them creep forward, only hand signals from now on.

The plan was essentially the same one Montoya and his people had used. Secure the bridge and communications stations, secure the engine room, corral the crew on the stern and then do a systematic search for Jessica.

While I was reviewing the plan in my head, a crewmember passed near where one operative was hidden. He stopped to light a cigarette, the match flaring, a machine gun slung over his shoulder. The operative used the moment when the crewmember was temporarily blinded by his flaring match to take him down. He silently dragged him backward, and in a quick motion, snapped his neck. He shoved him behind a crate, and I quietly followed. Two bad guys down.

Five members of the team entered the superstructure and climbed the stairs to the bridge. I couldn't see what was going on, didn't have a radio or anything, but when the guys moved forward, I followed in their footsteps quietly and rapidly. They moved in a piggyback motion, one person moving forward while the other covered. I was kind of stuck looking out for myself. Up ahead, as the first two passed a bulkhead, a door popped open, and another crewmember came out.

"Assiz? It is your watch. Assiz, you idiot, where are—" He caught sight of one of our guys and simultaneously tried to bring his rifle up to shoot, use his radio and retreat through the door. In his clusterfuck rush to do everything at once, he achieved nothing, and a silenced round burst through his throat, blood spraying in an arc, surging in time with his beating heart. As he sank to his knees, gurgling through the frothy, foaming blood coming out of his mouth and neck, another operative kicked him in the head to seal his fate. Three down. I wondered how many there were. The crew didn't appear to be particularly professional. I hoped it stayed that way.

We pressed on. The guys on the bridge radioed all secure. No casualties and no shots fired. There were only three people on watch on the bridge, so that was quickly taken care of.

I followed as we weaved in and out of containers stacked two and three high, each container made of steel and forty feet long by ten feet high. If they were keeping Jessica in a container, it could take a while to find her. About amidships, we came to a sort of clearing. A row of containers flanked the port and starboard sides of the vessel, leaving a space in the middle, away from prying eyes. Aha.

I tapped the man in front of me on the shoulder and motioned I wanted to talk and needed them to slow down and stop for a second. After the message was passed, the group of five agents huddled around with me in the middle. We crouched down close to a container to provide cover and security. Three of the five were facing outboard to protect our flanks, continuously monitoring the area.

"Make it quick," one of them said. I could tell they were annoyed I'd snuck on.

I motioned them in closer. "Those containers over there." I pointed at the ones in the middle. The containers in the middle were stacked two high, but arranged in a rough circle. "I don't know how many container ships you've been on, but there's no way a ship would have rigged them for passage from Corpus like that. It's a useless waste of space, and if they should hit rough weather, they'll fall overboard."

The operative caught on quickly. "If it's a circle, that means there's some space in the middle."

"Exactly. These are standard forty-foot containers, so you'd have to figure the circumference is about two hundred feet, give or take, the way they're overlapping. Stacked two high, makes them about twenty feet tall. There has to be a reason they would be like this. They may be trying to hide something. This isn't a regular stow plan."

"Okay. We'll check it out." He hesitated, and said, "I'm still not happy you're here, but thanks for the intel. The name's Wardwell."

Wardwell gave quick orders, and in a few movements, three of his team had scaled the containers and lay prone on top.

Wardwell held his left ear. "Team reports there's one, approximately twenty-foot, single stacked container in the middle of this circle formation."

"That has to be it," I said. "That has to be where they're keeping her."

He nodded and pressed his fingers to his throat mike, radioing instructions to his team. The three prone team members dropped down from atop the containers into the clearing. The next few moments felt like forever. I wanted to be on the other side of these damn containers, but there was no way for me to scale them.

There was still something bugging me, something else that didn't make sense. I walked cautiously around the containers, away from the team. I was mindful of the danger posed on board the ship, and I had my gun held loosely at my side, safety off, finger outside the trigger. What was it? What was bugging me? I stopped, crouched down and turned, some internal Spidey sense tingling. I was about fifty feet away, just over a container's length from Wardwell. Then, just as one of the sealed container doors cracked open right in front of me, I figured out what it was that was bothering me.

I felt like slapping my forehead with my hand. There had to be a way in. You wouldn't build a fortress of containers and not have a way in.

The door, the one in front of me, slowly inched open on well-oiled hinges. It was sheer dumb luck I was in the right place. I saw Jimmy's fat gut squeeze out first, followed a half second later by the rest of him, and then Ricky appeared. If there was ever any doubt we were on the wrong ship, it was immediately and irrevocably erased as their two ugly heads looked around, blinking in the darkness. They carefully stood up and took aim at Wardwell and his partner, still crouching where I had left them, not noticing me lurking in the shadows.

"Hey!" I said. "Fuckers! Over here." I didn't give Ricky a chance to turn more than a quarter before I shot him. I turned my aim to Jimmy, but my warning shout had got the attention of Wardwell, and Jimmy was soon leaking blood like a slapped mosquito.

I raced through the container door the two fishermen had opened and ran inside the container. A crude hole was cut through the sheet metal of the container, leading the way to the inner sanctum.

I carefully poked my head through the hole, not wanting friendlies to shoot me. The three operatives were exiting the twenty-foot container in the middle. They motioned me over.

"It looks like she was in here, sir," one of them said. "Or at least someone was, but there's no sign of her now."

My heart came crashing down. Switching on my flashlight, I entered. It reeked inside. Reeked of fear and sweat. I saw the makeshift torture chamber, crude chains hanging from a beam that matched the photo Black had sent me. There was blood on the floor. Not a lot, but enough. I hoped it wasn't Jessica's.

I wanted to collapse on the floor of the container. Curl up and cry. But I couldn't. Jessica was still out there somewhere. She still needed me. Not until I was certain she was dead would I ever give up the search.

The rest of the crew were rounded up and interrogated. They all pretended they knew nothing. Still at large were Black, George and Lewis, if he was with them. God help them when I catch them.

I walked back toward the bridge and into the captain's office. The captain of the *Bold Endeavor* was seated at his desk, hands secured in front of him. The same captain from before.

"Remember me? Where's Black," I said.

He ignored me for a moment and shrugged.

I slapped him in the face as hard as I could. "Listen, you pig fucker, I don't think you realize the situation you're in. We know how the guns were smuggled, and we've figured out how the missing people were frozen. Inside refrigerated containers, the anhydrous ammonia would freeze them, then the reefers would keep them extra chill. Very clever. We'll have a forensics team on soon, and the evidence will be conclusive. You, my friend, are going down for a very, very, long time." I leaned forward on his desk and looked him right in his eyes. "There won't be any lawyers for you, no protection, no trial, no rest, no escape."

The captain returned my stare. "I am international shipping cap-it-an. Protect-ed by international law. And you are not in US waters. Your threats," he shrugged. "They are idle. You do not frighten me."

I smiled, my mouth wide, exposing my teeth, garish. "I think you're forgetting one small thing, captain." I spat out the word. "You're now a terrorist, as is Black and his entire operation. So let me think." I tapped my fingers on his desk. His eyes flickered to them and then back to my face, gauging me. "Where do we send terrorists we capture? Hmm." I could see the light dawning like the early morning sun in his eyes. "That's right. You've got it now. That little slice of heaven in Cuba called Guantanamo Bay. You'll rot in there forever. Is that worth it, huh? Is it worth it to protect Black?" I slammed my fists down on the table, making his ashtray jump half an inch. "Is it?"

I walked out and slammed the cabin door, letting him stew for a minute. And myself. My anger hadn't been fake. I went to the galley and made myself relax, poured a cup of thick, black coffee, the spoon nearly standing up on end.

I didn't say anything when I came back in, merely walked over to the large cabin window and looked out, sipping my coffee, letting the aroma fill up the room. It didn't take long for him to bite.

"When you say Guantanamo Bay..." he said. "You are serious?"

I nodded. His eyes filled with fear. He tried to reach for a cigarette on his desk, some foul-looking Turkish blend. I walked over and knocked the pack out of his hands, cigarettes scattering, several rolling onto the floor.

"You might as well quit now. You won't be getting those where you're going," I said.

He stood up. "You cannot talk to me this way. I am not a US Citizen, and we are not on US soil when the vessel owners hear of this—"

"Sit down and cut the shit. I *can* talk to you this way. I *am* talking to you this way. Don't for one second think the owners of this boat are going to support terrorism, support you. They'll drop you so fast it'll make your head spin...give up Black. Once we have him, we can talk about what happens to you. It can be bad," I shrugged and gave him an olive branch. "Maybe it can be not so bad."

I could see his mind ticking over, processing the information. "Bad I know. What is not so bad?"

"Perhaps you can still be a captain? But you'll be banned from the US."

"So. No more America?"

"And no Guantanamo," I growled.

He shrugged. "Okay. I tell you. First though. My cigarettes? Yes?"

I pushed them across to him, helped him light one, figured the gesture might help.

He took a drag and said, "He has an island. Small. Not far from here. A launch picked him up a few hours before you got here. Took him, that crazy George person, and the girl."

I stiffened. "What was her condition?"

He shrugged again. "I am no doctor."

"Tell me how she was, dammit. Or we can revisit our deal."

"She was alive. That is all I saw." He lifted his hands in supplication.

I raised my hand as if to smack him again. He scooted back in his seat and hurriedly said, "I do not know, truly. I only saw her from a distance. She was walking by herself. She did not appear hurt. Her hands were tied behind her."

Oh, thank God, she's alive. My knees almost gave out at the news, but I still didn't have her back yet. I motioned him to a chart of the area, and he showed us where the island was. Wardwell called in for satellite reconnaissance, and we figured we could be there via our boats in about an hour. We made the remaining crew, the guys that weren't terrorists but deckhands and engineers, set the anchor, and when it was safely secured in the depths below, we locked them all in the medical office, the only lockable and sterile place on board that would fit them all.

Wardwell told me he wasn't pleased with me disobeying the order to stay put, but he appreciated the insight he'd given the team, so he'd think about my role when we got to the island.

The *Glorious* was still en route, with an ETA of about twelve hours. By that time, this should all be over one way or another. Hold on, Jess. I'm coming.

TWENTY-SEVEN

We were back on our two vessels, with zero casualties. The crew of the freighter was locked up, so they couldn't warn anybody. I was in the lead boat now, having passed some sort of test. Wardwell must have done his thinking quickly, and the group decided I might be more of an asset than a liability.

The coxswain turned into the waves and increased speed to thirty-eight knots, faster now we had a following sea. Wardwell hunkered down and gave us a quick brief of the upcoming operation. We didn't know what we were getting ourselves into, but had to assume this was Black's hideout and command bunker. He wasn't expecting any trouble, but he had to know he was on everyone's radar. So he'd have lookouts posted, maybe dogs and alarms.

We made good time to the island, and it was still dark when we were within sight of the target, although dawn wouldn't be too far off. For a personally sized island, this thing was immense. I guess crime does pay. Perched atop a small outcrop was a tropical-looking mansion, lit up like Bastille Day or the Fourth of July. Black was not bothered by any thought of secrecy. Which wasn't what we were expecting, but I should have guessed, as he was just that egotistical to think no one knew where he was. Anyway, that was good for us. It meant he didn't know we were coming. Or maybe it said he didn't care? I pushed the thought from my mind.

We were surveying the island from a distance through optics, expecting some reactionary or defense force. If Black could afford an island, he could afford to hire a team to protect him. He had the guns. Either they were way better trained than his regular guys, or he didn't have any, as there wasn't anything obvious.

With the engines of the forty-fives carefully burbling away at a little over idle speed, we approached the island on the darker side, away from the lights and mansion. The aroma of fried shrimp and the occasional faint note of big band music drifted across the water as we made our approach. Maybe a late-night party. The noise could be good cover.

They'd lent me a spare pair of night vision optics so I could see what was going on in the dark, but I still couldn't detect any movement. Our boat went first, paving the way for the other. If we encountered any enemy fire, they would know where to focus.

We didn't meet any resistance and beached our boat, raising the outboards at the last second, and securing the boat via a line to a friendly palm tree in case the tide turned. The tree didn't seem to mind the imposition. We signaled the other team all clear, and once they were beached as well, we moved out in teams of two.

Although I'd been given temporary honorary status, they still made me bring up the rear. I couldn't tell if that was a good thing or not, but the two guys in front of me were constantly monitoring our six, so it was a moot positional point.

We followed what could have been a goat path through the brush, careful to keep the noise to a minimum. We could hear the music getting louder the closer we got. It sounded like he was having a goddamn party. Maybe he was. He'd managed to sneak out of the country. Undoubtedly, he was exceedingly happy with his fat, tubby self.

My mouth twisted into a rictus of a bitter smile. I couldn't wait to get my hands around his fat neck and squeeze. I calmed myself. First, though, we had to get there.

We surged up a small slope, shale and sand falling behind us. Still no resistance. At the top, we lay prone and again assessed the situation. This was a lot for me. I'm more in tune with going in guns blazing, but I appreciated the steady-as-she-goes sentiment.

We couldn't have been more than three hundred yards from the house. For all its vastness, I couldn't but help admire the landscaping and attention to detail. As we had come up on the rear of the house, we could look down into the courtyard and the large pool, everything tastefully chic. My stomach rumbled as the smell of cooked shrimp hit my nostrils again. I could just make out a few scantily clad women frolicking in the pool.

There didn't appear to be any walls surrounding the villa, but there would surely be some motion detectors or floodlights as we got closer. Wardwell signaled for his electronics guy, who crab crawled up to us and hauled a small black box seemingly from nowhere and did his magic, looking through some sort of scope.

I surmised he was scanning the area, and then he held up three fingers. Three minutes? Three guards? Three motion detectors? I wish I knew what their code meant. It was a little like learning to read for the first time, but then being given a book in complicated French. You might stumble around and make the odd correct guess, but that would be sheer dumb luck.

"Motion detectors," Wardwell whispered, seeing my confusion. "He'll set up a jamming signal. Everything's all interconnected these days. Makes our job a whole lot easier."

We crept forward some more, keeping close to the ground. I tripped on some brush and went sprawling. I may have felt like an idiot for a moment, but it saved my life. I never heard the gunshot, more of an overhead echo, and then a *ka-thunk* into a tree behind me.

"Get down," Wardwell shouted to his team, landing in the sand beside me. My heart was pounding in my chest. "Terry, find the sniper," he said, and then to me, "How did you know there was a sniper?" I didn't enlighten him.

Someone, presumably Terry, elbowed his way across the sand, staying low, and set up his rifle. We waited for the shooter to take his next shot. The shooter waited, too. These were professionals. The music had stopped at some point. I'm sure gunfire wasn't on the party menu.

Terry, trying to draw out the sniper, sent out a three-round burst, aiming at the most likely area. One of his shots must have ricocheted off something as a narrow plate-glass window overlooking the entire length of the pool cracked and shattered. I could hear some muffled shouts.

The place lit up around us. Floodlights came on. Shots were thumping into the palm trees above and beside us, shredding foliage. Wardwell said a few things into his throat mike, and the floodlights went out one by one, as they were shot out by Terry. We moved now, the advantage of surprise long gone, having to make the best of it. I hoped Terry had taken out the sniper, but I didn't know for sure. More gunfire erupted from the mansion toward us. We dodged and dove, inching our way to the house. We couldn't afford to be pinned down. It was hard to figure out how many people were shooting at us, and then we heard the high-pitched whine of a drone. That couldn't be good.

"Goddammit, they've got eyes in the sky," Wardwell said.

The drones were too small to take out and too fast, but they were getting a real bird's-eye view. They didn't have the right tech on board to shoot at us. They weren't that kind of drone, but they surely had infrared or night vision. Someone in some control room could see our every move, and these little bastards were too small and too quick to shoot down. What was I saying about technology helping us? Ignore me.

Not having any other choice, we moved closer, some fifty feet from the house now. We were still taking fire, but from the angle we were now to the house, it was harder to get a cleaner shot. I saw a tinted glass door open near the pool and the barrel of a rifle nudged its way out. I patted Wardwell on the shoulder and pointed at the door. Two quick shots later, a human-sized shape slumped against the door and slid down, smearing blood along the glass, the rifle clattering to the floor. This was our chance to get into the house. Signaling his men, Wardwell and I rushed to the door, weaving and zigzagging. Coming up fast against the wall, I flattened my back, and shimmied up to the door, careful there was no one else inside ready to leap out. Confirming it was clear I was about to enter when I heard something skid across the nearby sandbank we had been on and land with an empty oomph.

One of our guys had taken a hit. I could see him trying to crawl toward us, but one of his legs was twisted weirdly.

Without thinking, I ran out, hooked my elbows under his shoulders and backpedaled. I knew this was hurting his leg like a motherfucker, but it sure beat the alternative. I hoped he thought the same thing as I dragged him and his bleeding leg toward the house. He'd passed out by the time I got back to the house, though it was only a few seconds. Probably a good thing. One of the other guys took over, opening his medical kit and giving him a shot of something.

I ran to the door, stepped over the dead bad guy, and almost shot my reflection in the mirror, my finger twitching on the trigger. I hadn't recognized myself. Covered in blood and grime, I looked like some deathly apparition ready to reap vengeance. I took a second to get a grip on myself, calm my raging heartbeat. The reckoning was coming.

Through the door, I found myself in a tiled hallway and, stepping softly, followed it to the kitchen. I could have easily tracked where I was going as the aroma of shrimp was strong down here. As I came through an archway, I heard an ululating scream and a massive meat cleaver swished through the air where my face had just been. The scream gave me enough time to avoid having half my face looking at me from the floor. The guy with the cleaver—June, he was not—ran at me again, a bloody white apron tied around his waist. À la Indiana Jones, I just shot him and dodged out of the way as he crashed into the wall. Score one for the good guys, well me, anyway, too bad about the chef. Those shrimp sure did smell heavenly.

I heard the pitter-patter of almost silent feet behind me, crouched and turned, my gun held in a firing stance. Wardwell skidded to a stop a few feet from me, his gun aimed at me, too. We slowly lowered our weapons.

"Got the drop on you," I said.

Wardwell grinned. "I knew it was you."

We left the kitchen together and went through what looked like a dining room. It didn't appear as if it had been used recently, and dust bunnies skittered around the floor at our feet. We rounded an archway, and I saw a winding staircase leading to an impressive landing. The staircase looked like it was made from marble. I idly wondered how Black had shipped everything here and got it built. There was the occasional sound of suppressed fire from nearby, so I knew the team was still fighting in close quarters.

We moved carefully, as silently as could be managed, shoes occasionally squeaking off the tile floor. I was on the third step up the stairs when I heard a scraping sound from behind me. Instinctively, I stepped to the side and crouched down, turning. George, that goddamned wraith, had a knife to Wardwell's throat. How did that happen so quickly?

"Shoot him," Wardwell gasped, struggling against George's grip.

I took aim but didn't have a clean shot. George was in too tight to Wardwell, using him as a shield. George smiled, the first expression I'd ever seen him have. This couldn't be good. He backed off down a corridor, Wardwell in a tight grip, subdued by the knife, scrambling backward, held in place by George.

Fuck.

I followed.

"George. Don't do this," I said. "Come on, George. I can get you out of this. You can go back to fishing. No one will have to know. I can fix it. You just have to stop now, George. Just stop. It'll be okay."

George kept moving. When he was near the kitchen door, he made his move. He sliced the knife across Wardwell's throat, shoved him toward me, and took off running. Shit.

Training kicked in, and I caught Wardwell, laying him down, applying pressure to his wound. George took off out the kitchen door. Meanwhile, Wardwell was struggling with me, and I had to play the delicate role of applying pressure to his throat to stop the bleeding without actually choking him. He continued to struggle, and then with one great heave, scissor-kicked his legs, bucked me off him and rolled away.

"Fuck. Off me," he said.

"I have to stop the bleeding. You're in shock."

"Not in shock, not bleeding." He sat up and pulled down his collar. There was a slice in the collar, but his neck was clean.

Sweet Jesus. George must have nicked the top of the Kevlar. If he'd tried to stab him, he would have succeeded, but a sideways slash like that and the Kevlar fibers slowed his knife down. Talk about luck.

Wardwell got on the radio and warned his men George was on the loose and most likely coming out the poolside door. I left him to them—Jessica was my priority. We started back up the stairs.

It was quieter on the second floor, at least compared to the chaos outside. "Turn the knob on the side of your night vision goggles two clicks forward," Wardwell said, quietly. "These goggles have a few different settings. They're next-gen goggles."

"Oh wow," I whispered. "You're all red and stuff."

"Yeah. Infrared. We can scan the rooms for heat signatures."

We crept by several empty rooms until the room ahead showed two heat signatures. One stationary, one scurrying to the side. We crept into position, one of us on either side of the door, and signaled to each other. I was to go low and left, Wardwell was to go high and right. If anyone was going to shoot us, they'd probably aim for the center of the door, and we could take them out without getting killed ourselves. At worst, they'd only have time to shoot one of us.

Wardwell took a step or two back and then slammed a booted foot into the door near the lock. It was only a normal house door, nothing fancy, and the wood frame split, the door banging open. We slid in, and I scanned the room. No shots. No one was firing at us. The room was immense and overlooked the ocean. A large king-size bed with red sheets occupied one end of the room through a set of double doors. On the other side of me was a well-stocked bar with a mirrored back, and in front of me were two oversized, comfortable-looking leather armchairs. In one was a disgustingly large fat man wearing a neon green set of velour pajamas. Where does he get this stuff?

On the floor, next to an ashtray that had been knocked over, ash besmirching the carpet was a still smoldering cigar, the thick stank filling up the room. In between the two chairs was a small square table, the tablecloth also on the floor, as well as the remains of two steaks, and two broken wine glasses, the red wine slowly spreading to form a sopping puddle next to the table.

I took all of that in at a glance, but what caught my eye was the thick steak knife jutting out of Black's massive chest. Blood was oozing from the wound.

"Jessica! It's Frank. Where are you?" I said, scanning the rest of the room.

I didn't hear anything. Wardwell went to look around, keeping one eye on the door. I made a beeline for Black. I could tell he was breathing, but shallowly, as his large chest was slowly rising and falling, the knife moving in concert.

I tapped lightly on the knife. Black's eyes shot open with the increased pain. "Where is she, Black? What have you done?"

He gurgled back to me, bubbles of frothy blood mixed with his spittle, his mouth working, but no words coming out. He also looked like he was trying to laugh. I used my left index finger and pressed down on the handle of the knife. It slid into him maybe half an inch, barely at all, but enough, and his laugh-gurgle stopped, the life leaving his eyes, his chest ceasing to heave. I stared at him for a long moment, the bitterness I had coming up as bile, and I spat in his face.

"Fuck you," I said. "Fuck. You." And I spat again, tapping the knife for good measure.

"Frank," Wardwell said, coming out from another room. "You need to get over here."

I followed his voice into the bathroom. In the shower was Jessica, wrapped in steam, sitting on the shower floor, arms around her knees.

I motioned Wardwell out and said softly, "Jessica?"

She didn't move. I opened the shower door and turned the water off. I grabbed a fluffy towel from the rack behind me, noticing it was a sick shade of green. I hated his awful color palette and wrapped the towel around her.

She didn't move, but her eyes flicked to me for a moment.

I stood rooted to the spot. "It's all right," I said. "Black...his crew, they're all dead. You're safe. You don't have to worry anymore."

Nothing. No emotion. She must be in shock. I knelt next to her. "Jess. It's me, Frank."

She didn't reply, just looked through me with a thousand-yard stare, semi-glazed look.

I tried again. "Black. He's dead. I finished it. He's never going to hurt you again," I said.

She paled, her eyes focusing for a moment. "Dead? I thought…"

"It's okay," I said, moving to her again, lightly touching her shoulder. "He can't hurt you anymore."

EPILOGUE

I don't remember how we left the island. Don't remember how we'd gotten back to the boat. It was a blur, a mental block, the mind shutting down to allow for recovery, perhaps the shock of seeing Jessica the way she was, beaten and lost.

Black's death, easy and useless, was almost a disappointment. The cold dish of revenge, once served, was more tepid than expected.

When the haziness cleared, I was sitting in a stiff plastic chair, my back aching, not sure how long I had been sitting, staring across at Jessica, who wasn't moving. She was lying in a hospital bed covered up to her shoulders with crisp white sheets, folded back with stark precision, her arms laying still and lifeless.

A nurse told me we were in a hospital in St. Thomas. Jessica had to be sedated. I beat myself up, sitting in that chair, glad for the discomfort and cramping, a small penance for not finding her sooner.

Different nurses came in from time to time, shifts changing, the hospital always moving forward, time always moving forward, but Jessica and I were stuck in a cocoon of solemn never-ending, never-changing, plastic chair hell. Well, I was in the plastic chair hell; she was in bed, but I'd swap her pain with mine in a heartbeat.

Her vitals were checked, blood pressure pumped and released, heart rate monitored by pocket watches and stethoscope. Notations scribbled with cheap ballpoint pens on a clipboard attached to the foot of her bed. I barely stirred. Jessica didn't move.

She was hooked up to various IVs, filled with clear liquids, some smaller than others, no doubt antibiotics, and pain meds. Her face and shoulders peeked out above the sheets and had some thick bandaging, small nicks, and cuts already healing. I remembered the bruises, the cigarette burns.

I was wallowing deeply in self-pity. I knew it. I could feel it, see it, but I didn't want to move. I felt responsible for this, for Jessica lying here, for what she went through. So, I stayed.

I told them I was her fiancé, not wanting to lie, but needing to know what had happened. She didn't have any family that could visit. Her brother was dead, and her mother with Alzheimer's. I felt someone should know, someone that cared for her. The doctors, hesitant at first, but when no one else arrived, they looked at each other, whispered and shrugged, gave in. It was an island, after all. They told me she hadn't been sexually assaulted, but she had been horrifically abused. They found burn marks, big enough to have been from a cigar, in places only the softest lace should ever have laid. Bruises from repeated beatings, some older, some new. Bruises on top of bruises.

Each bruise punched me deeper in the gut. My melancholy bottomless. They didn't want to send her home. Her injuries weren't life-threatening, but the doctors thought she'd be better off where she was.

The Coast Guard sent a chaplain, which was nice, asked if he could say a prayer. I shrugged. I'd take all the help I could get.

Night changed to day, the tropical light streaming through the blinds. Light fading, moonbeams chasing the sun. I sat through it all. I held her hand, motionless.

"Mr. Dalton? You should get some rest. Jessica is going to be sedated for quite some time," Doctor Adams said. "The mind is a fragile thing. It needs time to heal, as much as if not more than her body. We're constantly monitoring her, and when the time is right, we'll slowly bring her back, make an assessment." He rubbed his face, looked like he wanted to say more, but turned instead and left.

When the time was right, they'd bring her out of it and see if Jessica was still inside, see if the damage was permanent. Prepare yourself, they said. Is there anyone we should call?

Tobias had come to see us. Flown out especially. He was a bit confused as to how I'd ended up where I had, but he acknowledged that perhaps it was better he didn't know. Black was dead, Lewis was exposed, and Carter was found. He was good with that.

Tobias told me the *Glorious* had found George. Once they'd boarded the *Bold Endeavor*, the captain told them the same thing he'd told us, and they made best speed to the island. The *Glorious* had found George slumped over the wheel of Black's boat, puddles of blood seeping through a makeshift bandage.

He said they hadn't found Lewis. Yet. He was still in the wind, but they wouldn't stop looking. Somehow, he must have slipped out of the country. The last intelligence had him somewhere in South America. It was a big place, but he'd surface, eventually. The rat-fuck couldn't hide forever.

Tobias left. Other people came.

They told me to leave, get some rest. They gave me a pamphlet on surviving attacks. What a joke. A pamphlet on how to care for someone who was abused. That one I couldn't read didn't want to, didn't want to admit it happened. I felt reading them would somehow solidify it all, make it less a dream and more like reality. I didn't want this to be the reality. I wanted it to be a dream, needed it to be a dream. Just one fucked up night, surreal and bizarre, and I'd wake up in a cold sweat and shake my head. Drink some coffee, sit in the stern of *Serenity*, laugh at how ridiculous it all was. But no. It wasn't a dream. It wasn't one of those cheesy endings from a high school English class where the ending was a scribbled, 'and then she woke up and it was all a dream.'

Someone brought me a change of clothes when they realized I was never going to leave her side again. Others brought me food. Someone offered me a pullout chair to sleep on. You'll be more comfortable, they said. I didn't move.

I looked out the window and saw palm trees swaying in the island breeze. Couldn't work up the enthusiasm to give a fuck. Time went by.

When she first woke up, I was asleep, slumped over in the unforgiving hardness of my self-imposed plastic hospital torture.

"Frank? So thirsty."

I was immediately awake, brushing the sleep from my eyes, quickly standing, muscles screaming, contracting. I ignored it all, smiling through my tears. Hoping.

"Here. I'm here, Jessica. You're safe. Don't talk." I handed her a plastic bottle with a straw from her bedside table so she could drink. Images of Rivas flashed through my head. She took a few sips and then melted back into the bed.

"Jessica?" I said, but she was already asleep.

She didn't say anything for another two days. The doctors said that was normal. It was a good sign. The body resting after the sedation had worn off, repairing. More nurses, the occasional doctor, flitting back and forth through the door. Lights shining in her eyes, blood pressure cuff humming and inflating every quarter-hour, touching her, checking her pulse. Notes made, pens clicking, occasional brief, tight smiles, pats on the shoulder. We'll know soon, they said. So clinical, so efficient, just numbers on a chart. I'm sure they truly cared, but I was past the facade, past caring what they thought. I wanted my Jessica back. The waiting, and worrying, wearing me down.

I came out of my stupor, now there was some hope. Showered, shaved, changed clothes. I found the cafeteria and ate some soup. I'd gone to the bathroom, taking the time to assess. I looked like I'd aged a thousand years from what I remembered my face should look like. The tan had paled, the bags under my eyes heavy and dark. My skin was ashen, replaced with the color of the great unwashed and fluorescent light king. That was me.

When I shuffled back to the room, she was awake, and I stopped in the doorway for a second to take her in. Her eyes looked clear, those incredible brown eyes sparkling with tiny green flecks. The sallow reflection of hospital and pain, replaced by something else, something only a living person can give.

"Frank," she croaked. "What happened?"

"What do you remember?" I said, moving to the bed and sitting on the edge, taking her hand in mine and kicking my plastic chair away.

Doctor Adams came in, paged by a nurse. He was all business and smiles, motioned me off the bed. Checked her vitals, her bandages.

"Jessica? I'm Doctor Adams. Can you tell me your full name and date of birth? Where do you live? Who's the current president? Do you know where you are?"

"Doc, give her a chance, will you?" I said.

"Cincinnati," Carter said.

Adams frowned and looked at me, not sure how to take her answer, about to say something.

"It's okay," I said, smiling through my tears. "It's her. She's herself." Cincinnati was an old joke. She'd told me before that had been her safe word as a child. She was going to be okay. Adams said it would still take time and therapy. Time for the physical wounds to heal and hide, time for the emotional trauma to recede. She needed a stress-free environment, somewhere the brain and body could heal. He said some big ten-dollar doctor words, but I had stopped listening. I knew what she needed. She needed to be out of here, and away, away from it all.

Over the next few days, there were more assessments, travel preparations. Jessica told me awful things. Purging, mending. Things I wish I could unhear. But that was unfair of me. She needed compassion and understanding. It didn't matter a damn how I felt. It wasn't about me, none of this was. She said she remembered being taken, dragged from her car, something over her mouth so she didn't struggle. After that, it was a haze, snatches. Some real, some not. She felt the familiar rocking motion of a ship. Images of cigars, Black leaning in close and laughing. Pungent body odor, stale cigarette smoke. Peripherally, she knew what was happening, understood she was being abused, but the specifics weren't there. The memories might come back, or they might not. I was hoping not. It was probably better that way. I let her speak, let her get it all out. The sobs broke my heart. I held her.

As soon as they cleared her for travel, we set off for home, back to Corpus, a plan in mind. Jessica was on official convalescent leave, and I cashed in my chips with Tobias and took some extended vacation time. No one was going to argue with what we had been through.

We set sail two weeks later. *Serenity* was well provisioned and packed, fueled up and ready to go, thanks to Pete. Jessica cast off the lines while I spooled up the motor and we headed out of the dock and to parts south, parts unknown.

Pete mock saluted and waved as we motored past.

"Bon voyage, my friends," he shouted.

Jessica's light spring dress flowed in the wind as she stood on the bow, her hair streaming, shimmering like gold from the sunlight. If you looked carefully when she was close, you could still see the faint outline of the last of her bruises, barely showing.

It was going to be a long journey, a journey of discovery, a journey of forgiveness and healing.

I blasted the horn in reply and didn't look back.

FAIR WINDS AND FOLLOWING SEAS

Afterword

Dear Reader,

I can't thank you enough for joining me on this heart-pounding adventure in Dangerous Currents. Your support is incredibly meaningful to me, and I truly hope the story has left you on the edge of your seat.

If you found yourself lost in the twists and turns of the plot (damn that Black!), I would be immensely grateful if you could share your experience in a review. Your honest thoughts not only help me grow as a writer, but also guide other readers to stories they'll love. Every word you share makes a difference.

Frank Dalton will return in further adventures. Check where you bought this book, my social media or website below for details.

Stay connected for more thrills! Follow my journey on social media:

facebook.com/shippwrites

Instagram.com/shippwrites

For the most exclusive content and be the first to hear about my new projects, please join my subscriber list at www.ShippWrites.com

Thank you again from the bottom of my heart. Your support is the lifeblood of an indie author, and I can't wait to share more of Frank's adventures with you.

Jonathan.

Acknowledgements

This book is the culmination of all the knowledge I have gained over the last few years. It's a reboot of my first novel To Dance the Hempen Jig, but with a thorough emphasis on editing, quality and approximately twenty thousand plus, new words.

All of that requires time and money – it's not cheap or free to be an indie author (think editing/software/hardware/cover art etc.,) and to produce quality products.

Of course, none of that would be possible without the dedication and unwavering support of my family who follow me willingly into the storm.

Thank you for believing in me, and thank you for making this dream come true.

Jonathan

About the Author

Jonathan, a Chief Warrant Officer in the U.S. Coast Guard on the cusp of retirement, finds his true north in the world of storytelling. His desk, a microcosm of his dual life, is both a tactical command center and a cradle for his literary creations. Here, amidst the hum of duty and the clatter of keys, his faithful dog stands guard, ever alert for snacks.

His writing blends the thrill of maritime pursuits with the nuances of everyday life, capturing both action and introspection with equal flair. His tales are windows into worlds where duty collides with the narrative, and the high seas meet high stakes in prose. Rich in authenticity and peppered with humor, Jonathan's stories offer a glimpse into that world.

When not writing, Jonathan enjoys long walks and short naps—or is it short walks and long naps?—and the occasional moment of existential panic on how to use semi-colons correctly. Thank you for following him on this journey.

To find out more, follow Jonathan at:

facebook.com/shippwrites

Instagram.com/shippwrites

www.ShippWrites.com

9 781963 639018